I0764507

THE FINAL MASQUERADE

Novels by Dennis Bowen

THE WATER DIAMONDS
Book 1: International Thriller Series

THE BLACKSTONE PERFECTION
Book 2: International Thriller Series

THE CRYSTAL SEDUCTION
Book 3: International Thriller Series

THE REDROCK QUARANTINE
Book 4: International Thriller Series

THE FINAL MASQUERADE
Book 5: International Thriller Series

THE FINAL MASQUERADE

Dennis Bowen

The Final Masquerade is a work of fiction. Names, characters, places, and incidents are the products of the author's imagination or are used fictitiously. Any resemblance to actual events, locales, or persons, living or dead, is entirely coincidental.

ISBN: 978-0- 9979147-0-2

FIRST EDITION

www.DennisBowen.com

www.twitter.com/DBowenThrillers

www.facebook.com/DennisBowenThrillers

Book Interior Design by 52 Novels

ACKNOWLEDGMENTS

Thank you to the readers who have immersed themselves in my *International Thriller Series*. While I create the intrigues that span the globe and enjoy every minute of it, in the end, I write these novels for you and your enjoyment, it's that simple.

As with *The Water Diamonds, The Blackstone Perfection*, *The Crystal Seduction*, and *The Redrock Quarantine* those who offered suggestions and encouragement during the writing of *The Final Masquerade* deserve my appreciation.

For the fifth time, I express appreciation to Laura Taylor. Her editorial consultations have kept my manuscripts clean. Her mentoring has kept me off the stage, as she would put it. Last but surely not least, I value her as a colleague in this wonderful profession.

As in life, each successive endeavor—such as writing a series of novels—is built on what came before. Laura has provided just the right touch—a hand neither too heavy nor too light—in order that each novel is correct in presentation while preserving what I as a novelist have brought to the table. As before, any errors or omissions in *The Final Masquerade*, I claim as my own.

I extend my gratitude to family members and friends for their support, and to former colleagues, some of whom offered up their lives in the service of this great country, and whose presence in my life gives my International Thriller Series its noted sense of reality. Thank you to all.

—Dennis Bowen

CHAPTER 1

There was no doubt whatsoever in Magus Crayle's mind that the man standing across the bedroom from him was the Roman Catholic pope. Although his white vestments appeared soiled and tattered, he recognized Zoran on sight. Next to him, another man he knew only too well. The Elder, known outside his Illuminé secret society frame of reference as the Prince of Monaco, spoke.

"Remember my words to you, Mr. Crayle? You are, in actuality, three men. The first, a cold-blooded CIA assassin." He handed a device to the pope. "Here, Zoran. You do the honors."

Before Crayle could react, the pope pressed '1' and a sneer replaced his normally holy countenance.

With a snap of his head, the man with three lives rose from his bed, extracting a SIG-Sauer .40 caliber from under his pillow as he did.

"Give him his orders, Zoran."

The pope produced one mere sentence, which he followed with a sign of the cross.

Crayle walked from the bedroom toward the kitchen. A beautiful woman stood at a stove, preparing what smelled like eggs, ham, and hash browns. She turned just in time to see her husband point the weapon.

The two reports rebounded off the ranch house's flat surfaces like the mini-explosives that they were.

Boom!

Boom!

The impact on her chest flung her back against the frying pan handle, splattering food across adjacent walls.

Red fluid spurted from the wounds, decorating his clothing and his face in a deathly pattern.

One glimpse of her vacant eyes was all he received as her lifeless corpse fell forward onto the hundred-year-old floor.

For a moment, Crayle the assassin couldn't process what he'd done. What he'd been caused to do. He dropped the weapon, and scooped up the woman he'd declared the love of his life more than once.

It was dark and cold as he carried her into the back yard, laying her next to the waterfall built by her father. Next to his grave.

The Elder and the pope watched with interest.

Crayle prepared a new grave in the fashion of her Serrano Indian traditions, and laid her to rest.

"You can see now, Zoran, that his programming is complete. We can choose the assassin, the genius strategist, or the third Crayle. However, should we choose number three, he would come after us for a final time. Final for us. For obvious reasons, we must take care not to press the three on this device."

The original Crayle had been reprogrammed to remove compassion and caring by a crew of devious psychiatric researchers at Central Intelligence. That had facilitated Crayle Two to develop strategies utilizing minimized, tactical nuclear weapons that had killed tens of thousands of innocent victims in Marseille, Ürümqi, Beijing, and in Central Iran.

The two men re-entered the ranch house, exiting by the front door.

Crayle hardly heard their vehicle depart as he squatted—hands on thighs—and stared at the fresh gravesite. The one they'd caused him to create.

• • •

The devastating tranquility of the moment didn't last.

"Okay! Alright! Lock and load!" The voice of Lenny Lipschitz caused sweat-drenched Crayle to sit bolt upright in his bed. Prepared to defend.

Seeing there was no need, he rubbed the muck from his eyes, as if in preparation to fire laser-like death ray beams through the private investigator's head.

"Breakfast is on! Follow me!" Lenny spun on his heel and marched outside to a waiting table.

As the beleaguered spy stumbled from under the covers and through the living room, he caught a glimpse that caused his heart to skip. Stepping from the kitchen with two plates full of eggs, ham, and hash browns, was the woman he'd just slaughtered.

No red holes on her chest. Nothing but her butterscotch-hued skin and minimal Serrano smile.

"Have a good sleep, Magus?" she asked as she passed before him. "Better close that gaping mouth. It's mid-August. There are flying insects about."

He realized his mouth hung full open. He shut it.

"Might want to put on some clothes, too."

• • •

Crayle stepped back into the bedroom to face down his cherry wood armoire. He took a second to breathe deeply, hold, then exhale slowly through his nose. Three more times and he was good to go.

He opened both doors to face the same dilemma he always faced: which black shorts would he chose … and which black T-shirt to go with it. Color matching might be a problem for some men, but Crayle had it down. And whenever he had to dress up, he would open a bottom drawer, select from an array of equivalent black socks. Last step: slip on a pair, before inserting his feet into the usual ECCO Velcro-fastened sandals.

Today's regimen called for casual. No socks.

He dressed in less than two minutes. Although there were no battles to fight this fine day, and the smells wafting in through his open door portended pleasure versus pain, he would stay vigilant.

In a throwdown, even if it included the Catholic pope and the Prince of Monaco as tangos, he would have Ms. Crayle's back. And that was that.

He raised the back of his shirt and slipped in his black-toned SIG to complete the wardrobe.

Finishing his abbreviated routine, he shut the armoire and performed a Crayle-primp in front of a full-length wall mirror. He pushed aside a Serrano dream catcher in order to get the full effect..

There. Ready. All components present. Everything matched.

He turned to leave. He stopped.

Mmmm. Perhaps one more shot at the mirror.

After a number of scowls, leers, and panther-like exhalations, he was ready. Into the bathroom to run a brush through his mountain man hair, and then he exited to meet the others.

He didn't take time to proclaim the day one of peace and tranquility, perhaps he would see to that over breakfast. His memory restorations had brought no insights into any religious nature he might have had, but perhaps he could manage a prayer. It couldn't hurt to try, he thought. Could it?

His smile was his greeting as he crossed the living room and stepped out the cabin's sliding door.

CHAPTER 2

A casually dressed Crayle, wearing characteristic black shorts with a black T, joined his private investigator colleague at the deck table. Just in time for the P.I. to head inside to the bathroom.

A little late, it occurred to him that he was not in Hekka's ranch house as in the nightmare, but rather at the lake cabin owned by Jack Sommers. And that he, like Lenny, had left the cabin's sliding door full open.

"Magus?" Hekka called out from the kitchen. "The lake is beautiful and calm today. Like glass. How about you and Lenny move the deck down to the water's edge."

"If it weren't twenty feet square, and if it weren't made of hardwood, and if it weren't fifty feet down to the lake, and if we didn't have an eighty-foot Ponderosa pine to squeeze it around …"

"And we might trip over one of the gray squirrels," Lenny added as he returned outside. "And when the odors from your fine cooking waft out onto the lake, the fishermen'll be over here like stink on shit."

Hekka found herself using a butcher knife to stir the hash browns. "Gentlemen. It warms my heart that you have given my heartfelt request serious consideration."

"Do you realize, Darling, in another month or so, I will be celebrating the first anniversary of my crash on the Malibu Highway?"

"You'll have to speak up. I'm creating a lot of noise cooking our Serrano burgers."

He twisted his head toward the kitchen. "Are you telling me your tribe had its own burgers?"

"Louder." She produced a sly smile.

Crayle stepped inside. "Make sure Lenny's has the extra kick we talked about."

"I heard that," the P.I. accused as he, too, stepped inside.

"Lenny, you're sounding more accusatory every time we see you."

"I married an attorney—what can I say?"

"Now that we've lost track, let me remind you. I was telling Hekka it's been about a year since my crash. And following that, the anniversary of our first meeting."

"You mean the romantic one I arranged at the Tack Store?" She waved the knife through the air like a pirate with a sword.

Satisfied with her short career as a swashbuckler, the self-appointed chef emerged from the kitchen. "Yes, Lenny, the one where Magus was attacked by a man with a knife. One of Lalumière's men. And a second one with a silenced pistol."

Crayle added a smile. "And my Indian associate-to-be took him out with a ten-inch Bowie knife."

"Gives a new interpretation to a romantic encounter," she added.

Lenny nodded. "Yeah. You'll never find that method of meeting women on that new romance website I found … what is it … GetLaid.com?"

Crayle had learned over time to disregard Lenny-isms. "Regardless. We're done with those days. But forget that, I've been reading an international thriller with all manner of exciting chases, violence, sex, exotic locales, and so forth. I could write one of those. Without any more mayhem in my personal life, I'll need something to do. Lenny, I've got it. I'm going to become a bestselling international thriller writer."

"No, you're not," said Hekka, re-brandishing the butcher knife. "You're taking me to beautiful places all over the world. Places where there are no words for any of those activities you just mentioned. Only peace."

"Maybe writing would relieve the inner—what the Germans call—*angst* in me."

"Do you recall now how it is that you are fluent in German?"

"Don't you see?" said an animated Crayle. "I could research my stories as we travel. And I could write anywhere."

"Well, you'll have to promise me no more bullets, bombs, hand-to-hand combat high in the Eiffel Tower, and the rest," she cautioned.

"That's all finished. I promise." He turned to the P.I. "Give me a rundown on all the players, the happenings, et cetera. You know, the bombs. My memory is pretty much intact, but I still need a refresher from time to time."

"Got it. Here goes. The mini-nukes that went off were in Central Iran and Marseille and detonated by Lalumière, Western China and Beijing courtesy of General Li, Versailles thanks to Pattie, and Paris with the aborted attempt … to eliminate the French government … on the Eiffel Tower. Oh, and the one that dropped into the ocean off of Long Island from the Queen Mary 2, intended for New York City. How'm I doing?"

"Continue."

"Europe perp teams: Sylvain Lalumière, his son Jean-Marc, Pattie Norbrunn, the Elder known also as the Prince of Monaco, and the recently anointed Pope Innocent."

"Asia?"

"Chin Yao-wu, Li Ya-fei, Ling An-yee and the other eleven of Chin's adopted daughters."

"Well done. And other players include the CIA, French DGSE, British MI-6, along with President Stones and his NSA pals. And the in-flight French government, the imprisoned Communist Party Standing Committee. And Jack, ex-wife Marli, and new wife, Flori."

"Don't forget Phoebe's sister, DFM."

"Delta Force Mandy. Oh. I almost forgot. Alona said she'd help bring in the Mossad if what we have isn't enough."

"Please tell Alona to stand by on that one. We have our hands full."

"*Had* our hands full," concluded the conversation as Hekka delivered the repast. Having long ago spent a short Summer stint at a Big Bear Lake restaurant, she toted out all of the plates with both arms full and set them on the table, spilling nothing.

Without another word, Lenny finished first, checked his watch, and left for the airport.

"He didn't say goodbye, Magus."

"Gotta hurry over to Alona before she goes out of heat."

"I don't believe you said that."

Crayle pressed his index fingers to each side of his head. "Perhaps massaging my temples will exorcise Lenny from my brain."

Hekka cocked her head. "Good luck with that."

"Hmmm. Did you clean out Jack's old coffee mug before you loaded it up? It took him years to build up the flavor-enhancing scum."

"Didn't touch it. You know, you should have an official CIA coffee mug given all you've done for them."

"It doesn't pay to advertise. Besides, it seems that in my original incarnation with them, I went around assassinating people. Not the kind of image I'd like to promote."

"You can bet those people were evil. Otherwise, they wouldn't have been sanctioned."

"Sanctioned? Where did you hear that?"

"My father watched all the Clint Eastwood movies. Over and over. The Eiger Sanction, for example."

"Good save, my dear Hekka. I wouldn't want to think that your presence at the Tack Store—where I was the one sanctioned—was anything other than a coincidence."

"Where I thrust the Bowie through the back of the bad-intentioned killer's neck?"

He laughed. "They don't teach that technique at The Farm. Do they?"

"Nice trap, Magus." She smiled just a bit. "That's what they told me to say." It was her turn to laugh.

They clinked orange juice glasses as Crayle offered a toast. "May we never experience, or have to deal with, *company* affairs ever again."

"Here, here." They clinked again.

CHAPTER 3

It was a brand new day in the Big Bear Valley. There was a feeling among the area denizens that the place had been designed just to provide new days, especially when that's what people needed.

The birds sang.

The sky was clear blue.

A fresh breeze tumbled over the mountains to the west.

A couple of bushy-tailed gray squirrels sat on their haunches, as if pondering a future gathering of acorns for the winter.

The only element missing from the previous one was Private Investigator Lenny.

With another full breakfast of ham, bacon, eggs, and a Serrano burger fully deployed on the back deck, Crayle made his entrance, yet again clad in his signature black T-shirt, black cargo shorts, and favorite ECCO sandals.

"Sun's out. Light breeze. Late Summer. Another crappy, typical day in Big Bear."

Hekka pinched salt and pepper onto her meal. "Do you remember that our trip begins today?"

He took a seat next to her and forked in some eggs. "Trip?"

She'd become conversant with his Irish component that embodied devilishness. She played along. "Yes. A little vacation not involving cruise ships about to blow up or with Pattie Norbrunn as the tour guide. Without Lalumière and his son, Jean-Marc. Without the evil pope or Monaco prince. Without Chin masquerading as Emperor of China, along with Li and the daughters. Without—"

"Okay. Okay. I get it. Now, where was it we were going?"

It was the twinkle in his eye, not the sausage penetrating what Micmac would've called a shit-eatin' grin, that gave him away.

"We are driving to Las Vegas, Mister Crayle, there to reside at the Hard Rock Hotel, and participate in its incessant energy when not basking by each one of those beautiful, relaxing pools."

"So you're wanting a bomb free, bullet free period away from our fabulous team."

"Precisely. And I knew you would give me a ration—as Micmac says—so I put this on so you wouldn't forget."

She stood, dropping open her robe to reveal a barely existent dark brown bikini.

"Oh, I like that. Butterscotch and chocolate. Mmm. How 'bout we step inside after breakfast?"

"After breakfast?"

"Unless you have a little *al fresco* action in mind."

"It so happens that I need to run over to my ranch on the way to Vegas and see if the boys need anything. We'll be gone a whole week, and I'd like not to be taking anyone's panic cell phone calls."

"I'm sure your two brothers, having served as 101st Airborne Division Screaming Eagles paratroops, can handle it. I'm sending Lenny along, just to be safe."

"Forget our favorite P.I. I'm taking *you* along, just to be safe. Besides, got a call from our very favorite FBI Agent, Phoebe. Said we just had to see what Micmac has in his front yard."

"It's probably one of those chainsaw totem poles or animal figures they make from trees around here."

Crayle finished the meal in short order and headed for the cabin's sliding door. "I'll throw a couple of suitcases in the Cobra so we can leave directly from the ranch."

"Terrific. Down highway 18 and over to 15 north. I should drive, though. You have a nasty habit of turning into the Quarry."

"We could drop into the old subterranean CIA haunt cum hospital and see how Doc Rorschach is coming along with your mother."

"And maybe restore your memory that this little escape is about us. He said it is likely to take several weeks, and that he'd advise us of material progress. We can drop by on the way back."

"Deal." He disappeared inside, leaving Hekka with her thoughts. She'd no sooner schlepped the dishes inside, rinsed them, and stacked them in the dishwasher than she heard the Cobra rumble. When a man was ready to go, a man was ready to go.

Stuffing her Bowie knife inside her purse, she set security and stepped out to the awaiting Crayle. "Where's our luggage?" she said, mockingly eyeing the two-seater.

He nodded behind. "Boogie-bags are in the trunk."

Her thought process began to interpret its spy meaning of that sort of black ballistic nylon bag stuffed with operative goodies, but affected a smile instead. She hopped in.

"We have the first-tier essentials: handguns, ammo, pressure bandages, toothpaste, et cetera. I know a multi-story shopping center in Vegas with lots of clothes. I'll take you there."

A smile was all she needed in response.

Crayle drove left onto 18 West through the nearby village of Fawnskin, where the few townspeople out and about quickly gave notice to the rumble of the Cobra V8. Transit to the other side of town took no more than ten seconds.

Crayle picked up the pace. The breeze in the face felt perfect as they headed around the west end of the lake. The fishermen bobbing around in vessels ranging from skiffs to surrey-covered pontoon boats underscored the peaceful nature of Big Bear Valley.

To converse, they had to speak over the roar of the Cobra's engine, the wind, the birds, and other traffic.

"Look. There goes another squad of eagles' nest seekers. Off on a trail into the woods and hills. Adults. Children. Every year at this time."

"Better a real nest than the one the Aryans had you imprisoned in after the Helsinki kidnap."

At that moment, a pair of eagles passed overhead, also headed west.

"I believe they took the human activity we saw back there as their cue. They're headed home to pose for the inevitable shots."

"Shots would be an inappropriate characterization. Photos is better."

"You're right. Going to guns on eagles gets you serious down time behind bars up here."

"As it should."

As they drew abreast of Micmac and Phoebe's cabin, Crayle swerved onto the narrow shoulder, skidding to a stop. Between them and the residence sat an Abrams tank. While its khaki coloring might have been described as an earth tone by an aggressive realtor, the structurally sound former UDT man rinsing it with a hose and applying a fresh coat of carnauba wax would have been an environmental stretch.

"How's it going, Micmac?"

"Hey, Magus. Hekka. Everything's normal. What's up?"

"Normal with an M1A3 Abrams tank in the front yard?"

"It's kind of noticeable, isn't it?"

"They make a change to their hunting regulations up here?"

"Well. The Fall season starts soon."

"Going after big game, are we?"

Micmac produced a quick smile. "It's a new project. New weaponry. Can't talk about it, but it's really hot."

"I'll bet."

"Boys and their toys," Hekka observed. "Where's Phoebs? I want to take her shopping … with your money."

"What money?"

Crayle brought the conversation back on point. "C'mon, Micmac. Give."

Micmac glanced about and then up, as if able to detect satellite surveillance with the unaided eye. "You've got super-clearance with the pres, but not for this project. So here's the abridged version." He pointed to a hose stuck in the barrel's business end. "I've invented an internal coating to withstand abnormally high temperatures. Reduces friction at the same time."

"A reduction in friction should yield greater range. Correct? And the heat aspect?"

"The first is classified Secret, and you're right about the heat part. It's TS. Sorry."

"What's it doing in your front yard?"

"Phoebe won't let me bring it inside."

"Why don't you park it in the garage?"

"Been there with Phoebe on that one. Even if I widen the garage, she doesn't want me, or anyone else, parking their tank next to her 911."

"Yes," said Hekka. "She's worried you'll come home drunk one night …"

"Hey, I'm a retired sailor. I don't drink any more." He grinned.

Crayle grinned back. "And you don't drink any less."

"I heard that about the garage," emanated from the front porch.

"Oh, Phoebs darling. Fetch that little package on my work bench. Give it to Magus." He turned back around. "It's an update on the Vestige tracking chip. I want you to test it out."

"I don't know, Micmac. I had the first version embedded under my skin and TJ and his hit squad used the burst mode broadcasts that embedded themselves onto anything metallic to chase us through the Hollywood Hills to Malibu."

"Haven't you heard? We're living in peacetime now. C'mon. Please."

Phoebe trotted past the tank to the car, package in hand. "Here, Hekka. Just the right size for your purse."

"I'll take care of it. Say, we're off for a week for a little Magus and Hekka time. Give it a few days, then see if you can track us. It'll be worth your while."

Micmac stopped rubbing the wax as his head snapped around. "Did I just hear foursome?"

Phoebe rolled her eyes. She and Hekka spoke at the same time. "Sailor."

Crayle revved the Cobra V8. "Okay, guys. We're heading over to the ranch to check on her brothers, and then we're gone. See you later."

About a mile past the MacKay's place, they turned left, and drove across the bridge over the Big Bear dam. Their demeanor waxed light-hearted as the Cobra's performance exhaust announced their passage through the aptly named Boulder Bay, which led them into the folksy village known as Big Bear Lake.

BBL, as some residents referred to it, wasn't big enough to have suburbs. Rather, it possessed a number of enclaves, each unique in style, that existed on the west and east ends of town.

The Crayles passed numerous stores, patrons, and gawkers.

"Whoa there, Charley. Bring this sucker to a stop," Hekka called from the passenger's seat.

"What's the matter?

"New winter wear in the windows. Early bird sale. I need a new coat in case it's cold in Vegas."

"Vegas is desert."

He pulled over and stopped, anyway.

It took Hekka exactly fourteen minutes to run across the street, enter the two-story shop, try on and select a fur-lined, sheepskin jacket, pay for it, return to the car, and buckle up.

He'd admired her style as she'd exited the shop door, and waved her old jacket in the air, like waving a checkered flag at the end of a race.

"Well?"

"You look fabulous. The open front kind of shows off the bikini."

The pair continued to BBL's main intersection, and made the obligatory—if you don't want to drive off into the weeds—left turn onto Pine Knot Avenue. They made the right turn one makes before driving into the lake ahead, passed the fire station, and headed east from town. The road to Hekka's ranch.

CHAPTER 4

With the Cobra's engine held down on revs and set one gear higher than it otherwise would be, the Crayles had enough quiet about them to carry on a conversation and not disturb tourists and locals alike.

"After my mother's disappearance, my father moped a lot, but before you met him. He always said that when life gets really tough, it's okay to put a positive spin on things. Even conjure up memories."

"Memories have been a struggle for me."

"But you do remember our time in the Bavarian Alps, right?"

"The vacation?"

"Uh, huh."

"And you were just hanging around at Hitler's old hangout, the Eagle's Nest."

"And your friends brought you there on the maglev subway … so we could be together."

He remembered, indeed. Strapped to a gurney, he'd been transported at what seemed to be 300 miles per hour by the Aryan duo of Von Prem and Frau Doktor Mengele via a secret, near vacuum tunnel. He'd killed off a couple of their captors, and rescued Hekka's naked body hung from a meat hook high overhead. "Those were the days, weren't they?"

Though she sat there buckled in, she started with some moves, as some music with a major beat played in the distance.

"Remember, you've got our kid in there."

"We're just a few weeks along. No problem."

"Just be careful, that's all."

"How about we put those darker reminiscences aside for now?"

"It's a deal."

"You have the gift of intelligence, Magus. You got into the CIA and they sent you to school. Mathematics and that strategic methodology based on ..."

"Applied General Systems Theory."

"Yes. Then they sent you to China and France to develop the Blackstone Strategy. An in-depth, perfect plan that couldn't fail."

"I find it difficult to appreciate what I accomplished."

"Those bad people—the Illuminé moles—were responsible. You couldn't have known about their plot."

"If I was such a genius, why didn't I figure it out?"

"Because focus on the task at hand and the forms required for a fail-proof plan to overthrow not one, but two countries must've consumed every waking moment."

"You're making excuses for me."

"You know what happened." She became uncharacteristically animated. "Lalumière's gang tried to kill you. Right here in Big Bear. Remember TJ, the triangle-jawed triplet? And it wasn't just to remove evidence either."

"What do you mean?"

"The top people—the Elder, Chin, et cetera—were not only aware that you knew every detail, but that you had the capacity to create a counter-strategy if you remembered their scheme."

He placed his finger in his ear, furrowing his brow. "Just a second. Rorschach finally has the cochlear implant working. He's talking too rapidly. With the Swiss accent. He does that when he's upset or excited."

He listened, thrumming the car's engine down a bit more.

"Oh, good. Your mom's recovering well."

"That's more than good, it's great. But I still don't like him having that thing in your ear canal. I remember a movie …"

• • •

Just east of Big Bear Lake village, their progress came to a halt. Up ahead, a construction stoplight manned by men wearing orange reflector vests held up their hands and a sign reading DETOUR. They directed cars one-at-a-time into the Big Bear Convention Center parking lot and through a huge, corrugated rollup door in a large corrugated structure. On the building's side, the word *Oktoberfest* portended the upcoming annual bash that attracted revelers from as far away as San Diego and San Francisco.

"There will be oompah bands, lederhosen, dirndls, sausages, and beer, Magus."

"It's not even September. Why are we being directed there?"

"You are relatively new to the Valley. Fall is upon us. That's when all the roadwork is scheduled in snowy environs like ours. Last year, at this time—you'd just been brought here by Jack and had no memories. Because of your crash in Malibu."

He drove them across the parking lot and through the large door into the festive-decorated building.

Ahead, three cars blocked passage through a similar door on the other side. As the Crayles came to a stop behind a row of hair dryer stations, the three attendants stopped what appeared to be a set-up operation.

Hekka glanced around the converted warehouse. "Check out the stacks of boxes with the image of a beer stein on them. I'll bet they sell a lot of them. Those appear to be the glass version. They have earth-ware versions—one liter each—called *Krugs*, as well."

"We should stay. I lust after German beer. Especially the dark."

"Competition disallowed." She pointed at herself. "The lust stops here."

"Noted. But—"

"No buts. We'll quench your thirst when we reach Vegas. At the Hofbräuhaus. Okay?"

He was amazed at how quickly she could draw her Bowie to underscore a point. "Promise you won't forget."

"Promise."

"Oh, I noticed them setting up an EMT station outside."

"They get busy during the festival. Somehow, things are kept under control."

"Since we started all this, I feel that I'm getting the foreign things I helped start under control. Then, poof. Gone. Chaos."

"Maybe we should send in Big Bear's finest. EMT, CHP, Sheriffs, doctors, nurses, and so forth. Send 'em overseas."

"We've waited long enough." He did something he normally wouldn't do. He pressed the horn button.

"*Hiss!*" went the Cobra.

Again.

"*Hiss!*"

He turned.

There sat his wife, weaving her head from side to side as if to tame the beast. He realized she probably could tame a venomous snake. After all, she'd tamed him.

No sooner had he returned his attention to the cars blocking his progress, than one attendant leapt over the Cobra's trunk, pulling a hair dryer bag over Crayle's head. As Hekka turned at the commotion, a second woman did the same to her.

As soon as the pair of assailants cinched the bags at the neck, the third started the flow of gas.

In what seemed like only a couple of heartbeats, the blocking cars in front vacated the scene.

The large doors in front and behind slammed shut.

CHAPTER 5

The Crayles awoke in the large metal room secured to tie-down rings above and below.

Crayle groaned. "They beat us unconscious. Nothing broken here. How about you?"

Hekka uttered a companion groan. "Yeah. I'm okay."

"They've suspended us with these bungee cords like this because of what happened last time at Eagle's Nest and *Rotfels*. We got away."

"With our hands stretched up toward the upper ring, and our feet to the lower one, we can't move."

"We've beaten death a number of times before. This time, I'm not sure."

"I have pertinent experience hanging onto the quarter horses in their left and right skits and scats. Strong thighs and all."

She leaned his way, imparting a pendulum motion.

"Let me see if I can swing over and wrap my legs …"

He glanced above them at the suspension element. "They must have a meat hook business."

Hekka gave her body a twist. The rings swiveled so that she now faced toward her husband.

He followed suit.

"If I push up with my arms, and down with my legs, and then backwards … I come within a few inches of you."

Arching her back, she tried again coming ever closer.

That she never called it quits had always been a source of admiration for him of his strong and resolute complement in life. He replicated her efforts and, after three more times, they pushed their heads forward.

Just as their lips touched, a rusted iron door—matching the rest of the cold, dimly lit enclosure—burst open.

The man leading a squad of four heavily armed men—all clad in lederhosen—was familiar to the Crayles. They'd encountered him during the beatings just two hours earlier.

"Very clever. We bind you in such a manner that you cannot possibly move and you manage a kiss. Quite touching. If you wonder why it is I, Aryan Number Two, that is taking care of business, our Number One is presently encumbered with unleashing the small nuclear devices supplied by the dimpled operative, Pattie Norbrunn. I believe you know her, in all senses of the word."

"We've met."

Hekka closed her eyes.

"The sumptuous repast you consumed prior to your beatings served two purposes. The last meal of a condemned man and woman, and it made the subsequent beating more effective."

"A pity all that good food had to mess up your floor."

"It is well that you have retained your sense of humor. It will become a necessity in your final days."

"Days? What do you need from me that will take days?"

"Not a thing. Our leader has decided that you shall die a natural death. Along with your lovely wife."

"Strung up like a bow string doesn't strike me as all that natural."

"Oh, I almost forgot. We are not heathens, Herr Crayle. While beating your wife, I exercised care in not punching her in the abdomen." He turned, motioning his men along, and started for the door.

Crayle's eyes snapped to meet Hekka's. They pleaded.

"Magus … our baby is fine."

At that instant, the two-inch thick boiler plate that comprised the walls turned bright red, creaked and groaned for a couple of seconds, and began to melt. The roof sagged in enough for Crayle and Hekka to begin unlacing their bonds.

Before the Aryans could react and shoot their captives dead, an Abrams M1A3 tank pushed over the molten wall and ground to a halt.

Men in Navy blue popped from behind the oversized weapon and engaged their enemies for less than three seconds before all of the Aryans were dead.

Two of the tactical operatives ran to the Crayles and released them from their bonds while the others crouched down to provide cover.

The hatch popped open, revealing a familiar face.

"Micmac!" Crayle cried out. "What in the world are you doing here with that Army tank?"

"You do what you gotta do. I had to field test my depleted uranium blanks. They created the heat to melt the steel. It's a little side thing I'm doing via Mandy. You know, former Delta Force? Army? It's for heavy-lifting hostage rescue. Besides, Phoebe's getting her hair done, so I had to stand in for her and her Glock."

"Who are they?" Crayle waved at the black ops team.

"Well, you have your Sixers …" He referred to the British Foreign Service nickname. "… and I have mine. Meet SEAL Team Six … retired."

"We'd love to stay and chat, Micmac …" Hekka said as she and Crayle climbed into the Cobra. "… but my brothers are expecting us at the ranch. I'm hearing sirens, so please be sure to give the sheriffs, the ATF, Homeland Security, and any other interested parties our regards."

She turned to Crayle, who fired up their sports car, drove around the tank, and through the building's gaping hole. Outside, they smiled and waved like Hollywood stars at scores of stunned onlookers. Back on the main road, they headed east.

"Twenty minutes," Hekka said as she laughed.

CHAPTER 6

Nearly 6,282 miles east of California's Big Bear Valley, the morning sun edged its way into view over Italy's Apennine Mountains. Neither its beauty nor its glare were visible inside the sumptuous top floor apartments of the Apostolic Palace that sequestered the two partners in crime.

"It is most uncomfortable for me to sit here and witness a naked man stepping into his briefs. That they are black instead of white is the only positive."

"White is for the external world. Black, some might say, reflects my heart."

"What some might say does not concern me. What does concern me is what you just told me just a minute ago."

"How so?"

"That it is not even remotely likely, Zoran."

The Elder walked to the closed and shuttered window as if he wanted more than anything to open it to the ever-adoring crowd below them in Saint Peter's Square.

"All I said was that Magus Crayle is probably having nightmares regarding his slim prospects of destroying Illuminé … and us."

"If he were to destroy you and I, he would effectively destroy our organization. Those in high places and dangling at our fingertips would become like a snake without its head. They would cease to slither."

"I would appreciate other symbology, Elder. Snakes give me the creeps."

"I feel so close to my dream. So close. Without Crayle and his gang of miscreants, I shall have it."

"Well, he's destroyed every one of Lalumière's hit squads. The triangle jawed triplets—all killed. And recently in the Big Bear shootout at Micmac's cabin, their father. Still, our hands are tied. I can't send Vatican forces, and you can't send your elite troops from Monaco. We must continue to utilize outside forces such as the Aryans."

The Elder winced at the memory induced by the pope's remark. In May, just three months before, Crayle's team had easily rendered his entire elite guard force unconscious in the successful rescue of the spy and his wife from his own Imperial Palace. That he almost had been eaten by the team's demon dogs hurt, but not as much as the assault to his ego.

"Patience is our savior, not our master, Zoran. I anticipate we will shortly hear of a victory far away."

"By the way, I've been wanting to thank you for the birthday present." He tilted his head toward a second-century table with the referenced item on top. "A Kiväări long-range sniper rifle under a Vortex Razor 5-20X scope mounted via a LaRue Tactical QD. In .338 Lapua Magnum, a combination unlikely to be beaten. The appropriateness and the love imbued in it nearly brought tears to my eyes."

"The weapon had just arrived for my royal guard unit. You might say I swiped it."

The pope, still in his underwear, produced a solemn version of the sign of the cross. "You are forgiven, oh Prince. I accept your gift with grace and humility."

"Did you ever kill them by that means?"

"The political leaders? Most of them succumbed to poisons I acquired during my travels. That those potions were peculiar to various parts of the world made any tracking or profiling of me next to impossible." He motioned to a Renaissance-era pot next to the rifle. "Please, have some more tea, Elder."

"Thank you. Perhaps later. Since the tragic loss of Cardinal Fratze, it seems your only remaining colleague is his peer, Alighieri. Given that you require atheists of the cloth, do you have difficulty moving Illuminé faithful into positions close to you?"

"Faithful? You have quite the sense of humor given that you are the leader of the most profound group of atheists on Earth." Waiting for a response, the pope took a glass of clear liquid, then using the Elder's tea spoon, mixed in a line of white powder from a 535-year-old mirror. He glanced back at the Elder. "An old favorite. Rum and coke."

Two heavy knocks reverberated from the pope's chamber door, followed by the re-entry of the pontiff's most trusted assistant.

The Elder spoke first. "Cardinal Alighieri. It has taken a while, but I trust you have the news we require."

Pope Zoran was taken aback that the Elder seemed to have commandeered the cardinal without asking and without an inkling of warning. The strength of the man's reach was, at once, impressive and frightening.

"Elder … Your Eminence," effused the out of breath cardinal. "I fear the news is not good."

The Elder's visage moved from measured smile to glower. He hardly needed to hear more.

"The team sent by our affiliates, the Aryans, failed catastrophically. I've personally reviewed the streamed video of the encounter in Big

Bear Lake village—the Aryans had an excellent plan, spoofing a Bavarian drinking song band. With Lederhosen and—"

"There is no excellence in failure, Alighieri," admonished the Elder. "Von Prem read me in on the operation beforehand. In Germanic fashion, success was assured by attention to detail and—"

"I am sorry to interrupt. They had re-routed the two Americans into an enclosed building, and had them captured. That is when the tank arrived."

"A tank? Surely—"

"Again … sorry to interrupt." The cardinal rightly feared that his insubordination might overtake his report in the eyes of the two most powerful men on the planet. He'd seen what the pope had done with a silenced pistol to Cardinal Fratze. "It was the UDT-SEAL man. And he had a tank that spewed metal-melting flames."

The pope turned to the Elder. "He's off his meds once more."

"No. I am beyond sane," the cardinal retorted. "Here. Look at my Holy iPad."

The two Illuminé principals put their skepticism on hold, reviewing the video three times before the pope flung the device into his fireplace. "Can no one kill this man? If there were a God, I'm sure even He would fail."

"Easy, Zoran. Since our belief is in disbelief, there is no god. It is we who will have to see to Mr. Crayle's last supper." He turned to the cardinal. "You may go now, Alighieri."

Once the cleric shut the door behind him, the Elder continued. "Von Prem has failed. I will deal with him. With the upcoming Formula 1 Grand Prix—rescheduled from last May's debacle to September—I have my hands full. Perhaps you can see to the demise of the Crayle team. After all, you are the pre-eminent assassin on this planet, Zoran. Having taken out world leaders in the past, this assignment should be a piece of cake."

Zoran thought back to simpler times in his native Croatia. To an earlier time when he could have prayed for divine assistance, and then for divine forgiveness. Before he became an atheist. Before he joined Illuminé. "I will see to it forthwith, Elder."

"One last item. Have you heard from my daughter or Lalumière? I last made contact with them in the Caribbean. Some bump in the ocean. St. Lucia, if I recall. Something important, Pattie had said. Something I would be proud of. Have you heard?"

A shake of the head and a shrug of the shoulders was all the semi-nude pope could manage.

With that the Elder left in the same manner he'd arrived: disguised as a monk with ancient leather-bound scriptures in hand. The hooded cloak, the full beard, and the stooped figure he manifested disallowed any observance that he was not only the head of the globe's most dangerous secret society, but also Head of State of the Principality of Monaco.

CHAPTER 7

On the same day as the pope and Elder conducted their *tête-à-tête* at the Vatican, Sylvain Lalumière found himself in a very different kind of place. The ceiling was composed of several angled panels, each depicting ancient religious rites in gold and red tones, then surrounded with more gold and small windows to the sky. The panels formed into a grand cupola with larger windows and, yes, more gold.

Having returned his jaw to the closed position, he checked out the ground-level adornments. One large framed window with thin intervening framed panes provided a 360-degree view of expansive grounds.

Then there stood the centerpiece. Gold statues from a world far from Lalumière's. Far in distance, far in culture.

"This palace is appropriate for a king, but it is not French. Where have you brought me? South Asia? India?"

"I'm sure you recall, I exfiltrated us from Saint Lucia by hot-air balloon, having thwarted Magus Crayle and his team's attempts to deny us our destiny. We landed safely at L'Espérance airport in Grand-Case. Air traffic control there must have lost their documentation for a balloon approach. They said 'winds southeast, runway 30' but we didn't need the wind in our face, we needed it behind us. 'We'll take the other one,' I said. They said, 'Twelve?' It was fun watching fixed-wing aircraft flying in circles, staring at us the whole time. It's a wonder they didn't collide. Anyways, a taxi delivered us to the capital, Marigot, for lunch—"

"Yes. I remember that. Pizza at a place run by an expatriate French Canadian."

"And in the capital city of Saint Martin, the French side of that island. Are you keeping track of all the French, here?"

"You promised we would fly to France, and you gave me a sedative that I might sleep and awaken in my new kingdom."

"Well, we finished our pizza and beer, and departed Saint Martin. Some very unique weather came along—due to global something or other—and blew us to this place." A horizontal stretch of her arms indicated the palace.

"And what is that noise? It's driving me crazy."

"It's not noise, my dear. It's chanting."

At that moment, the chanting along with cymbals, drums, and a gong entered the room. A group of bald-headed men dressed in saffron-colored robes picked up the volume, in case the Frenchman possessed a severe hearing deprivation.

Pattie moved closer rather than compete with the din. "As fortune would have it, we landed in this remote, safe location that is home to the Krishnas. They call it New Vrindaban. You dwell in the Palace of Gold."

"But inside of France, correct?"

"Uh, not exactly. But part of the French and Indian War was fought here, so the French aspect is in place. We're in the panhandle of the great state of West Virginia."

"Ahhh?" screamed Lalumière.

"Almost heaven, it's been called."

"Since I feel half dead, it does seem apropos."

"No, silly. Almost heaven, West Virginia. As in the John Denver song."

"I know no one named John. And I've never been to Denver."

Pattie craned her neck. "Thanks, God."

"There is no god."

"Uncle!"

"I am your husband."

"Uncle means I give up. But only just for now. Here, come with me." She yanked him behind her. "You need to actually see the splendor."

Outside, the effect was immediate on Lalumière. The beautiful garden, protected by a surrounding palace wall, had been kept to perfection. A tall, three-tiered, circular fountain pointing into the heavens served as the central focal point. Like most every other item, it too was of gold.

"Over the walls, you can see the Appalachian Mountains. They—"

"I feel not the wealth of this place …" the Frenchman interrupted. "… but rather its richness. It is difficult, you know. Monetary wealth is not a prerequisite for richness in one's life."

"One more word and you'll be wearing one of those robes. C'mon. Back inside."

Pattie sat him down in one of the golden chairs. She did notice that a calm had come over him with just a short exposure outside.

"Here, Sylvain. While you slept, I procured some take-out from Grandma Jo's Polka Dot Restaurant in Moundsville. It's just south of Wheeling on the Ohio River. If it weren't for the security risk, I'd take you there for supper." She pulled two Styrofoam boxes from a paper bag. "Two eggs, meat, home fries, and toast. At $3.60 each, best deal in town."

The Frenchman devoured the meal in short order.

As if on cue, the Krishnas showed up with a post-breakfast concert.

Lalumière ripped apart the take-out box, pressing the halves to his ears. "Ahhh!"

Pattie waved the well-intentioned musical act away and extracted the doping device from her purse. She dialed in an hour and supplied the CIA beta-test drug which had worked perfectly before. Sure enough, the Frenchman fell asleep for precisely one hour. He awoke in the midst of perfect calm.

"Here, Sylvain. Here's some tea the Krishnas prepared. It was truly nice of them."

"No. I don't want whatever it is in those Styrofoam cups. I'm sure it isn't French Roast. I want that."

"Darling, I asked them for the non-alcoholic drink of our homeland …"

He popped the plastic top and took a gulp. "Agh!" He spat. "This is from the cat box. It is no more French …" He glanced at her.

"Than me? Maybe I wasn't born in Holland after all. Maybe other things I've told you aren't true either. I am a spy, you know. We make things up."

"Where are these Krishnas? Perhaps they can beseech the Buddha to spirit us to Versailles," he said, oozing sarcasm.

"Actually, they were enamored with our balloon. They took it up for a spin. Haven't seen 'em since."

"A divine wind has taken them away, no doubt."

"Don't fret, *Liebling*." She lowered herself between his knees and started with his shirt buttons. "Monika Rikki has been in contact. The bad news is that Jack Sommers is back at the *company* in Neil's old billet and has sanctioned me. A hit. But Doctor Rikki has enough savings in her special psy-ops piggy bank to transport us to Europe, diplomatically and medically."

He took a sip of tea. "When?"

She'd proceeded down to his belt. "Tonight." She began to devour his sensitive parts as the drug she'd placed in the teapot began its assault. The increased blood flow would be good for him.

• • •

Just after the sun called it quits for the day, Lalumière awoke. Pattie sat across from him in a gold chair.

"You are always putting things in my drinks."

"For your own good."

"I'll bet that's how your American husband died. Am I right?"

"You mean Deputy Chief of Mission Randy. Forget about him. You and I are king and queen. That's all that matters. While Versailles is being rebuilt for us, I think we should reside with my father. We will be safe from the CIA."

Before falling asleep from the drugged tea, he got out a few last words. "Yes. At Monaco Palace. Brilliant."

"Yes. It is."

Sylvain Lalumière struggled with his eyes. They closed and he pressed them back open. "Just one more question. How will you navigate us back to France?"

"I'll just take a look around to see which way the wind blows. Hey, how do you like that? I took that from L.A. Woman. An ancient Doors song."

"Doors? My son listened to a French group. *TÉLÉPHONE*, they were called. I preferred the French talking songs called … I can't remember. Here." He handed her his phone. "Contact your father. Ensure he will attend our upcoming formal coronation in Paris. And his friend, the pope. They must both be present."

"How about inviting the old French government? Those who would've died had our Eiffel Tower bomb been allowed to function."

"Yes. Allowed to function." He nodded for the final time. "That damned Crayle."

CHAPTER 8

With one more near-death experience behind them, Magus and Hekka Crayle continued east in the red Cobra, its two wide, white racing stripes pointing the way. Suspiciously silent in the village behind them, there now was a total absence of sirens. It was as if a carefully planned kidnap and torture interrupted by a steel-melting, flame-spewing military tank was insufficient to catch any prolonged attention of the Oktoberfest revelers or the laid-back locals.

Hekka pointed to a wooded hill on their right. "That's where a light plane went in. It lost power after takeoff, and hit there amongst the trees."

Crayle glanced left, checking over the lake for incoming.

"My father and I were right about here when it happened. We were lucky they missed us. He stopped and we ran up there."

"Could you save anyone?"

She shook her head.

He caught the motion in his peripheral vision, and pulled over.

A pair of fidgeting hands in her lap assured him he'd done the necessary thing.

She followed him in exiting the Cobra.

"C'mon." He led her up the hill about 100 feet to a patch of broken, charred trees. From this point on, he knew she would take the lead.

Hekka knelt. He joined beside her. Long black hair blew against him as she began a song. In the native, unwritten language of her Serrano ancestors.

After ten minutes of paying their respects, they continued toward her ranch. Death, especially tragic death, wound one's mind down to a numbed state. She didn't speak again until Crayle negotiated a quick right-left past a small wooden store.

"We'd come here, my mother and I, to shop for antiques. Usually while my father was over at the lumber yard stocking up for his next project."

The deaths she'd witnessed as a youngster on that hill precluded a smile. One that would have accompanied memories of times with her parents.

"Doctor Rorschach told me he was cautiously optimistic about your mother's recovery. When he releases her, it might be helpful to bring her to that store. Fond memories, especially with someone she loves, should help her."

She knew he was right. But the car that crashed into her mother in Helsinki erased her memories, a tragedy that never should have happened. If only her father had gone along. The strength that had gotten her through all those tough years on the ranch won out. She'd chosen to make the journey alone.

Those thoughts, the kind that linger to the point of mental nausea, were interrupted as Crayle drove past the exit to the little burg called Sugarloaf.

"I can almost hear Micmac and his band as we experienced them all those months ago."

"I can almost hear Phoebe's internal vibrations when she took her first look at him."

"Couldn't have been all that Bud Light, could it?"

"I believe she had both short term and longer term need."

"They seem to be happy enough. He gets to tinker about with tanks and depleted uranium liquids, and she's got …"

"Him."

Another couple of turns and a mile further, and the Crayle's pulled into the ranch's dirt driveway.

CHAPTER 9

Sylvain Lalumière, the ersatz King of France, stood up with a start. Being well over six feet tall, he banged his head on the curvature of the private jet's fuselage. He reseated himself and turned as if for some degree of comforting to the petite, dimpled woman sitting a couple of feet away.

"Where am I? I feel sick."

"As I promised, heading to La Belle France. You've had a nice sleep. Remember that CIA device where I dial how long for you to be out? It works to perfection. I'll file a report to the Science and Technology Directorate as soon as I get Wi-Fi service."

"You cannot file with them. You are rogue. They will track you and kill you."

"Actually, they'd kill us both. You know, I've needed love all my life. Why can't they just love me?"

"The CIA loves no-one. You killed one of their middle managers, Neil Wohlford."

"But they discovered that he was an Illuminé mole. Doesn't that make me a hero worthy of their love?"

"They kill people. They don't love them."

"I kill people, too. We're family."

"You have promised me that the killing is finished. Except for Magus Crayle."

Yes. Having dispatched Lalumière's son, Jean-Marc, off a rope bridge in St. Lucia, she had just one to go. "We agree completely." She wrapped her arms around his neck. "And I'll hold the collateral to a minimum. How's that?"

He blinked.

"Here. Sit up on the basket rim so I can get into our very large suitcase. Time to suit up."

"Why am I sitting in a hot air balloon basket in the middle of our Falcon 7X private jet?"

"I had promised you a flight from Saint Lucia to France in a balloon. Although I retrieved our lighter-than-air craft from the Krishnas, there just wasn't enough time. So I stowed the balloon aboard. Our ride in this basket is symbolic."

At this point, he knew it was fruitless to pursue further questioning. He glanced down at his clothes and saw the worn and soiled garments of his alter ego, Mitim. A touch of his face and he felt the beard that matched the outfit. And her in her nun's habit. The future did not appear bright.

Pattie interrupted his train of thought with, "Land ho!"

He twisted his head around to follow her gaze to the bulkhead-mounted television. The forward-facing fuselage camera showed a runway in sight. "Mitim again. Hmph. What has come of all those performances on the river boat? On the Rhône? You said I had acted my part as a modern version of the Man In The Iron Mask brilliantly. And here we are in a CIA jet, sitting in a hot-air balloon basket, prepared to land someplace that, I am assured, is not France."

"All we did was important, but it's a lot of water under the bridge."

"Like the one in Avignon. *Sur le pont …*"

"*Buzz!* Love your intelligence and your sex. But singing? You need to keep the day job."

"Louis XIX is my new day job."

"True, true, true."

"Wait a second. I thought you wanted me to be Emperor, like Napoléon, and you would be my Josephine."

"It doesn't matter now. With Jean-Marc dearly departed, the line of succession is you, then me."

Their conversation was interrupted by a landing that could have been more smooth. The basket toppled, tossing its contents onto the deck. In short order, though, they deplaned into a muggy day.

"You are correct, you know," he said sadly. "With him gone, emperor or king doesn't matter." He mopped his brow of the humidity. He would never see his son again. But his two daughters at school in Switzerland, perhaps.

The crew extracted the balloon, set it up, and placed a newly-drugged Lalumière into the basket. He awoke to the realization that he'd been transported inside a yellowish-tan building. A very old one.

"You've brought me to a suitable place, am I correct?"

"Of course. It's our last stop before our return to Versailles. And our thrones."

"Then, finally, I shall become a true leader of all France."

"When Versailles has been rebuilt for us. As you may recall, my little stunt with the bomb took it down to ground level."

"Surely my countrymen realize the magnitude of what is to happen. They will finish the reconstruction soon."

"Magnitude or not, they are still French. This may take a while."

"Waiting drives me crazy."

"Do you recall what I said?"

"You've said many things."

"I have one more to kill. Mr. Crayle."

"You can't leave me here."

"This place is special."

"It is just another island. It is not Versailles," he complained.

"The island of Sainte Marguerite is the last place they held the original Man In The Iron Mask, from whom you take your acronymic nickname. You've visited all the rest. Here, my Mitim, then king."

She'd left him incarcerated before.

He knew the fear. His pulse surged. "This place is abandoned! I will starve!"

"I've arranged for your food, drink, and satisfaction."

"We are married."

"Think of her as a consort … for the king."

He calmed just a bit. "How long will you be away?"

"One week. Approximately."

"You don't know where Magus Crayle is."

"Of course, I do. I'm a spy. Remember?"

"He is very good and very smart. I can't lose you. Forget him. Stay with me."

"No can do. If I don't get him, he'll get us. Look. Here's some backstory on him. He tested an IQ of 153 at age 13. Genius."

"*Formidable!*"

She spread lotion on his arms and legs. "There. That will help you stay moist until I return." She took his hand and pulled. "Follow me."

He struggled as she led him to bed.

"No," she admonished as he indicated amorous intent.

With care, she laid him down, his Sleep Number preset to 92, just as she had at the Château D'If not far to the west. She kissed him on the lips as he lost consciousness.

• • •

Pattie caught the next ferry across the bay to Cannes and then a cab to Nice. The airport had been re-stabilized and was soon to open to general aviation. Just ten months after the mini-nuclear blast at Marseille, she and her Dassault Falcon 7X departed for the long flight west.

Having observed how long it took the French to repair the major airport made the Versailles rebuild appear years in the offing. But that only achieved importance if she survived Magus Crayle.

CHAPTER 10

A distant 2,390 miles southeast of Sainte Marguerite Island, itself next to a large body of water, the ruined capital of Iran was just retiring for the night. In response to repeated and escalating violations of their nuclear weapons embargo, the new American president, Kimbel Stones, had proven himself the polar opposite of the previous do-nothing president by leveling all governmental structures and killing much of its governing body.

The one building that remained standing, 200 years old, now housed the remnants of government. Within, two men had garnered an enclosed basement room that had been, due to the absence of Islamic lucky numbers, swept for listening devices an arbitrary four times. A third man in attendance would journal and relay any orders from the country's leader.

The heavy oak doors had then been closed and sealed. A private force headed by a former U.S. special forces lieutenant—one whose violent actions against Iraqi civilians had earned him a dishonorable discharge—stood guard.

"Shall we converse in Farsi?"

"The walls speak Farsi. Another language."

"English is best."

"We are both fluent."

They each nodded affirmation.

"What is your interpretation of your title, Your Eminence?" queried the nuclear physicist known as Navid Mohammed.

"Ayatollah means Sign of God," said the older man. "It also means Miracle of God. I prefer the latter."

"As long as our people, the Shia, believe it, they will follow."

"Quite true. We could discourse forever, but we've already done so long enough. Time has come for the great event."

"Our ally is prepared. She will—"

"She? A woman? No, no, no, It must be a man. It is our role to avenge Allah, or, at least, to appear to do so. Women are to bear children and to provide our sexual satisfaction whenever we have the need or desire. The Qur'an supports me on this." He turned to his aide. "Bring a suitable one to my bed chambers. A virgin. She must be a virgin."

"Yes, Grand Ayatollah, Great Miracle of God. As you command."

"But the virgin is for later," said the cleric. "For now, let's discuss the future of our great country."

"It is simple. In spite of my inauspicious birth circumstance as a Saudi, I aspire to greatness. Perhaps not to the greatness that you have already achieved, but my own, and with my signature on it."

"Where all would say, this is the work of Navid Mohammed. *The* Navid Mohammed."

It pained the ayatollah some to apply salve to a lesser man's ego, but this particular lesser man could help make Iran great again. As the country had been as Persia. He produced a smile. One that indicated he knew of the other's worth.

"Thank you for your confidence in me, and your belief in me. I am humbled."

"You do understand, Navid, that I dream to rule the entire middle east. A nuclear capability, deliverable anywhere I choose, is a requirement, not a pipe dream."

"Then we shall travel forthwith to the special location of which I have spoken. It bears material relevance to your dream."

CHAPTER 11

The red Cobra wound its way east from all signs of civilization toward the more rural setting of Erwin Lake. When they pulled into the Poppi ranch, Crayle half-expected Hekka's brothers to have established a perimeter, given their Screaming Eagles military training. There existed no howitzers, machine gun emplacements, or spools of razor wire.

As they walked to the front door, he gave a glance at the waterfall her father had built for his wife, who, at the moment, was being cared for at the CIA's underground Quarry hospital.

For a moment, he recalled his first intimacy with Hekka. The night illuminated by a wolf moon. The tingly splashes of ice-cold water on their entwined bodies came to mind. Hekka's look told that she read his mind, all the way to the sordid details.

Without knocking, she preceded Crayle inside. Her two brothers didn't look up from the game. The Cowboys and the Redskins stood locked in a 21-21 tie in the fourth quarter. "Go Redskins," they shouted in unison.

Hekka reached up and ran her hand through Crayle's hair. "No scalping parties … if the Redskins win."

"Go Redskins!" shouted Crayle.

"Guys, put the game on hold for a second."

Their heads spun her way with a 'you gotta be crazy' look. After several seconds, the older one complied.

"After all this time, you haven't been formally introduced to my husband. So here goes. Brothers, this is Magus. Magus, the older one is called Reko, meaning watchful and vigilant." They shook hands. "The younger is Aatu, the noble wolf."

Reko added, "Our parents struggled with a name that combined Finnish with Serrano so much that they just gave us Finnish names. They work well in any case."

Crayle affirmed the brother's conclusion with a smile and a nod, then turned to Hekka who seemed to be in a hurry.

"Magus and I are headed on a little vacation. To Vegas. He has procured Top Secret passes for you to the Quarry where mom is being treated." She handed them a piece of paper. "Here are GPS coordinates and instructions for ingress-egress. You'll need to check in on her—she's still frightened and disoriented from her experience in Helsinki."

"Right after the game," said Aatu as he pressed the *Play* button.

• • •

The football game ended well and no scalp was taken. The Crayles said their goodbyes and stepped outside.

"One moment, Magus. Here, come with me."

She took him by the hand and led him around to the back of the house.

He should have thought of it.

Before he could punish himself, they came into sight of the corral and the horses. Her quarter horses. She didn't need to smile for him to know of her love for the beasts. The animals, fast and quick, obeyed her every command, verbal or physical.

"Come here, Precious," she called.

A mare responded immediately, trotting to where they stood.

"You, too, Pecker."

A stallion strode over, taking a place next to the other. He nuzzled her a couple of times to show his affection.

"Pecker?"

She shrugged, much like the French, and stroked the muzzles of both horses. Then, with a sigh, she took Crayle's hand, and the two retreated back to the car.

It seemed like old business when the Cobra headed north, then down the treacherous switchbacks of Highway 18 from the Big Bear plateau past the Quarry, that topside appeared like any other quarry. All of that changed if you knew the way in. They glanced over for a moment. Then back to the road.

Hekka switched on the XM-Sirius radio setup and cued up some Classic Rock. She knew what her man liked.

The long drive across the low desert valley below and then through a cluster of mountains took them at last to the California high desert town of Barstow. Crayle pumped gas at the truckers' favorite, the Flying J station, while Hekka ordered a couple of plates of food at the attached Denny's. An hour's drive across the hot and dry high desert brought them to the east-California village called Baker. Not just another place for truckers and travelers to refuel, it was famous for its 134-foot thermometer and its entry-way north into the world-famous Death Valley.

"That name sounds more suitable today to Big Bear Valley than the placid valley just to the north."

"In olden times, it caught out the settlers in their wagon trains. No water for the horses or livestock. Or the people. There's a place that is below sea level, but just the normal amount of death these days."

While Crayle replenished the supply of gasoline to the ever-thirsty Cobra, Hekka stepped into the Country Store to purchase several packets from the wide variety of beef jerky and a couple of lottery tickets. Waving them at him as she returned to the car, she indicated, "I do intend to get lucky on this vacation."

He nodded his assurance of that outcome, and they headed east on the long, boring Highway 15 toward California's border with Nevada. Toward the ultimate vacation and party city known to the world as Las Vegas.

CHAPTER 12

Small by stature, grand by power, the man stripped the workman clothes from his body and replaced them with his usual attire.

"There," said the man who'd handed the clothes to him. "You now look to be a proper ayatollah."

The Grand Ayatollah, one of a few with that lofty title, nodded to his body guard, who fired a bullet into the man's head.

"My people would recognize me if I were in servant's garb. Now, how do we enter into the bowels of this place?"

"I am sorry," said the bodyguard, pointing to the dead man. "He was our guide."

The only other element, other than the platform on which he stood, appeared to be a car. They entered and pushed the only button on the dashboard.

The car moved forward slowly, then attained maximum momentum as it descended a downward ramp.

"Oh! This is like Disneyland," shrieked the ayatollah. "Pirates of the Caribbean!"

The car pulled to a soft halt 130 feet down. Another platform and more guards. Vetted once again, they moved to a second car. This process repeated three times until they had dropped far below ground level.

"I know the answer, Uncle."

The ayatollah felt his own brilliance in hiring his nephew. Total familial trust, and Yousef was both intelligent and insightful. "And what question was that?"

"Each segment of the ride drops forty meters. Four drops: 160 meters. 520 feet American."

Fortunately for the nephew, there was no one left to shoot him.

"Why do you mention them, the Americans? They are the bane of Iran."

"To beat them, you must know them. You told me this as a child."

He would have responded had not his view through the iron-barred gate ahead not disturbed him.

Navid Mohammed represented a distraction as he put the finishing touches on his creation. He looked up to see the grand ayatollah stepping through the gate toward him, smiling from ear to ear.

"Navid, my son. I came at once." He turned to his bodyguard. "Stand at the gate, Yousef. See that we are not disturbed."

Wanting in his entirety to see why his uncle had gotten up at such an ungodly hour, Yousef obeyed.

The ayatollah moved to a two-inch thick table made of cut crystal with an elliptical pedestal at its center. Normally, the beauty of this magnificent piece of furniture would have dropped his jaw.

Navid stood aside, waving his arm at the centerpiece. "Behold. This is my latest creation."

The cleric felt a severe headache coming on. Perched on the support sat an English-style rugby ball. Not impressed at this early hour, he turned to summon Yousef.

"It's a bomb. A grand bomb for a grand ayatollah."

The cleric turned back, the headache displaced by disorientation. Then, he understood. "In the guise of the bomb brought here by that Chinese man several months ago. General Li."

"Yes, but this is my—our—very first nuclear weapon. What do you think?"

"Congratulations to Allah and to you, Navid! But we must test it. Yet, if we do it in our country, the Americans will know within milliseconds. And the Israelis milliseconds later. What do you suggest?"

"In all humility, I have developed the perfect plan. As you are singularly aware, my brother, Hamid, was assassinated in Monte Carlo last year. His mission—a personal one—to destroy the Frenchman."

"Yes. Lalumière required such destruction. Our intelligence service ascertained he was the man who detonated the Chinese weapon brought to our central Iran facility near Fasd. He'd worked in a French water company that had provided the tunnel and water to supply our covert nuclear project there. Your brother was killed before he could accomplish his mission."

"There is more. Hamid learned through our resources that this evil man was under the protection of the State of Monaco. And its prince."

"Why was I not informed of this new intelligence?"

"We had to be sure of his involvement, and, to do that, we had to identify the assassin of my brother."

The ayatollah's brow furrowed. "You have this?"

The smile gave Navid away. "Yes!"

"Take me through it, step-by-step. I must know every aspect before I act."

"Very well, Ayatollah. When Hamid and I washed up from Saudi onto Iranian shores, we were adopted. I have a half-cousin in the intelligence community. One related to my adoptive father serves in Nefaq—the MOIS Department of Discord. Disinformation. The other, on my adoptive mother's side, serves in the Quds Force of the Islamic Revolutionary Guard Corps. The IRGC. Foreign intelligence.

They have patched up their parental differences and work together quite well. The domestic security force, Basij, was not involved."

"They cause nothing but damage to our worldwide image."

"With due respect, Ayatollah, I've heard the Basij pray to Allah for guidance as to which hand to pleasure themselves by."

The men shared the humor.

The cleric knew why he liked Navid. He had couched the humor to perfection and caused himself a brief indulgence. A smile. "Tell me of the intelligence."

"Quds acquired surveillance footage at the time of Hamid's execution. They learned that a red-headed Monegasque prostitute last saw him alive in his Fairmont suite in Monte Carlo. Utilizing facial recognition algorithms, she was identified leaving the room next door."

Navid assured that the ayatollah had absorbed the intel, adding drama with a brief pause.

"Then the body, tossed from his own balcony, and discovered by a yachtsman and his wife, washed onto the rocks, below the same balcony. The authorities easily determined cause-of-death, a slit throat, but hushed it up due to the potential public relations nightmare. My Nefaq cousin put that together with U.S. Embassy intel—"

The ayatollah grew frustrated and angry. "Enough! Enough! Do you know who she is?"

"A woman who masquerades as a travel agent at the American Embassy in Paris, who researches her accommodations all over Europe, assassinated our assassin."

"I'm losing patience …"

"CIA."

"The CIA killed your brother."

"It gets better," Navid assured.

CHAPTER 13

The ayatollah had stepped into the secure executive bathroom not to relieve himself, but to congeal his thoughts. He had learned over his lifetime that the *I win, you lose* approach to problem solving tended to create more negatives than positives. The best solutions had everyone winning, though he suspected Navid's motives to be purely personal. He returned.

The younger man could contain his secrets no longer. "As I spoke earlier, this identified woman is CIA. The teaser is this. The 'it gets better' I indicated before is as follows. She's the descendant of the infamous Dutch spy, Mata Hari."

"The one who dressed and danced as one of our kind? That's your bombshell?"

"No. This is my bombshell. She's the daughter of the Prince of Monaco."

The ayatollah sucked in his breath. He brought his hand up so quickly that Navid ducked back. In vain. The fingers stopped at the cleric's chin as he calmed, and considered.

"Oh, I see. So the prince harbored this Lalumière character at the palace due to a connection to his daughter. When your brother, Hamid, travelled there to kill him, it was the prince's daughter who did the deed for which you require revenge. This is most difficult to believe … and to process."

"Exactly. We also determined that Lalumière is of the secret society, Illuminé."

"And the rest."

"And this connective tissue infers that the prince is also Illuminé. Perhaps it's chieftain?"

"That, my young friend, is intelligence."

"Q.E.D."

"What?"

"*Quod Erat Demonstrandi*. Latin for *that which was to be proven*."

"Your extensive education is showing. Being Muslim, Latin was not my most favored discipline."

Navid's eyes glistened, demonstrating his pride. That aside, having the bomb was not sufficient. It had to be demonstrated.

"Can we test our atomic bomb here in Iran, Ayatollah? Or, should I ask, how deep must we go for such a test to be undetected by our enemies?"

"The Americans and their allies have sensing equipment in India, Turkey, Iraq, and Saudi. Plus several amongst the Indian Ocean islands. We can't dig deep enough."

"And the Emirates?"

"No. The Emirates have severe wealth going on. They wouldn't jeopardize that for anything."

"Surely not for the Americans, but what about for Allah?"

"They are Sunni."

"Their Arab affiliates murder innocents every day."

"Damn the Arabs! They are God's mistake."

"God doesn't make mistakes, Your Eminence."

"I appreciate your wisdom, for a young man. We have supported the Arab terror organizations for many years, and with great wealth at the expense of our people."

"When Arabs fight Israelis, or when Arabs fight Arabs, they have no energy remaining to fight Shia. Our new bomb ends that dynamic. Once we prove to the world our capability, the Arabs will leave us alone. At that point, our wealth shall remain here."

"Your wisdom is exceptional. When you've exploded this device of Allah overseas, you shall return as a hero. You will build more bombs for our arsenal, as well as for the guarantee of a peaceful future that they will presage."

Navid produced a brief bow. "It shall be my honor, Your Eminence."

"Of course. So, back to our dilemma. Where to test?"

"The bomb you see before you is the answer. The ultimate answer. We test it in Monaco. If it works as designed—and the timing is perfect—we rid ourselves of my brother's assassin. In addition, we remove the Illuminé leader whose minion Lalumière betrayed us by a remote detonation of the Chinese nuclear device at the Fasd site. And we eliminate future interference in our—I mean, *your*—goals for domination of the Middle East. It will be one step closer to the goal line."

"I shall provide you my answer within two seconds. Yes!"

CHAPTER 14

Having expensive cars pull into the port cochère was no big deal in Las Vegas. Still, onlookers always checked out the occupants for celebrities, just in case they might spot one. The Crayle's red Cobra, with its two wide white racing stripes, received more scrutiny than most. They pulled into the valet parking lane, and the driver turned to his passenger with a serious smile.

She'd seen the giant Les Paul model guitar above as they'd approached and, given her staid and restrained background, was more than a little impressed with the ostentatious entry.

"We're staying here … at the Hard Rock Hotel?"

"You bet."

The valet's smile matched Crayle's. She glanced up from the high performance tires. "Michelin Sports all the way around," observed the platinum blonde. "I promise to be gentle with it."

He handed her a folded $100 bill, numbers up. "Yes, be gentle."

He pulled their luggage from the tiny trunk which amounted to two boogie-bags and a couple of umbrellas. Inside, he registered as Mr. and Mrs. Thomson. "Without the P," he advised the clerk.

Hekka was only half-surprised by the name change. After eleven months, she'd become accustomed to the spy game intruding into their lives, even on vacation.

They arrived in their Rock Star Suite minutes later and while Crayle stuffed the bags under the bed, Hekka plopped into a funky Swedish-modern red chair.

"They're in all the rooms," Crayle said, wishing he hadn't.

She swung the chair his way. "*All* the rooms?"

He figured the best non-response was a shrug.

"Aside from the TV blaring our favorite classic rock songs," she shouted, "I feel immediately at peace, for a change."

"The TV makes it nigh impossible for anyone to eavesdrop."

"Like when we're on that huge bed making babies?"

"I caught that back at the Oktoberfest building. Congratulations to us. I doubt we'll be making more babies for a couple of months."

"Oh. Did the government shorten the gestation period?"

He laughed. "I'm relaxed, too."

"I'm betting that the entire world is relaxed without us and our friends running around causing mayhem."

"I feel a declaration coming on. The world is now at peace at least until our vacation is over. One week, right?"

"If Chin's people don't come and grab us. You still owe him the Redrock Strategy."

"I can work on that down by the pool. Or one of the several pools. The bad news is that I'll have to deliver it in person. Wanna come?"

"First, I'm not letting you out of my sight." She turned sideways and pulled him to her by his belt. She pried the buckle loose and finished her thought. "Second? Yes, I wanna come."

An hour later, they sat on two lounge chairs at the Nirvana pool. It resembled a tropical paradise with palm trees and foliage obscuring an upper secluded area behind them. He pecked at a tablet computer. Its case allowed it to fold in an upright position with a small keyboard in front.

"Dear Chin Yao-wu," Crayle began.

"Emperor Chin sounds better. Try that."

"Check the situation over there, would you? I'll need to capture the immediacy of his circumstance in this cover letter."

Hekka checked her Smartphone. "Whoa, check this out. All the focus is on the rebuild of Beijing except for the old government's palatial digs. I'm guessing that the oppression embodied in the Workers of the World Unite mantra doesn't extend to the elitist leaders."

"That's a good take on that setup."

"It seems, all taken into account, that things are progressing smoothly in the first months of Chin's reign."

"I'm not seeing any strikes by the masses or anything like that. It says that Chin's massive successes in the stock market have led to economic policies that already are turning the country around."

"People tend not to strike or riot when there's money in the bank. Anything about the southern islands the communists were contesting with the Vietnamese?"

"Apparently, Chin and his crew have dialed that back. Peace has broken out in the Far East."

"Then we can truly relax. Finally."

"C'mon. Let's jump into one of those cabanas."

"Can we just jump in?"

"It's easy. You just look like you know what you're doing. Exude confidence."

Inside, they found a couch, a refrigerator, and a flat-screen TV. Crayle pulled a couple of Heinekens from the fridge.

"When Lenny and I escaped Big Bear, I drove the Cobra full throttle down the hill. The original Triangle Jaw he dubbed TJ and his crew gave chase with their arsenal of Hemi-powered black Chargers, but we made it."

"How'd Lenny like the ride?"

"We clung to the edge of a narrow road tacked onto the side of a very steep set of mountains. White knuckles for him for thirty or so miles."

"I would've thought he'd throw in the towel after that."

"I didn't know 'til much later that his involvement was all about his dad."

"Yes. Murdered by the same TJ that chased you. Over a thumb drive."

"That drive contained all the plans I had created as Master Strategist For The Overthrow Of Governments."

"Your second incarnation."

"It's tough having me times three. As distinct personalities, probably doable. With the Rorschach memory restores, they collide."

"Where'd the doctor get all those memories in the first place?"

"I must've been inside some manner of experimental program for quite awhile. Years, even."

"Does the CIA grasp the concept of boundaries? Of what is permitted by moral standards?"

"That, dear Hekka, is the great unanswered question. Morality versus the public well-being."

"Will it ever be answered?"

"Don't know. 'Til it is, we do what we gotta do."

"No, no. We did what we gotta did."

"No wiggle room?"

She extracted her Bowie from its sheath and thumbed the blade sideways.

"None."

A young man entered, ostensibly to take drink orders.

"Sir? Ma'am? You'll have to pay for this cabana in order to …"

He noticed the knife. Then, Crayle cleared his throat.

Reluctantly, he glanced from the threatening ten inches of steel to the hundred dollar bill waving in the air.

"Yes, Sir," he said. "I'll see that our records showing Mr. and Mrs. Smith as having reserved this cabana are updated right away."

He backed out.

"Mr. and Mrs. Smith," said Crayle. "Weren't they spies?"

CHAPTER 15

It had been a while since he'd been to Las Vegas. Sitting out by the pool at the Hard Rock under clear skies with the sun beating down worked wonders with a messed up attitude. Add a well-prepared Mai Tai or two, and a beautiful woman, his wife, applying layers of Hawaiian Tropic oil to his body, and the world gravitated from mayhem and discord to peace and harmony in short order.

As if on cue, a line of Hawaiian Tropic models, at the hotel for the annual pageant, paraded by. They strutted their stuff in bikinis for the first time since the sponsor dropped that aspect of the contest in Australia, 2012.

"For the record. I'm not noticing," Crayle said with a lame attempt to hide a grin. "I am sure, though, that they are all old and fat."

"Don't be afraid to say what you think." Hekka's own lame attempt came at surveying the area with no apparent success. "Wouldn't you know? I left my knife up in the room when we showered for lunch. If you have more to say, would you please run upstairs and fetch it? It's already sharp. Now, where were we?"

Crayle craned his head back, peering up as if through the blue atmosphere to a higher place. "I could use a little help about now." No response from above. From elsewhere.

At first, he ignored his phone, placed on a nearby table due to the incapacity of his Speedo swim briefs. The buzz of its incessant vibrations called to mind spending fifteen to twenty minutes in the company of one Lenny Lipschitz. Sometimes just ten. And like Lenny, the irritation would refuse to go away until he dealt with it.

He glanced over to Hekka, who met his eyes with her unique, penetrating stare.

"Hello," he said in annoyed fashion, anticipating as well as hoping for a wrong number. The voice on the other end put him on alert.

"Oh. Chin. I didn't expect a call this soon."

He wrapped his towel around the microphone end of the phone to suppress the sounds of people having fun. He pressed his lips close to prevent eavesdropping.

"Yes. I'm making excellent progress with the new strategy. I should have substance—the problem attributes, the option selection criteria, and the external solution constraints for the generation of successful alternatives—oh ..." He glanced at Hekka. "... next week."

The new Chinese emperor had acclimated to his new lofty position, and didn't feel that speaking with his version of a Sun Tzu/ Lao Tzu combination as would equals was appropriate. "Mr. Crayle. There are already rumblings with respect to democracy and, rather than simply crush the perpetrators as did my communist predecessors and emperor namesake, I wish to promise the people excellence in governance the likes of which has not been seen. No bothersome, time-consuming elections replete with easily discernable lies and other deceptions to take the mind of the people away from what is important. And a BMW or such in every garage. An adequate strategy will not only allow me to promise, but also to accomplish exactly that."

"I agree. Those are my marching orders. I see no reason why you cannot promise and deliver to that promise within a three-year period."

"So, prosperity, harmony, and balance are attainable to the extent that your systems methodological analysis has brought you thus far. Excellent. I have pressing events to care for between now and next week, anyway. How about next Thursday?"

Exactly what Crayle had feared. A deadline. Soon.

"You wish me to send the Redrock Strategy to you next Thursday?"

"Oh, no, Mr. Crayle. I expect you to present it in person next Thursday. Here."

"Of course. Allowing your enemies even the slightest access to a transmission of the document would be unacceptable." And so would showing up with it not completed, he thought to himself. "And I should be able to answer any questions you may have when we meet. Just to let you know, I'll need to focus heavily on this to get it done. I'll be incommunicado until I see you at your Hong Kong palace."

He winked at Hekka as he waited a second for pushback. "Alright. Next Thursday then."

Chin clicked off.

Crayle stood. "Here, Hekka. Keep my lounge chair warm. It seems I need to run upstairs for my work documents."

"Keep your chair warm?"

"We're going to Hong Kong. Next week."

She started to object.

"You'll have your week's worth of vacation in Vegas as I promised. Then it's back to work."

As he slipped on his robe and headed off toward the hotel entrance, her mood shifted from bright to dark. "I can tell I'm personally going to have to see to the closure of these foreign involvements. It is clear that quality time with Mr. Crayle will evade me until I do."

• • •

The Hawaiian Tropic contestants made another round of the Hard Rock's pool area.

"Yes," Hekka said. "Yes, ladies. Young, nubile … and not pregnant." She looked down at her protruding belly, then back. "Your time will come."

Crayle hadn't taken thirty steps toward the hotel before his phone rang again. He checked caller ID this time. FOREIGN CALLER it said. He continued on as he took the call.

"Chin? Again? It's still not quite ready."

"Since we will be out of communication until next Thursday, per your request, I need to feed you some of your precious intel."

"What do you have?"

"The new airport is on Lantau Island, Mr. Crayle. The old, Kai Tak, is now the cruise ship terminal. A small passage of time, and what was there is here, and what was here is there."

"That sounds Chinese inscrutable to me. But, I get your point. With the post-explosion reconstruction going on in Beijing, the majority of new economic activity has moved there, but the seat of government remains at your palace in Hong Kong. Government: Hong Kong. Economic action: Beijing."

"The point is this. The people of my country do not care in the least who is in charge. It's an ages-old Chinese trait. Give the masses the rules, and they're fine."

"You're saying they are not communists, democrats, capitalists, or even royalists, but are apolitical in the Western sense."

"Precisely. A place to reside, food to eat. And manipulating their children to the best schools to guarantee their economic future, and the ability to see to their parents latter years. Oh, excuse me one second."

Due to the excellent connection and the quality of modern Smartphones, Crayle could hear both sides of the conversation in Chin's chambers. He stopped just before entering the Hard Rock Hotel, where the sounds of Rock 'n' Roll, at volume, would terminate his ability to converse.

"Li, I am issuing a new directive. My six daughters, who guard the communist Standing Committee that we've imprisoned at hard labor in Hainan, inform me that they have nearly completed the creation of my terra cotta warriors. Therefore, I direct you to transport them here. Since my Caterpillar tractors have already been delivered to Beijing for reconstruction, your huge transport plane should be perfect for the task. It would be comforting if you lead this operation yourself. None of the warriors are to be harmed in transit. Do you have any questions?"

"This is good news," Li responded. "Very good news. I shall see to the warriors, see that the Standing Committee is sealed below ground in their work cavern, and return the daughters to your palace. When this operation is complete, I will attend to the nuclear bombing of Hainan, which will then be blamed on the Vietnamese, as we've planned."

"I almost forgot. Yes. Ensure that all of our attack forces are at the highest state of readiness along the border. Following the Vietnam attack ruse, they must be prepared to invade. First the north to take back what the Tang Dynasty lost, then the south. We'll need the warm water beaches to replace those lost on Hainan. Agreed?"

"Yes, Emperor Chin. My Lightning Strike forces are poised to make Desert Storm appear to have been a much protracted engagement. Soon, Chinese will replace English as the most sought after language in the Vietnamese schools."

"Well put. Please now. Go. And report our successes as they occur."

"Perhaps we will toast with your best Scotch."

Crayle heard China's top general depart the room.

"Are you still there, Mr. Crayle?"

"I am. And I heard your conversation with Li, as I'm sure you intended."

"In your role, you need to know everything. Once we have Vietnam, there are more fish to fry, as you would say."

"I have anticipated those moves in the Redrock Strategy. I am certain you will be impressed."

"I've grown used to being impressed with your work. I will see you soon."

Chin rang off. Crayle caught movement to his right. Hekka, exiting the hotel and bearing his work books, looked fabulous. Her bikini seemed to be at odds with the slight paunch forming at her midriff.

Within three minutes, they'd situated themselves back inside the cabana.

She placed the spiral-bound binders on his lap, then moved up for a kiss. "There, author Crayle. You have been given your first deadline. Perfect experience for when you pen those spy novels you spoke of. As for me, I'm going for a swim." She turned on her heel and headed to the pool.

"That little guy in your belly needs to get used to the water. Micmac will want to prep him for the SEALs."

"*She* … is going to have nothing to do with violence," Hekka threw over her shoulder.

"Our child is getting a toy Bowie knife for his or her first birthday."

Unaccustomed to the vagaries and displays of the Anglo-Saxon race, Hekka turned, held up her hand, and with the other, pressed all fingers down … but one.

"Love you, too," Crayle said as he chuckled.

CHAPTER 16

Hainan Island, just offshore of the south coast of mainland China, was a special place. A good sized territory, it sported beach resorts such as the four-mile white stretch of sand at Yalong Bay on its southern tip, along with a non-combative population that suited those in power.

The terra cotta mine workers, consisting of the seven man Communist Party Politburo Standing Committee, stepped out of the mines into welcome sunshine. As was the custom with them, their leader and former party chairman, Po, spoke first.

"I believe we so-called Chicoms can escape from Hainan across the narrow straight at Haikou to the mainland. We next continue north to hide and gather resources at Guilin."

Their work in the Terra Cotta mines complete, the question for the remaining former Chicom leaders was what manner of termination would befall them. Certainly, the warriors had to be transported to Hong Kong, positioned to be buried along with Chin when he'd observed his final sunset. The components would be assembled by experts, and then closely guarded. Or so they believed.

"These are for Chin's grave. Just as the first Emperor Ch'in ordered in the Second Century BC."

"What of *our* graves, Po? We are nearly done here. When we finish this new set of Terra Cotta Warriors for him, we become disposable."

"I vote for a work slow down," said Premier Wong.

"That is good. He needs us for this. If he kills us all—no warriors will be transported to guard his tomb. If he only kills a few—as an example—it slows everything down."

"He is neither old nor feeble. He can wait us out on that one."

"Escape seems to be our only alternative. We have been in this place since the Beijing bombing. Wei, you are from this area of our country, what is our best option?"

"We require a means of killing the Chin daughters who stand guard."

"We can lure them into the mines. Then, seal them in."

"Right after we—"

"Wo! We will not harm them. I have thought this through. Since we have spent our off hours at this facility's library, I have discovered the ethnic makeup of Hainan Island. And the mainland north of here."

"I have seen the indigenous peoples through the fencing. Bright colored clothing and head gear. Dressed as them, we would stand out."

"Precisely," said Po. "Hiding in plain sight."

"Still, taking down the daughters would prove fatal. Despite their youth, they have all mastered at least one deadly martial art."

"That is a critical observation. We all survived and prospered with our wits and our words. Jackie Chan we are not."

"I believe that Jackie still resides on the south side of Hong Kong Island. Perhaps Yu should give him a call?"

The men shared a brief chuckle. They all knew that Chin had made his fortune in the world of the capitalists, not communists like themselves. In his case, opportunity had proven the trump card.

CHAPTER 17

It is clear, Chairman Po, that General Li is responsible for our common predicament."

"When we ruled from Beijing before its bombing, he pressed us repeatedly for a mission to the Uighur sanctuary province. Not long after the trip, we witnessed the nuclear explosion estimated at five megatons in the Xinjiang capital city, Ürümqi."

"Yes. He had previously reported to us that something serious was afoot, and it was he who surmised that the Muslims had acquired an unstable nuclear device from the Iranians."

"Given the blast that had previously occurred in central Iran, all of the world bought into that conclusion."

"We have it on record that both he and Chin visited Beijing the day we suffered a similar explosion. In the old bomb shelter tunnels of the Underground City. At one blow, he eliminated most of our communist leadership, and pointed his finger at the Uighurs."

"I hate to admit it, but his strategy was brilliant."

"You must not use that word. The philosophy of communism does not allow brilliance from other than the power elite. Us."

"When we capture Li and his puppeteer, Chin, we shall force them to divulge which of them devised the plan. That individual shall suffer most before he dies."

"I have studied both men in depth. I cannot reconcile what has befallen us to either of their minds. I am led to suspect a third party."

Before the men could experience further deep though on the subject, they heard a roar approaching from the north.

Their heads swung skyward.

Mouths dropped in disbelief. Perhaps a hundred yards away, a giant tubular square sat suspended in the air by huge rotors at each corner.

Because the dryness of a prolonged drought had turned the brush and foliage of the island to fire tinder, Li's flame-spewing drone, on trials under the control of Gao Bo-da, encircled them with a ring of fire.

Sounding like an ancient god, a speaker offered them a lift out as swirling winds danced twenty foot flames about them.

In spite of the panic and fear, they recognized Li's voice.

He promised that, if they agreed to serve Chin's need in transporting the warriors north, they would be set free. After that job was complete, they would be offered administrative positions, but with the same juicy perks of government-funded gambling, fat bellies, plus booze, drugs, and ladies. Before they could reminisce with their individual versions of the juicy perks, the reality sank in.

One: if they tried to escape, the unheavenly device above would turn them to cinders.

Two: they had no other choice than to comply.

The members of the Standing Committee looked at each other, then nodded.

Po glanced up at the drone. "We will do as Chin requires."

As the drone retreated a distance, its fanning of the flames ceased and they soon died down. The Standing Committee trudged back into the mine.

Only one of its number saw through the Chin promise. Po knew that, once the job completed, they would all be put to death. Chin's false sense of security could be turned to advantage. He, Po, had a Plan B.

CHAPTER 18

Mick Mackay, the only one watching the muted television, read the subtitles as the French newscaster blathered on.

"Looks like they're upset about losing Versailles. The government in exile is promising to bring in a restoration team from the States, since we seem to be restoring stuff all the time."

Hearing no response, he continued. "I mean, what've we and our team done? Staged an assault on a château in the eastern part of their country, blown up their second largest city in the south, nearly blown up Paris, and—oh—the Monaco assault doesn't count, technically, not being part of France. So that's it. If they want to bitch, we should go back and ..."

Micmac felt—before he noticed—the glare. Three sets of eyes. Searing eyes. "Hey, lighten up. Lenny's with Alona back in Amsterdam still trying to fence our stones, and someone has to take over."

"Lenny wouldn't have touched that line," Phoebe admonished. "You know anything about diamonds? Maybe we could arrange a swap."

"Ouch. Of course, you would have the P.I. here instead of me."

She stepped up her glare a notch. “My statement was rhetorical.”

“I’m not too sure Alona would consider messing around. Um, maybe.” His grin wasn’t returned.

“Trust a sailor to start a hole, and then scrounge for a bigger shovel.”

“I meant … I … crap.” Micmac clammed up.

“Changing the subject, I just know Jack wants us to be involved again.”

“Not on my watch.”

“This just sitting around when there’s serious work to be done sucks. I’ve never had a challenge this tough.”

“I’ve checked it out. Easy as falling off a bridge.”

“Terrific,” Phoebe exclaimed. “We have someone with experience,” she added, referring to their recent experience in St. Lucia, when Pattie Norbrunn literally threw Micmac from a hundred-foot-high rope bridge into the soup below a waterfall. “I need to calm my nerves here. I’m going to go clean my weapon.”

“We don’t have a bidet.”

“I’ll ignore that. So where’s Lenny … and our diamonds?”

“Y’know, you’re right. He should’ve returned by now. Bad pennies do that, I hear.”

“It bothers me when he’s around, and it bothers me even more when he’s not. Where is …”

• • •

“… that little twerp?” Alona checked each room in their Amsterdam walk-up flat to no avail. She checked next door with the pretty blonde tactically positioned in her window seat, brushing her hair, and arranging her blunt-cut bangs. Sharing space with the building’s hookers, Alona had become friends with several. It wasn’t a stretch for an attorney who’d defended a few back in San Bernardino, California. Before she’d moved *up the hill*, as the locals said, to Big Bear Valley. As she turned to traipse back to her apartment, she spotted Lenny waltzing by the outside window, blowing a kiss to the blonde.

By the time he reached the front door, she held it open for him.

He glanced back at the blonde. Then at Alona. "It's nothing. She reminds me of my sister, that's all." Had he not sounded and appeared like a seven-year-old caught with his hand in the cookie jar, he might have gotten away with it.

"You don't have a sister."

"But if I did …"

She motioned him in the door, latched onto his arm, and led him into their temporary abode. Pointing at their bedroom, she said, "Sex. Now."

"Don't you want to hear about our diamonds?"

"Turn me on. Tell me while you're getting undressed."

He began to disrobe. "You should be proud. I've got a probable for our one-pound bag of D flawless, one carat stones."

"How much?"

Having beaten him getting naked, she stood, hands on hips, anticipating his usual malarkey.

"Would you believe $12,240,000 U.S.?"

"Divided by …"

"Divided by the three, that's $4,080,000 per couple."

Pushing her lips to one side, she glanced up at the ceiling and re-did the math. "$2,040,000 each."

"What each. You're stuck with me. Remember?"

"And I've still got Jack Sommers' Black Card for my wardrobe needs. Ummm, feelin' good. You're gonna remember this one."

Before any salacious activity could take place, Alona's phone rang.

"Hi, it's Phoebe. I just noticed you'd called. Thought I'd toss one back your way."

"Undress slower," Alona whispered in Lenny's direction, then stepped into the living room.

"So. What's up?"

"I just needed someone to talk to. Nothing serious."

"I can hear the need in your voice. Go."

"It's Lenny. It's not like he goes around whining all the time, but …"

In the background, Phoebe could hear a door open and someone walk across the room. Then, "Whine. Whine. Whine." She heard a door close.

"What's that all about?"

"He's decided that informing me, often, about his feelings on this or that just puts me into auto-tune-out mode. That perhaps I don't appreciate the gravity of what he's complaining about at any given time."

A door opened again. Again, the pacing across the floor. "Whine … whine … whine." Another door closure.

"That was him?"

"Uh, huh. Since I'm not getting the drift of his misery, he now just uses the word whine."

"Oh. That can't possibly be annoying. I'll be right over."

"To Amsterdam?" Two seconds later, Alona got the implication of support. "Phoebe, I don't need someone to commiserate with. Really."

"Commiserate? I'm bringing my Glock."

"It's okay. I …"

"Whine …whine … whine."

"How fast can you get here?"

As if there wasn't enough happening, Lenny's Smartphone rang. The naked P.I. ran back into the living room and answered. Ten seconds later, he produced a monotone from beneath a blank look. "It's Magus. Saddle up. We're going to Hong Kong."

CHAPTER 19

That the Hong Kong customs officials allowed the Crayle team, consisting of himself, Jack, Hekka, Micmac, Phoebe, Alona, and Flori, to enter the Special Administrative Region confirmed the reach of U.S. President Kimbel Stones. That they also let in Lenny Lipschitz went beyond.

The excursion in from the Hong Kong International Airport on Chek Lap Kok Island lasted even longer thanks to Lenny's constant observations as to how the inhabitants viewed through the windows of the bus did things wrong.

Many on the public shuttle spoke English and appeared to be harboring crouching tigers and homicidal dragons to eliminate the obnoxious foreigner before he could cause real damage. The team's welcome had not been enhanced when he scratched his side, causing his sidearm to fall to the floor.

"*Ni hao,*" said Lenny with a sheepish smile as he returned it to its proper confines. Hello, indeed.

In less than an hour, they reached the North Point district of Hong Kong, and their operational headquarters, the Harbour Grand Hotel, without further incident. Lenny falling asleep was credited.

Once installed, two-by-two into their rooms, they caught the upper floor elevators to the 41st floor club, *Le 188*.

While the incredible view from the horseshoe-shaped, glass periphery was inviting, they gathered on the less distractive couches and chairs of the rectangular inner terrace. Their conversation took a break each time an airliner flew over—given the open-air ceiling structure.

Jack provided the sitrep. "Okay, we're here under the beneficence of Emperor Chin. Magus pulled strings for us since Chin needs him. We're officially here as tourists. I'm sure you all checked that box on your immigration forms according to my instructions. Right, Lenny?"

"I sure did, boss. So, if Magus needs a rescue up at the Chin palace, we just continue on with our Suzy Wongs just like tourists."

"No Suzy Floozy for you, my fantasizing twerp," said Alona as she twisted his ear.

"Ow. How am I supposed to hear what Jack has to say?"

"Shush, you two. Or I'll use you for decoys," said Jack. "We all walked through customs wearing concealed weapons. That should tell you something."

Following Micmac's lead, they each activated motorized, hand-held fans, not so much for the air flow as for the noise to defeat curious patrons or listening devices for which Hong Kong was famous.

"I can't hear. Can you speak up, boss?"

Jack pointed at Crayle, who'd pressed his earflap closed, allowing excellent hearing under adverse noise conditions.

"Oh. Yeah." Lenny followed suit, as did the others.

"We're taking the tube—the MTR it's called—into town, then up to the Victoria Peak viewing platform. We'll use that to assure that there are no tails. It's only a short hop from there over to Chin's palace. First, I need to know that you two, Lenny and Phoebe, will have each other's backs in a throw down."

"Only if she's naked and bends over."

Crayle arrested an initial move by Micmac. "Lenny's good. Phoebe?"

"Yeah. If he's gonna get done, it's gonna be me."

Crayle took a long, soothing breath. It had already been a long day.

"We are going to get a nice meal, now, and rest from the long flight, although those lie-flat seats were just shy of miraculous."

"Yeah, boss. Push a button, turn up the TV, and off to snooze land."

"Good thing the flight attendant quieted that sucker down before the other passengers could form an attack group." Phoebe winked at Crayle.

"Hey, it was Daffy Duck. What wasn't to like? Some ethnicities …" He dragged out the word. "… just don't have a sense of humor."

"Alright, back on track. Get a good night's sleep. We rendezvous at 8 A.M. in the café for breakfast, MTR, tram trip up the hill, and then Hekka and I will head in. We'll need the rest of you close by, and armed, in case Li tries something."

"I'm in," said Lenny. "Let's go get some vittles and meet back here for the 9 P.M. show. With the buildings all lit up, and the tall Kowloon one with *WOOF! WOOF!* text messages running up and down, and the laser show."

Crayle remembered the show. Ling had brought him to *Le 188* when he'd been in Hong Kong to develop Chin's original strategic plan, the Blackstone Strategy, a few years before. "Okay. Food. Show. Sleep."

They exited through the only point of ingress or egress and returned in an hour. The show, with green lasers emanating from the north bank of Victoria Harbour, proved spectacular as was the 'texting' Lenny referred to from the 100-plus-story International Commerce Building in Kowloon. Hong Kong under night lights was the spectacle residents and visitors alike expected each night. They were always awe-struck, regardless.

CHAPTER 20

Eight thousand life-size terra cotta warriors do not all fit in a gigantic-by-nature C-5 Galaxy air transport. Guarded and directed by several of Chin's daughters, the Chinese Communist Party elite, its Standing Committee members, had utilized three fork lifts and several hours to load the plane. They flew with it to an abandoned airport under the command of General Li's special forces in Hong Kong's New Territories.

There, the pilot backed the aircraft to a hangar just larger than Chin's target location in Xian, and unloaded each batch. Consistent on every flight, daughters ushered the seven aft to sit in the tail on quite uncomfortable cushions.

Guards fifty feet away armed with AK-47s kept an eye on them while sharing war stories. Add the roar of the four jet engines, and the Committee enjoyed relative privacy.

Wong, in effect second-in-command to the chairman, spoke in a somber tone to his comrades. "This is the final trip. We have brought all of the warriors. Chin will be satisfied. I'm hoping he does not send us back to Hainan to while away before we succumb to boredom."

Chairman Po voiced his perspective. "Chin will have the warriors for his afterlife. I'm afraid he will no longer have any need for us."

A hush fell.

Except for their heartbeats.

Wong broke the silence.

"His hero, Ch'in Xihuangdi, was said to be most ruthless. He would win a war with an opposing nation, then execute their armies. In very cold blood."

"I'm afraid we are our own worst enemies," Po observed. "That is the same manner in which we have dealt with enemies of the People's Republic. Especially our own citizens. A bullet and a bill."

He referred to the practice of shooting captured dissidents, firing a bullet into their brains, and then billing their relatives for the cost of the bullet.

"I mentioned, if you recall, while we labored in the mine that I had a plan."

"Chairman Po. Now is a good time to reveal that plan."

Po smiled. "We shall do as the Americans say. We shall make lemons into lemonade."

"How so?"

"Since time is of essence, I shall be succinct. Wu. You are experienced at the graduate level in electronics. Zhang. You are experienced in all manners of the utility of light. The two of you will form Team One with Wong as your leader. Cheng and Yu will support Team Two leader, Wei.

"Wong and Wei, you shall support your teams as their spotters, supplying GPS coordinates of our targets. In addition, you are to observe the effectiveness of our assault and feed that information back to each of the teams and to myself via our secure communication system. In summary, there are two teams of three, plus myself as supreme leader."

Po anticipated the questions that followed.

"How do we escape from our captors? They are heavily armed."

"And where do we go if we do get free. And how do we get there?"

"And what do we do when we are finished?"

A confident Po read them in. "If you will look behind you, you will see that the guards are here no longer."

"They must be outside, ready to shoot us if we try to escape," proffered the intelligent one, Wei.

"Ah, not so," said Po in a soothing voice. "Money has changed hands and agreements reached. I would not depart if I thought otherwise."

The rest exchanged glances. They knew Po to be a straight up guy. And, they had little choice.

"Follow me," Po said. He didn't bother to mention that the money exchange and deals made had General Li's mark all over them.

• • •

Once outside the hangar building, a driver in a black suit and balaclava drove them from the airfield to a safe house east of Kowloon City. There, they met people they had never expected to meet in their lifetimes. The premier spies of the old China. Their China.

For the next several hours, during which their escape had still gone undetected, specialists provisioned and trained them with weapons. Pistols, short versions of AK-47 automatic rifles, and the rest.

"That all of our weapons are silenced indicates a surprise attack," Wei observed.

Po nodded in the affirmative, and continued. "Whether there will be one or several attacks will be revealed to you at the last possible moment."

"What if something should happen to you, Po?"

"Hope that it doesn't. You should know about such practices by now. For security purposes. It is critical, since there are just seven of us, that we all survive. These loyal members of the spy service have provided plans that, when enacted to the minutest detail, will yield that degree of success."

"And when we are finished with the usurper Chin?"

Po produced an all-knowing smile. He had prepared and honed his pep talk over the several flights from Hainan. He deployed it as one would a weapon. "We shall return to our proper places. To the very summit of the land of our birth. We shall return to Beijing and begin anew. Gentlemen, we shall stage a renaissance that Chin could only promise, but never deliver."

The men attempted to check each others reaction before adding their own.

"Now, if there are no further questions, it is time for myself and Team One to board our boat. We shall lay siege to Hong Kong Island. We shall create history."

Hooded, the covert types led them into a set of two vehicles, quite similar in appearance to the American Chevrolet Suburban used in that country to smuggle people across its southern border.

The waiting boat also bore a resemblance. It appeared to be a junk of a bygone era. Po hoped that he had instilled in the men a sense of urgency and pride, but secretly wondered if all seven of them signalled the essence of a bygone era.

• • •

Looking like the image of the past it was, the boat under full red sail motored across the harbor and tied up in the Hong Kong harbor, roughly halfway along the north coast of the island. The separation of teams had been by mission and, since each member was readily identifiable to the public, Team Two stayed in their vehicle with blacked-out windows, and no member of Team One was allowed topside on the junk until the darkness of the early morning, when the two teams would insinuate themselves into an otherwise peaceful, but quite frenetic environment. Hong Kong.

CHAPTER 21

Since most of the Chinese spy agency's staff had quickly converted to a Chin philosophy, it was up to the spy liaison to track down someone in Hong Kong he could trust with his life. Although he expected a warm greeting, the man was unduly surprised to be hearing from anyone in the Standing Committee. He subsequently procured two more under his command whose hearts remained indelibly linked to the banner of Communism.

In a clone of a red body, gray roof cab with blacked-out windows, the three members of Team Two made their way to a location just east of Kowloon.

There, in the municipality known as Hung Hom, they broke into the computer mechanism and power generator for the four green lasers.

• • •

In the early hours of the next morning, Po, by himself but with his sniper rifle case, stepped ashore. He took one of the ubiquitous red and gray cabs to his destination.

Under orders from the Chinese spy agency, the cab proceeded past the Admiralty district and through the partying Lan Kwai Fong district. Up the side of Victoria Peak, he reached a perfect vantage point from an area known as the Midlevels. From there, he'd have a perfect sightline, especially with his starlight night-vision scope, to take out any who might escape the palace. Po recognized that every member of the Hong Kong assault team realized it would be difficult to identify either Chin or Li in a monochrome green image, but to the man each wanted to be the one to take either, or both of them, down. Those acts would conclude a rather brief insurrection by the stock mogul and his traitorous general, and enable the Standing Committee's path back to power.

For now, he waited to be joined by Team One once they finished their first mission below.

• • •

Team Crayle, fresh from the 41st floor Le 188 and a fabulous meal, headed outside the Harbour Grand, turning away from the harbor. They headed up Oil Street to Electric. There, across the street, was the proprietor of the corner auto repair shop, trooping back and forth from his rollup-doored shop to an orange Lamborghini parked part way up the block. They traded smiles, but something was wrong. Not with the repair man, but with Lenny. He forged ahead at a pace exceeding normal.

"Slow down. We're still suffering jet lag back here."

Lenny threw some words over his shoulder. "I gotta see something. It's important."

"We need to stick together …"

Lenny broke into a run.

"Get your ass back here," Phoebe yelled.

"I'll be quick, Magus. It's important. I read that Jackie Chan did a scene from one of his movies up there on Fortress Hill. On that street up above the subway station."

"Important?" said Phoebe. She turned to Crayle. "I can stop him."

"Don't push it. I'm close to saying yes."

Lenny sprinted across the main thoroughfare, King's Road, nearly getting hit by four cars and two rickshaws. To the right of the subway entrance, there was a one-story elevator and to its right, a tri-directional, zig-zag stairway with a striking, multi-toned mosaic facing of stone tiles. Since pedestrians had stopped for a smoke and blocked the stair entrance, the Jackie Chan fan nearly ran over a couple with a baby stroller as they exited the elevator.

Quickly, he was inside and up a level. Half way. The rest of the journey required either fifty or so cement stairs on the left or an up-escalator on the right. He knew Crayle was on a short fuse, so he sprinted up the escalator. The pent roofed glass cover kept off the bird crap and the drizzle that began to fall.

The remainder of the team, being somewhat more careful, negotiated the main street without incident. Since the smokers had moved on, they started up the stairway to fetch the errant P.I.

• • •

Lenny reached the street at the top of Fortress Hill and swung left. Beside the usual shop signs in Chinese, one with English translation jumped out. Oils of Pleasure Softened. Forgetting the revered Jackie Chan, he ran inside, causing the proprietress to reach under her counter.

After a couple of minutes interspersed with his exceptionally limited Chinese, the proprietor's daughter interceded. Her graceful interpretations produced the desired result. Lenny stormed out with what he hoped to be his salvation. The owner had mixed several lubricants that she guaranteed would mitigate desire in sexually overactive parties. Perfect.

Having scored what he characterized as a life-extending essence, he headed back.

• • •

Waiting below, the patience of the team had worn thin.

"We're going up. Phoebs. You've got our six. Hang out down here in case he takes the elevator again and we miss him."

She nodded, turned her back to the wall, and pressed her right foot flat against it. Her short skirt and halter top provided the shapely blonde working girl cover she'd used before.

Micmac took point, the Crayles and Alona close behind. As with Lenny, the team's zig-right, zig-left stairs only took them halfway up Fortress Hill.

Just before they rounded the last corner, Micmac's fist flew up into the air. He jumped back behind the stairway wall.

Po's three-man hit team opened fire with automatic weapons from the bushy hillside just above. They jumped onto the upper landing, and resumed fire.

Phoebe spun away from the wall, extracting her Glock. She could see her team hunkered down, but not the perps. No shot.

The father of a family of five hammered the *Close* button in the elevator. Every one in the vicinity ran for their lives, jumped into stores, or dove under parked cars. This manner of violence was not usual for Hong Kong.

Pieces of concrete flew in all directions as the team hunkered down.

Under her breath, Phoebe spoke for them all. "Lenny!"

Crayle pulled them together. "He's up there. Dead or alive, we have to take these guys out."

"He's got that micro-Uzi, Magus. If he's alive …"

• • •

Back to the top of the upper stairway, Lenny opened the sex-oil bottle and took a sniff. "Ooh!" his head snapped back. Before he could replace the lid, he heard, then saw, the onslaught below.

He stepped left and pulled himself atop the escalator's pent glass roof, spilling some ingredients onto an already rain-wet surface.

A fifty-foot slide on oil and water covered glass at a forty-five degree angle would have been tough in any circumstance. Lenny slid with the bottle under his arm and his Uzi blazing.

• • •

"Ahhhhh!" came a shout from above.

The team peeked.

Lenny.

Sliding down the pent glass roof above the escalator.

Micro-Uzi on full auto.

The three hit men of Po's Team One dropped like flies. Weapons clattered to the stone surfaces and blood poured.

Lenny realized there was no stopping.

When the family of five had arrived on the lower street and heard the shots, they'd run for the sanctuary of the subway next door. The elevator was programmed to return topside at this time of day.

Lenny flew from the escalator's roof covering, bounced once on the landing, and crashed into the now-open elevator door. He had enough left to punch the Down button.

The rest of the team, which survived by ducking on the tri-echelon stairway, had beaten a retreat to street level when the shooting ceased.

When the door re-opened, there was the team, grabbing up Lenny and dragging him into Fortress Hill Station.

Alona winced as they moved quickly across the tiles. "What is that smell?"

Weapons stowed, they each assaulted a turnstile with their Octopus proximity passes and, in seconds, boarded the next train headed west. Toward Central.

• • •

The train moved at a fast pace and, like the station, was spotless inside. The Crayle team was packed closely just inside the sliding doors where their leader pulled them even closer.

Lenny, not yet having had a chance for a bow, spoke the first word.

"I swear there had to be 100 stairs up above the zig-zag part. Alongside the escalator."

Then, Alona. "He said I swear. That's code for divide by two."

"We can crown Lenny later."

"Where's my two-by-four," Phoebe wondered.

They caught Crayle's intensity and lost the banter.

"Listen up. Before we entered the station, I noticed something. The green lasers across the harbor had swiveled to focus right on the palace. The attack on us wasn't isolated. I'm dividing us into two strike teams. Team 1, consisting of Hekka and Lenny, will follow me. We're heading up to the palace. I expect we might run into more of them up there. Team 2 will have Micmac, Phoebe, and Alona jumping out at the next stop, Wan Chai, grabbing a cab, and taking the tunnel under the harbor. Micmac has the lead on this one. Direct the cab to the source of those lasers, then do whatever is necessary to remove the threat. Questions?"

No one had time. The train pulled into Wan Chai Station. Team 2, just about one minute old, was out the door.

Team 1 continued to Admiralty Station, exited, then headed uphill to the Victoria Peak tram. Crayle knew the way.

CHAPTER 22

The enhanced laser attack on the palace had caused serious damage. The beams had probed windows as if to try and blind the occupants. But, at precisely 9:23 P.M., the lasers mysteriously snapped off.

Chin walked across the ancient rug and then retraced his steps. In the Fortress Hill aftermath, the Crayle team rested in silence on period-replicated sofas, loveseats, and chairs. Disarmed, a quiescent Communist Party Chairman Po sat next to them.

Crayle needed to fill in the emperor. Not just for the intel involved, but also as a means of decompression. "We call this a sitrep, Chin. Here goes. Once we were attacked, I figured there might be an assault set up for the palace and that the hit on us was to preempt our team from screwing it up. I figured the viewing platform near the palace would be perfect for checking the area for Tangos."

"That term is unfamiliar to me. Please explain," said Chin.

"Tangos. Targets. With just three of us in Team 1, we spread out through the crowd. It was Hekka who made the big score." He glanced over at Po.

"Yes. A sniper rifle in a long case had been prepared for me. Someone had printed POOL CUE on the side as if to explain its odd shape."

"There's a rule in the covert community, Po. Never allow your disguise to stand out more than that which you are disguising."

"Your wisdom comes to me a bit late, Mr. Crayle."

Hekka picked it up. "I saw a number of people turned away from the light show. Toward a bank of air conditioner units. With all the hubbub created by the weapon's at Fortress Hill, I decided on silence. I drew my Bowie."

Crayle smiled inside. He knew that she'd weaved through the maze of industrial strength A/C units in total Serrano stealth. Po didn't know she was there until the sharp blade indented his neck.

Po nodded his absolute agreement. "Your Bowie impressed me a great deal. At what point, Ms. Crayle, does a knife become a sword."

She smiled her minimalist smile. "You have a point, Mr. Po. A ten-inch blade is a bit large. But, like me, speaks for itself."

That they had survived Fortress Hill, had split up, and that Team 1 had located Po before he could snipe anyone was not the night's only miracle. At that point, Crayle Team 2, consisting of Micmac, Phoebe, and Alona, waltzed in pushing the three manacled members of Po Team Two ahead.

Chairman Po's head fell to his chest.

"I appreciate that your Team 2 has contained the attack with lasers and detained those responsible," Chin said. "I believe these here constitute all that your entire team didn't terminate. In other words, you have accounted for the entirety of the Standing Committee. Please, all of you, take a seat."

Every one found a spot.

"Micmac, fill us in on your little north-side operation," Crayle directed.

"Wilco, Magus. After the subway, we grabbed one of those gray/red cabs. The driver said he wasn't licensed to take us through the tunnel. It took 5,000 Hong Kong Dollars to fix that little problem.

When we emerged on the other side, I told him, where the green lasers were and, thank God, he knew. He kept repeating what he was doing as if he were nervous or something. Bottom line, we found 'em, surrounded 'em, and they gave up without a fight."

Chin knitted his brow. "Surrounded? With a team of three?"

Micmac shrugged. "Phoebe and Alona kept them under gun, and I opened the utility pedestal, shut off the power, pulled their jumpers, and tossed the power back on. Poof! Instant back-to-normal, automated, green laser show."

"Actually," Hekka added, "Magus and I were together when we were ambushed. Lenny here took out our three attackers all by himself."

Phoebe choked out, "He saved your lives and, in so doing, probably saved ours."

Vice Premier Zhang, sitting next to her, bared his teeth and gave a growl.

Her response was a right hook that landed squarely, and knocking the man out cold.

Chin produced a surprised, "Oh," then considered what Lenny had accomplished. "Perhaps he would accept a position with my imperial guard. It would pay extremely well."

"No, no. We need him, Emperor Chin."

Micmac pressed the back of his hand to Phoebe's forehead. "No fever."

"I'm not sure I understand," Chin said.

Crayle stepped in. "There were some initial issues between these two. As you can see, they've been resolved."

Out of Chin's view, Phoebe caressed the slide of her Glock with her fingertips.

"The status on the ground," said Lenny, "is that your Warriors are here and safe over on the Kowloon side. Your lives are spared, and we are fine. So, what's next?"

Alona, sensing that her husband could indeed snatch defeat from the jaws of victory, latched onto his ear, pulling him toward the door. “Come with me, darling. You need to go to the bathroom.”

With the two of them through the doorway and into the hall, all those remaining heard was, “Sex? In the Imperial bathroom?”

“Quiet!”

“Whine.”

The laughter shared by all was genuine. The last bit of tension released.

Chin regained composure first. “With the threats gone—at least for the moment—we can all get some rest. I suggest you stay here at my palace, or I can have one of my daughters—former daughters—convey you back to your hotel.”

“Thank you, Chin. We’ll pass this time.” He remembered his previous stay. He and Ling had come close, too close, to behavior neither would have chosen. “And by your leave, Chin, please have your guards toss these four into your new dungeon. We’re going topside for the remainder of the light show.”

“Then enjoy the evening in peace. I’m sure that somewhere—not here, but somewhere—there is trouble brewing.”

CHAPTER 23

Pattie walked into the Sainte Marguerite Fort Royal sporting a very big, dimpled smile. With everything proceeding as planned, she had to bring Lalumière up to speed. Quickly.

She stumbled past a dead jailer she'd left behind last time.

"I am so sorry, Sylvain. I have travelled everywhere, looked everywhere. But no Jean-Marc. No body that we could bury on the hallowed grounds of Versailles and to which we could often pay our respects. But I shall not give up."

Lalumière, bone weary from his latest incarceration, sat up on the edge of his sleep number bed and ran his tired fingers through his unwashed, shaggy hair. "With my coronation and installation as the new king, I will use those powers to find him. I must."

Pattie hoped the resources employed wouldn't look in the river on St. Lucia. Jean-Marc's assisted tumble from the bridge might be traced back to her. "First, we must see to the coronation in Paris. To that end, I have made arrangements with the pope to attend, and we'll furlough the top government types from their imprisonment in the Conciergerie, or wherever they happen to be incarcerated at this time. They will sign over governance to us. At that point, they will no longer be of use."

"I would love to have public beheadings at the behest of Madame Guillotine, as their forebears did to my ancestors."

"Hmm. Well, the masses believe these leaders have torn France to shreds. And they're right. Beheadings. Hmmm. I'm liking that."

He stood, reinvigorated by the thoughts screaming through his brain. "I must prepare. A shave. A bath. Appropriate clothes."

"No, no, no. You must listen to me. As you are, everyone could recognize you. With your beard and your filthy clothes, you look just like their hero of months ago. The Man-In-The-Iron-Mask. Like Mitim. I hate to do this, but I must."

She placed the original iron mask on him, kissed the mouth opening, and took a picture with her Smartphone. "There. Call the jailer if you need something."

"He's dead."

"Unfortunate." She creaked the iron door closed. "You'll last a week, my darling. You can think of me." She checked her cell phone for a signal and dialed. Five rings.

She recognized the voice at the other end.

"*Bonjour*, Pattie."

"*Ni hao*, Annie."

• • •

The ferry ride from the island to Cannes was short and uneventful. From there, it was a short ride to the newly refurbished and open airport at nearby Nice. Her private aircraft, courtesy of the imprisoned Sylvain Lalumière, awaited and, she was informed, already contained her special guest.

"You must be Navid," she said, extending her hand to the European-suited gentleman before her.

Fortunately, the cabin attendant had advised him to stand when she entered. Such deference-to-a-woman protocol was unknown in his religion, but he could tell things might go much better if he made the exception.

"Business time, my new friend. I have two bombs of my own. It turns out that I have plans for them. But I don't really need yours, so I'm doing you a big favor. One that you'll need to pay back. Otherwise, I could put you out there on the tarmac, and do this by myself."

Navid kept his hatred for the murderer of his brother deep inside, under control. He looked her directly in the eye. "You can run, but my one megaton bomb will kill you."

"You'll die, too."

"I will die in honor, avenging my brother, Hamid. Paradise is my destiny."

"Here's the problem. There are gradations of Hell. Your religion says so. Right?"

"That is correct. You are stalling."

"Then, because everything is symmetric, Paradise has levels, too. If you avenge Hamid's death, you get Level 1."

"Yes."

"I can set you up for the highest level, and you don't even have to die. Later, but not now."

"You do not understand Islam … but I will listen."

"One: you have a one megaton device. Really cool. Each of my bombs, however, have five megatons of radioactive destruction. Two: you don't know if yours will work. My Chinese bombs will. They've been used before."

"I can kill you just fine with a single megaton. More would be overkill."

"Here's my proposal. Don't kill me. Kill Israel."

Navid, fully committed and having cleansed prior to his arrival, stopped dead. Pattie watched him think.

He would take her far more powerful nuke back to Iran, affix it to a ballistic missile with the requisite range, and become hero of the century for his native country, Saudi Arabia. And his adoptive country, Iran, as well. He would reap untold rewards here on Earth, then ascend at a much later date to the premium aspect of Paradise. Perhaps Hamid had been weak, permitting this spy-woman to slay him.

"Sorry to interrupt, Navid. I need to know if you're all in."

"Yes. I do not play poker, but I am, as you say, all in."

Pattie flashed her dimples. "Buckle up."

CHAPTER 24

It was good to have friends in the Kremlin. Especially when the president of Russia began his adult career as an assassin for the Committee for State Security—the KGB. All things considered, living outside the realm in relative obscurity worked quite well when the absence of same would bring her into direct conflict with that particular assassin.

The czarina was lucky to be alive as it was. When she'd met the previous December with the prince pretender to the throne of France, Jean-Marc Lalumière, he'd used his thoughtful present to her of ancient Russian dueling pistols to thwart an attempt on her life. The source of the orders was not at all difficult to ascertain.

But there was something new afoot. No one would expect a woman in her position to have any manner of spy service at her disposal, but that notion was far from the reality. She'd just heard there would be a meeting of the heads of state of Europe at the Disney-like castle in southern Bavaria. The additional rumor was that the Russian president would shun the meeting, instead opting for a bare-bodied horseback ride with his favorite journalists in attendance. They, like modern journalists across the globe, were, in American terms, in the bag. They'd say anything his press director told them to say.

"What do you wish, Madam?"

"First, I want to know what you think of my plan for the great Russian president."

"Yes, Madam."

She studied her top advisor, Dmitri. Dmitri Khrushchev was dear to her and someone she trusted explicitly, implicitly, and all other ways possible. Although a bit stiff, he was a man of questionable lineage, and possessed an excellent mind and a feel for things politic. Besides, he had the height and bearded countenance to be mistaken for the second coming of Rasputin. What was not to like?

"We will role play. Use your imagination. Ready?"

"I will try."

"Oh, Dmitri. I've heard the worst news. The president is dead. Say it isn't so."

"Yes, Your Highness, it seems he slipped and fell. An unfortunate accident."

"I suppose it was the faulty scaffolding that caused him to slip."

"Fortunately, the noose was well constructed and held tight."

"He will be missed."

Dmitri nodded his concurrence. "Given that Russia now has no president, I've arranged that we move out of our apartments to new quarters."

"Oh, I hope it's not one of those renovation projects you seem to favor."

"No, Your Highness. It's move-in ready, as they say."

"What city this time?"

"Saint Petersburg."

"I'll miss—"

"You'll love it. Just outside of town."

"You're serious?"

"Catherine's old place."

"I couldn't have dreamed. Oh! I feel good. Come provide your services. Oh!"

"Madam, it's only been a couple of hours."

"I'm channeling Catherine and her appetite already. Come to me."

He stepped closer, not knowing what to expect. He was relieved when she formed a dialog chute between them with her hands. Lest the Russian walls have ears.

"I should attend the gathering at Neuschwanstein."

"You could mingle with the presidents of the major countries, except the French. Their hierarchy still seems to be missing. You require that level of intercourse to prepare the world for your ascension to the governance of Mother Russia."

"I belong there. Once the thugs are removed, and Jean-Marc reminded me as to how the task was accomplished in Beijing, we must be prepared to step in."

"Must also not forget our history, Czarina. The Swedish queen has regained the real throne in that country, and the Swedes have a long history of reaching out beyond their shores. Our raw materials would be within their grasp should the current leadership suddenly fail."

"Thinking at this level is onerous. Please check the samovar … I could really use some hot tea."

"As you wish." He moved off to prepare a tray for them both.

"Moscow has to go. Disappear. Unless we can catch the president and the rest of his crew out in the woods with their hunting rifles."

He brought the tray, handing her a tea glass encased in a sterling silver holder. "We'll travel incognito, as always. I will see to the forged invitations. I will also plan our escape. Once your presence is known …"

"I'm expecting to meet a person there, Dmitri, who can arrange the carnage in Moscow. I cannot yet give you a name."

The sage advisor tried not to appear shocked. How had she arranged anything without his knowledge? How? How? How?

"Please don't fret. This way, if you're captured and tortured, you will not have the knowledge they seek. Compartmentalization, the British and Americans call it. At least, I believe that's the term. Oh, we must leave soon. Please, prepare our trip. Our time has come."

CHAPTER 25

At the palace in Stockholm, the new queen stepped from her bedchambers. She talked the talk, walked the walk, and exuded all of the confidence required to run a country as its monarch. It was no small help that the previous government had put all of their eggs into a socialistic basket. Of the three classifications of the populace—rich, poor, and middle class—they'd managed to run the rich out of the country, leaving themselves to saddle the middle class, the only ones left with any money, with the bill. Over time, several decades, bringing home the bacon for one's family and for that of someone you didn't even know—grew thin.

Her mind turned to a queen of times long passed, Christina. Like her, she'd pursue her fervent desire for education. Five foreign languages. She stopped there. The last time she'd used her French was with her French lover. The young man had caused her to feel like a queen, indeed. He had also informed her of a looming threat from Russia. It seemed someone named Anastasia was about to seize power there.

Her favorite subject, history, had taught her that in 1709 the king of Sweden lost a battle to that country. The loss was so huge that it terminated the Swedish Empire while Russia's began. She would be sure to watch out for this czarina.

A moment passed, and she thought back to her lover. She pined. The news of the death of Jean-Marc Lalumière in the Caribbean had crushed her heart.

Not one to drown in her sorrows, she tugged a peach-colored ribbon that seemed to disappear into the ceiling. This would be simple. Once her chamberlain had responded by stepping inside her chambers, she would place her order. It took him three minutes this time. He was a leftover from the constitutional figurehead monarch of before. She was not pleased.

"Yes, Mum?"

"We wish to have Kobe steak, rare, with the lingon berries on the side."

"Anything else, Mum."

It was as if he searched with purpose to find her last nerve. "With shrimp, east Australian shrimp, fresh off the barbie."

"That is quite humorous, Mum. Perhaps you take your new position too seriously."

"Do you see this?" She'd picked a decorative item from its display place on the wall. "A relic of our Viking history."

"It is an old battle axe." He failed at squelching a laugh.

Thunk!

"What do you think of the old battle axe, now?" She gave a vigorous, scolding wave of her royal finger at the major domo, back pressed to the wall, as he tugged at the blade embedded in his chest.

"Perhaps you will better respect your superiors in your next life."

The man didn't disagree as he thudded to the floor.

The queen picked up her phone and dialed. To whomever responded, she said, "Yes. We require … come tidy up."

"Uh, Mum? There's someone outside."

"Then bring the person inside."

Appearing to have been beaten senseless, the tattered man was helped oh so carefully through the palace from its rear entrance.

He noticed that each room was replete with what he considered measured opulence. But such was the grand style in Nordic Europe.

Once delivered to her chambers, the queen was entirely without words for an extended moment.

He'd fallen into a chair.

In the next instant and with her mouth open, she ran across the room, pulled up the tall man, and helped him onto her bed.

"Jean-Marc. They said you were dead. My darling, what happened?"

He seemed groggy as would someone who'd had very little food, and who had travelled a great distance to find his way to her.

She listened, he spoke.

"I heard them. The ones who found me. The woman and her two children. I was the third one they'd found on that single day. Some kind of record, said the doctor. I was most fortunate. I asked about the others, and he described them. It was that Crayle associate, Micmac. He's formidable and still out there fighting against my father and his beloved Pattie."

"And the other?"

"It was her. Pattie. After trying to murder me, she's still alive."

"I believe I shall be of assistance. But first, you need to rest. I will see that you have everything you need. Food. Clothing. We must, however, keep you a secret. I am most fortunate that you did not die on that day. I am not going to have you vulnerable again."

Jean-Marc nodded gingerly. Any movement caused pain. And he had to take care that he didn't break any of the stitches holding his body together. Still, his mind progressed to a time when he was back in order. And able to track down and redress his issues with Pattie Norbrunn. He only knew that it had to be before any coronation. The good news? She didn't know he was alive.

He would acquire his much needed rest, then cement his relationship by taking the queen to bed. At this point, it was easy for him to liken what had become of his life to a chess game. "Knight to Queen One."

At that point, sleep would wait no longer.

• • •

Many hours passed before Lalumière's son awoke and felt up to the task. He completed the effort in much less time. Quite pleased, the Swedish queen lapsed into blissful, royal slumber.

Jean-Marc grasped his shoes and padded to the door. Absolute silence. He'd done the deed. Cemented a relationship. The door creaked ever so slightly.

"I don't recall dismissing you," came the queen's soft voice.

"Oh, the treaty," he responded.

"Forget the treaty for a moment. I've been a lady in waiting much too long. Get over here, Prince Jean-Marc. I'm ready for another royal screwing."

"Over Denmark?" he grinned.

"Come here."

CHAPTER 26

With regard to Pattie Norbrunn, there always seemed to be some cryin', dyin', or goin' someplace. Enough to make her feel like a country song. She'd taken the ferry from Sainte Marguerite to the French Riviera mainstay, Cannes. Then, finished the journey from the nearby, newly renovated, and reopened regional airport at nearby Nice to Salzburg airport, for easiest access to Hitler's infamous Eagle's Nest. She thought about the Prussian. About Otto Von Prem.

Pattie knew exactly what Otto wanted. She could help him place one of the football-shaped bombs beneath the Neuschwanstein Castle. When the European leaders, minus the Prince of Monaco, convened for their little love fest at the castle, the bomb would remove them from the playing field. Most notably, the chancellor of Germany. The political door for the Aryans would swing wide open.

Speaking of doors, she knew she couldn't just go waltzing into the castle like a sexy American tourist because security for heads of state would be at maximum. She opted for the back door approach. So, she'd flown into northwest Austria to affect a covert arrival.

From the Salzburg airport, a one-way for both she and the driver to the entrance at the old Hitler perch, Eagle's Nest, concluded normal means of travel. Her companion-in-crime, Navid Mohammed, turned grayish at her dispatch of the cab driver, but he'd known he was out of his element even before he'd arrived. His ride, one of the ubiquitous to Europe Mercedes ES-350s in silver, moved to the parking lot's edge for the return trip scheduled later in the day.

"You have your package?" she asked with her trademark dimpled smile.

"Yes. It is quite heavy and much less powerful than the Chinese bombs."

"And apparently invisible."

"It is in the car."

"Do me a favor, Navid, and go get the bomb. Please?"

He stalked off at a gait reminiscent of Olympic race walkers. The otherwise empty parking lot and the closed entrance indicated that the former Führer Adolph Hitler's Eagle's Nest mountain retreat was involved in a private ceremony today, as the signs down the road indicated.

The door creaked open followed by an eerie voice from within. "*Komm herein, Frau Lalumière. Guten Nachmittag.*"

As she stepped inside, she returned the greeting, albeit in English. "Thank you for inviting me in. Good afternoon, Herr Von Prem."

"Who is that man with you? He looks like a scientist with the lab coat and all."

"Oh. That's Doctor Ehrlichman. I brought my own nuclear scientist just in case."

"I believe that to be unnecessary. The two bombs you brokered from that Chinese General Li are quite simple to engage. I have the special remote control and the instructions in English, at which I am quite proficient."

"Last time you and I were in bed, I understood you quite well."

"Mmm. That man appears Middle-Eastern. Ehrlichman?"

Pattie had worked the backstory with Navid over and over until he got it right every time. "His father was German. His mother, a Persian immigrant. They're both dead."

"So much for racial purity. When we have control, all of that will change. Drastically."

Because Von Prem's wife and daughter had been struck and killed by a Turkish immigrant driver, his repressed anger emanated from every word when illegal infiltration into his country was the subject.

The doctor, who rolled his square-sided, air transport case inside, felt the same way about Germans. Still, he managed a smile and then followed the pair to the elevator and down to the maglev transport system.

Once inside the airlock tunnel, the transport vessel propelled them at nearly 300 miles-per-hour under the German alps to the cavern beneath Neuschwanstein Castle. The one known to the Aryans as *Rotfels*.

She didn't know it, but it was the eponymous name that Crayle had given Chin's new strategy. For good cause.

"Welcome to Redrock, Doctor Ehrlichman. Please make yourself comfortable. Pattie and I have a little work to do." The doctor looked in wonder at the red-hued walls, recognizing at once that it was embedded in its entirety with investment quality rubies.

The doctor found only one large bed, plopped on top of it, and was asleep in less than a minute.

"He's not been sleeping well."

"And the cause for his insomnia is …"

"No. Not me. He's stressed out a bit. You see, the two of you have a lot in common."

Von Prem bristled.

"So, Otto. What are you going to do with all of these rubies embedded in the walls?"

"Later about the rubies. The doctor?"

"It turns out that I lied about his heritage, and his name. He's Navid Mohammed."

The Prussian reached into a desk drawer for a weapon.

"He's from northern Iran. As you should recall, your Aryan DNA slides all the way from Northern Europe to the north of Iran. In a word, he's Aryan, too."

"I have no relationship with this man."

"Hear me out, Otto. You want the European leaders dead. He wants the European leaders dead. He's actually your assurance that these bombs I sold you go off as planned. He's your insurance policy."

"Why do I need such a policy? As you pointed out, they've been used without failure in Central Iran, Marseille, western China, and Beijing."

"How often do all the leaders get together at one time?"

"Almost never."

"It happens that I know the next time they'll be together …" She didn't provide that the new Chinese empress, Ling, had provided the intel. "… and, believe me, you want to get this done now."

"Very well." He checked his Rolex. "It will be noon soon, and they will be in place. I have calculated the positioning of the bombs, one held in reserve, so that we shall be safe here, but the castle and all who are there shall perish. Because your bombs expend no radiation, I shall rise from the ashes like a veritable phoenix and declare myself the new chancellor of Germany."

"You're sure about that placement? I don't want to go out of here looking like yesterday's toast."

"We Germans are quite precise." Followed by Pattie, he plopped down on the edge of the bed, careful not to disturb the sleeping Persian, and pressed *Play*.

Nothing.

He pressed again.

Nothing.

Since Pattie had conducted the transfer of the bombs in the first place, she was the only one in the room not shocked by the non-outcome. "Press *2* for the backup."

He did. Then *Play* again.

Nothing.

Furious, he threw the remote against the wall, sending a cascade of about three hundred thousand dollars worth of rubies in all directions.

"That Li has done this. He has kept the real bombs for himself, and has given me these … these …"

"Duds? That's what they're called. Duds. Oh, how awful."

The doctor had lapsed into a snoring episode probably due to the absence of any excitement.

Otto banged the base of his palms against his head. As if more was better, he did it again and again.

Pattie moved next to him, wrapping one arm around his waist, and pressing her other hand over his thigh. "There, there. Mama make you feel better."

Von Prem lashed out, sending her half way across the chamber and landing in a heap.

"You have a temper, don't you?"

"Look at the big screen. They are shaking hands and departing. They are pulling away in limousines that should be mine." He jumped to his feet. "I have my grandfather's MP40 Schmeisser." He ran to a desk and yanked the submachine gun and two 32-round clips from within. "I shall run up and kill them all myself."

Pattie dialed one hour into her sleep-inducing CIA tool and jammed it into his arm. In seconds, the Schmeisser fell to the floor. Then the clips. She guided him onto the bed next to the doctor, then stood back. A quite unlikely pair.

• • •

Precisely sixty minutes later, Von Prem's eyes flew open. He sat up, looking in every direction possible. Then the big screen. Empty. The parking lot was vacant, though in the distance one could see tail lights. That was all.

"I have failed. My own people will feed me to a shredder. I …" He felt the bed bouncing. He turned to see a stark naked Pattie jumping up and down in the middle. Crazy Pattie.

"Like I said, I know when they're getting together again."

"It will be years. Years!"

"A couple of weeks."

The startled Prussian gasped the obvious question, "Where?"

Pattie fell down onto her knees. "Do me, Otto. Then I'll tell."

As always seemed to be the case, Pattie had taken a very strong man and turned him to her purpose, with little apparent effort.

"But I have no bomb?"

"Another good reason that you need Navid."

He glanced over at the heavy rolling case the Iranian physicist had brought along. Then, back to Pattie.

"Yup. It's in there."

"What is next?"

"First, there's Paris."

"*Mein Gott!*"

"Yeah. My God."

CHAPTER 27

The events of Hong Kong were now history. And news of the Russian czarina, the Swedish Queen, and even the tribulations of European leaders at Neuschwanstein were effectively unknown in the locale Magus Crayle, Hekka Crayle, and Lenny Lipschitz called home. They had learned over time to tune out the rest of the world whenever the rest of the world didn't show up on their doorstep. Figuratively or literally.

The Crayles decided to spend the day at the Fawnskin cabin, clean the place up, prepare an appropriate meal, and enjoy another beautiful day beside the beautiful lake. Hekka's brothers were more than competent at managing the quarter horses at the family ranch and the growing list of clients. In a weak moment, they'd asked Lenny and his wife to meet them for a peaceful Big Bear lunch.

If a bad penny shows up and causes trouble, then Lenny represented that characterization. Apparently, Alona was busy prepping for an upcoming case. She sent her regards. Lucky Alona.

"Hey, rock 'n' roll, Magus. Rock and roll, Hekka."

Seated in the Crayle cabin's living room, Hekka continued to slide her Bowie's blade edge on the sharpening stone. "Good to see you, Lenny. Is your butt still sore?"

"No. Well, a little. The slides we had during my school days didn't really prepare me for that little James Bond bit in Hong Kong."

"Hmmm," Crayle mused as he reassembled his SIG-Sauer. "Do you recall in which Bond story he slid down the glass, pent-shaped roof of an escalator, splashed with sex oil, in order to take down three BG's with automatic weapons? In the rain? And in so doing, saved the rest of his team?"

"Alright. Alright. I played a little loose with the truth."

"Didn't Alona tell you there were times that you should remain silent?"

"She has used STFU a few times." Lenny pouted for a few seconds.

Hearing no more pushback, Crayle turned to a new subject. "Sitrep, Lenny. Where do we stand? Whassup on the Internet?"

Tick, tick, tick.

"It says that the new Swedish Queen is off to a controversial start. Her country has dumped the constitutional monarchy crap, you know. It says, she disemboweled the socialist regimen, so now everyone has to carry their own weight. It pissed off the deadbeats."

"Not too interesting now that Jean-Marc's gone. What else?"

"Over in Russia, that old czarina chick has some serious support."

Hearing no response, he checked further. "Ooh. That Disney place. Neuschwanstein."

"So."

"I remember. Swimming that gorgeous lake with the babes."

Hekka glanced his way. "If Phoebe heard you refer to her and her sister in that manner …"

"I'd just blame the testosterone, like I always do."

"How far does that excuse get you with Alona?"

"She doesn't understand me."

"Forget that, Lenny. What's the intel?"

"It says all the European heads went there to agree on how bad all their countries are doing, and that there were a couple of bombs that didn't go off."

"It would be difficult to narrow down the suspect list on that one."

"It says a forester noticed someone placing some things in nearby trees just before."

"Who is this mysterious, omniscient 'It' that knows all these things?"

"My tablet. It's like, God."

Hekka pursed her lips. "The same God that just can't wait to have his way with you?"

A moment of silence.

"That's rhetorical, Lenny," Crayle added.

"Wait! It says more."

Simultaneously, the Crayles counted down from ten.

"Wait! I have to scroll down …"

The Crayles reset and restarted their mental counters.

"One of them was short, like me. She saw the guy and smiled."

"This sounds like a soap opera. Did he recognize his long lost sister?"

"Alright, alright … she had dimples."

Hekka put down the knife, locking eyes with her husband.

"Crap!" they said.

She glanced back and forth at the two men.

"We're done …" she announced in a tone that seemed to channel Alona in her absence. "… and so are the burgers. You two. Outside! Now!"

CHAPTER 28

The next morning in Big Bear produced no sirens, no screams, nothing other than peace and calm. The Crayles slept in and Magus might have slept on into the next day had it not been for noise emanating from the kitchen.

"Must be lunch time," he muttered as he wandered into the living room. He provided a long stretch and yawn in case the other party wasn't aware that she'd drawn him from a dead sleep into the world of the living.

Not being quite awake, his brain wasn't in full function. Mistakenly, he made great effort to whiff today's lunch fare, and then channeled Lenny.

"Oh …" He stretched again. "I think I'll have my Serrano burger the same as yesterday." He thought. "Hey, I believe I just created the first line of my first novel. What do you think?"

Hekka stopped in her preparation of the day's lunch. She turned and shook her butcher knife at her husband, then started to laugh. What had been pent up, came out. She laughed until tears flowed. She dropped her knife and grabbed her face, as if to halt the expression of emotion.

"I apologize for getting you to laugh too much. It breaks with your Serrano stoic nature—the one you possessed when we met."

Back under full control, she produced the requisite stoic look. "So, we Serrano Indians are all alike."

"Excuse me a second. I seem to have stepped on a verbal land mine. It only partially exploded, so would you help me diffuse it?"

She peered at him with no expression whatsoever.

"And Indians? What happened to Native Americans?"

"My brothers served with the 101st Airborne in wartime. They said that the Native American term was created by an old white man, who worked at an East Coast newspaper. I'll have you know that many of we *American Indians* served honorably in many American wars."

"Did you have to deal with skin color issues as a child?"

"My father was wise. He taught me three things about assessing people: ignore the tone of their flesh, see what's in their mind, and last, see what's in their heart."

"Wise, indeed." Before he could continue, he felt a special vibration in his trousers.

Hekka heard the buzz. "Take it outside. I know it's the president. Just tell him thank you, but no."

Crayle headed outside.

Hekka arrived seconds later. "Mind if I listen?"

She leaned over and pressed *Speaker*.

"I just wanted to tell you how happy I am that you made it through the mayhem in Hong Kong. Ambushed by the Chicoms. As I understand it, that was awfully close."

"Lenny saved the day."

"Wow, that makes twice. Once at Lalumière's château many moons ago, now this."

"Thank you for the thought, Kimbel."

"Well, hi there, Hekka. Good to have you both on the line."

"While we have *you* on the line, and that *you* promised us a while back anything we want, how about some backstory. We know how you attained your current office—vice presidents move up when a president commits suicide—but how about before? How'd you get to V.P.?"

"I have a National Security Council meeting in fifteen. I'll be succinct. After I was saved from certain death by an even more certain CIA operative, codenamed Magic Man ..."

Hekka noticed Crayle's eyes flip northward as he began to whistle.

"... on an island on the Bering Sea, he and I lost contact. I migrated to a far friendlier workplace in Maryland where I was given a desk job."

"NSA HQ. Not your everyday desk job," Crayle observed.

"In response to an emergency call from someone on the West Coast, I took a little leave and headed out to San Ernestino."

"We know the place. On a bluff overlooking the Pacific. Nice. Let me guess that you were helping a friend."

"Long-time friend. Korean army pal of my dad's. Vietnam."

"I'm feeling a link, here."

"Did some work for a local newspaper. Ended up as Mayor Stones. I left out a few details, but we're short on time."

"What about the NSA? Did you quit?"

"They kept calling me back from what became a hyper-extended leave. I got embroiled in politics, and so successful in actually fixing things, that I made the ticket for the White House race."

"You don't seem a match for the left-leaning previous president. Why'd your party pick you?"

"It's easy. He appealed to emotions. To the ideologues. I appealed to rational intellect. Together, we covered the spectrum. Or so they thought."

"It seems that, the farther left or right of center are one's politics, the more one must appeal to emotions rather than logic."

"Well done, Magus. Studies have shown that, in a throwdown, emotion trumps logic every time."

"You don't have to worry about annoyances such as contradictory facts."

"That's it. Hey, gotta run. Best wishes and enjoy your vacation. And stay out of trouble."

Before they could respond, Stones clicked off.

Crayle looked up from his smartphone. "I think we should go back to earlier times when Big Bear and its surrounds were Serrano only."

"*Au contraire*. Why go back before the white man came and killed all the bears he didn't scare away?"

"I imagine he killed many of your people—is that correct?"

"Many? His weapons were too much for us. Too many rifles and pistols and too much ammunition. And mining explosives that also served military purposes."

"I wish it hadn't happened, but that was a different time."

"You make an excellent point. Since I joined you, I've learned a great deal about peaceful coexistence."

"I have a feeling this conversation has just taken a turn south."

"More like east and west. We've managed to engage in several firefights, blow up tens of thousands of people along with their cities . . ."

"On the positive side, we did prevent the nuclear destruction of New York and Paris."

"I see your point. We brought those residents peace by causing one mini-nuke to explode in deep water off Long Island, and by defeating Lalumière's crew atop the Eiffel Tower amidst thunder and lightning, not to mention the New Years fireworks. Hey, wait a minute. We didn't receive the Legion of Honor from the French president."

"An oversight. But President Stones did award us all the Medal of Freedom."

"Yes. I almost forgot. In that covert cathedral hundreds of feet below ground. Otherwise, people would have noticed our heroism and service to country."

She placed a plate of freshly-shredded hash browns, a sauce-topped bison burger, and a buttered and peppered ear of corn before him.

He started with, "Oh, this is so good. You sure there were no Caucasians in your family tree?"

"Only Indians."

"Clearly my ancestors didn't kill yours, so what was the secret for survival? They were out-gunned and everything." He scooped more food into his mouth. "I think the Serrano cooked some food and made peace with the white males that way."

"We were very good at extracting herbs from plants in the valley. We learned to blend them. Some became flavoring, some became medicines."

"And the rest?"

"We'd substitute them into the trappers and miners food supplies—one at a time in order to control our experiment. Then observe their effect."

"You used the intruders as guinea pigs?" He glanced at her semblance of a smile.

"If those who ate a specific blend died, we knew we had an effective poison. By the way, how's that burger taste to you?"

CHAPTER 29

The ayatollah was certain of one thing. He needed Navid to build future bombs. Members of the bomb team admitted that Navid had kept a vital secret to ensure his own longevity. He turned to Pattie, or the woman he believed to be Pattie.

Instead of her favorite nun's habit disguise, she'd donned a Niqab face scarf along with an Abaya full-body cloak. It was perfect for all but the most fundamental Islamists, and it defied facial-recognition systems as an added bonus.

"Plan A always gets the attention. But you must also have a Plan B. I have an eternal pipeline to nuclear bombs, but I'll need something in return for providing that option. A retainer, sort of."

He knew from Navid that a female CIA agent had killed the physicist's brother. Hmmm, he wondered. Her?

She'd stepped into the bathroom and returned looking quite different. She bore the attire and likeness of the infamous World War I spy, Mata Hari. The music seemed to emanate from nowhere as she danced the dance. The one which had enticed so many into betraying their countries.

He admired the face, the figure, and the moves.

"We are cheating on the latest embargo. I have plenty of personal cash stowed in Switzerland." He even named the private bank.

She recognized it immediately. Kobler's bank.

He could tell. "You've heard of it?"

"Quite." She also remembered explicitly her killing of the banker, and stealing of the proceeds. In short order, the pair were naked in the sumptuous bed. They progressed as one would expect. Nearing completion, she began to sing.

"*Ayatollah don't come, la-la, la-la. Ayatollah don't come, la-la, la-la. That ain't the way to have fun. No-oh. That ain't the way to have fun.*"

He apparently was not a good listener.

After an hour of rest, Pattie slipped once again into the bathroom, along with her overhead-sized suitcase, and donned her 'fun' clothes. She returned to the bedroom.

The CIA's Science and Technology Directorate had added Velcro attachment for moments such as these. To the Persian music with a more visceral beat in the background, she removed her nun's habit, the one that would have opened eyes wide among guards and staff in the anteroom.

"We're going to do it on your prayer rug."

"I cannot." The cleric tilted his head heavenward. Then back. He watched.

"The entire planet being in turmoil and all, I believe he is, at the moment, watching elsewhere."

"The rug," scowled the ayatollah, "is out of the question."

"Another topic. I'm afraid your chief nuclear physicist vectored off to Paradise in China."

The man's mouth dropped open. His face paled. He gasped. "Terrible, terrible news. He was germane to our effort."

"That's the bad news. Oh, do you need help with your vestments? No? Okay. Here's the good news. I've located a replacement for you, should you lose your nuke guy. A veritable expert in the field you require."

"You know an Iranian nuclear physicist that I do not?"

"Not exactly, but better. His name is Doctor Ernst Von Braun." She waited until she recognized a glimmer in his eyes. "That's right. Descendant of the namesake nuclear guy that engineered America's first atomic bomb."

Now naked, she lay on the rug, and produced her dimpled smile.

"Come and get it."

• • •

A seeming half-way around the world, the now-rested Crayles' continued vaction of relative peace and calm in Las Vegas came to an end.

"That's my damn phone again. Every time it vibrates, something has gone wrong."

The phone's vibrations had it skittering across the hearth and over. Hekka snatched it in mid flight. "Here." She tossed it to him. "Probably an old girl friend has tracked you down. I'm off to the ladies room. Keep it brief … and don't promise anything." The hint of a smile traced across her lips as she left the room.

Usually by this time, the caller had been shuffled off to voice mail. The vibrations persisted.

"Crayle here."

"Don't hang up, Darling."

His breath caught in his throat. He choked out "How—"

"Yeah, Hon. This is Pattie."

He managed a cough in response.

"I've got an 'in' for an American spy over here in Iran. Needs to be able to fake nuclear physicist expertise of the first order. How's your German accent?"

That was it. She'd clicked off. He checked caller ID. "Iran caller" was all it said.

"Crap!"

"What was that, my love?" Hekka re-entered the room. "Another 'but wait!' junk call?"

"Yeah. Junk call."

CHAPTER 30

The time had arrived for Magus Crayle's presentation to Chin. The twelve-hour flight West produced no new personal trauma or global mayhem. So far, so good.

Spy and strategist Magus Crayle and Chinese Emperor Chin stood before a wall-sized one-way window, gazing at the bustling city of Hong Kong below. The mid-day temperature of eighty and one-quarter degrees Fahrenheit was middling in every way. It closely matched the average for late Summer, early Fall.

"Look at all of them," Crayle observed. "They move about as they did under the Communist Party for all those years."

"It is the nature of we Chinese. We've been ruled by warlords, emperors, and the communists. At least the latter had an ideology and could promise their people a Worker's Paradise."

Crayle leaned back, taking a long pull from his forty-year-old Scotch.

"How'd that work out for the Russians?"

"You're correct, of course. Seventy years of absolute rule … no paradise."

"In America, we have a Bill of Rights. The rights are considered inalienable."

"I'm not familiar with that word *inalienable* in English."

"It means no one or no entity is allowed to displace the rights from the citizens. The Soviets alienated every one. The power elite—so characteristic of radical and extreme ideologies—used barbed wire, walls, land mines, machine guns, and even vicious dogs to prevent the recipients of their benevolence from running away."

"Our communists did a better job."

"They did. Still, guilt by association isn't a benefit, according to the human rights crowd."

"So what might I do, Mr. Crayle? The people ignore me or fear the unknown—what *can* I do?"

"After blowing up the government in Beijing and imprisoning the surviving politicians on Hainan Island, you became the only game in town. Trouble is, the town is a Special Administrative Region called Hong Kong. No cachet, I'm afraid."

"But my palace is here. I made myself here." Eyebrows raised, he glanced at Crayle. "You have an answer. I can tell it."

"Xian."

"Capital of the first empire. So what?"

"The empire of Ch'in Xihuangdi. Where it all started. He conquered and combined. Brought solitary order."

"As did I." Chin thought for a second, caught his breath, slapped his hand onto his breast, and gasped. "My God! It's brilliant! Masterful!" His head spun to Crayle. "You've done it again!"

"Let's take a break. Back here in fifteen?"

Chin's head still bobbed up and down. "Oh. Yes. Fifteen."

• • •

In another part of the palace, Empress Ling felt somewhat of a prisoner whenever she experienced extended stays. She asked the Captain of the Imperial Guard for a two-person escort. She was going out. To his protest, she merely held up a hand.

As she exited the palace proper into the courtyard, she noticed someone familiar. She walked to the young woman's side.

White daughter, wearing her eponymous cheongsam, stood in the vacated palace courtyard, head hung low.

"I'm sorry that you are so sad, Irene. Please accompany me."

Each of Emperor Chin's former daughters had taken an English name, as had become customary in the general population. Black daughter, born Ling An-yee, merely Anglicized her given name to Annie.

Outside the palace walls and after the eight-minute tram ride downhill, the two and their bodyguards walked silently to a nearby street.

"Please tell me what it is that absorbs you so. But keep an eye out for the left-handed traffic." She pointed to a sign painted on the street next to the sidewalk.

White managed a brief smile as she read, "Look Right!"

"Forget that I am now Empress. Speak to me as a sister would. As you've sought my council in the past."

"That's just it. You are Empress. I dare not."

"I could order it. Speak freely."

"I wear the imperial color and expected to become … I mean …"

"… the Emperor's wife. Ah, I see. Imperial White was the empress color. He chose me though my color, black, was wrong, but an emperor can do that. Break tradition."

"I do love you, Annie. Still, this saddens me."

"Hmmm. I've got an idea."

"You do? Already?"

"Chin will require a concubine."

White's countenance flashed from destitute to elated. "You are right! I shall bear the royal successor. A son." She went to wrap her arms around Ling, who held her at a distance with a royal stare. "There will be other concubines, and I will suggest the daughters of majority for that role."

"I shall have the first son, Empress. Quick! We must return at once!"

Forgetting her station for a moment, she grasped Ling's hand, pulling her toward the tram.

Ling used her death touch skills to press between the actuating tendons on the back of White's hand and send a shock. The fingers sprung open.

"There is no hurry. The other contestants for concubine have returned from their Hainan assignment. I will assure they are held in medical check before they are allowed to roam freely in the palace."

"You will do that for me?"

"Of course. You are my favorite. Come with me. We are having a drink to celebrate our brilliance."

White stumbled over a threshold as she checked the sign above. Hard Rock Café.

Through the door, they heard a band at the far side of the room performing a sound check.

"As you know, I attended university in the United States at USC. There are alumni groups all over the world. I've asked those in Hong Kong to join us."

Not used to being out of Chin's Dragon Building or the Palace, White produced a sheepish wave at the raucous crowd arrayed at one of the tables.

"One, two, three … *ni hao*," they chorused.

"*Ding, ding hao*. I'm doing fine," Ling replied as she and White took their seats. Then, with a wave of her arms and a wiggle of her hips, sounding just like Jack Sommers, she yelled out, "*Rock and roll!*"

• • •

Chin had sat impatiently in his meeting room, waiting for Crayle's return. He wanted to hear the master strategist's thoughts more than he wanted the world's juiciest steak. A poker-faced Crayle entered, noticing right away Chin's eagerness to engage.

"The move will be complex, Yao-wu. In a week's time, I'll have the transfer design down to the detail level. Of course, Xian does get quite a bit warmer than Hong Kong in the Summer, but the ancient Summer Palace received very little damage due to the nuclear blast in those tunnels beneath Beijing. It's still good for a little R and R."

The notion had taken hold. An excited Chin followed the logic. "We'll keep the Hong Kong palace for my retirement."

"For that, you'll require a successor."

"Yes. A son. Where is Ling?"

"She's seen to that issue, Chin. It falls on your first concubine, White, to produce your heir."

"Ling did that? She doesn't mind?"

"White is the imperial color, she told me. The perfect solution."

"My head is spinning. What to do?"

From behind a set of ornate cardinal and gold drapes, Ling stepped out. "This way, Emperor Chin. White awaits."

• • •

After one week, Crayle's team arrived and his completed design for the move to Xian progressed into implementation stage. It was agreed that, for security purposes, they would forego the otherwise requisite pomp and circumstance of the emperor's departure from Hong Kong.

All passengers save Ling, her entourage, the surviving four Standing Committee members, and a guard force that stayed behind, flew north in one of General Li's finest available personnel transports. The general's C-130s had already been dispatched to Beijing, just one hour and fifty minutes by air from Xian, clearing bomb debris. Li had given Chin his promise that Chin's own Terra Cotta Warriors would be placed next to those of the original Ch'in, but would be protected utilizing all modern defenses against deterioration.

The team brought the emperor, secretly, to their base of operations, the grand Sofitel Xian on Renmin Square. The ride to the room was silent and once inside, Lenny attached his tablet to amplified speakers via Bluetooth, and initiated Chinese operatic music—almost impossible to defeat with even the most modern surveillance gear.

It didn't take long at all for Chin to pine for his empress, who remained behind. Her absence, clearly devastating, he vowed to rectify at the first opportunity. He spoke in private with Crayle.

"I'd chosen her to be acquired from her orphanage where she'd faced the aging problem. The older an orphan, the less likely to be chosen. Clearly, the spirits had been in good mood as her selection was not to peasantry, but to the rarified status of stock market mogul, Chin Yao-wu. Me. Such good fortune. A superior private education. Safety and security. Even an International Relations degree at the prestigious University of Southern California. She'd kept in close contact with Red daughter, who'd studied at the cross-town university known as UCLA, but maintained primary focus on her positioning among the twelve daughters and life after the mandatory separation from the Chin family that would occur at age twenty."

Crayle, a good listener among his other talents, said nothing. He knew all about Ling's Black daughter days and more. He checked the time, excused himself, and walked through a common door, which he closed to obtain a modicum of privacy.

• • •

Back in Hong Kong, Ling followed her own thought processes, which were more related to current affairs than Chin's.

She placed the call.

The one person, whom she figured could help her, answered.

"Thank you for arranging a phone meet before you left. I need to talk, Magus."

"Our connection is secure, and I'm ready to listen. Please."

"I feel betrayed by Red, but understand her. In an orphanage, you learn to look out for yourself. That's what she's done. With me as Chin's favorite, Li was her best second choice. She's off somewhere with him and I, for the first time, am alone."

Crayle nodded his understanding, but responded, "That's behind us. The reality on the ground here in China is that the removal of the leaders with the 'get ready' bomb in Xinjiang and the 'main strike' on Beijing, left a power vacuum. Not good in Chinese culture. Chin stepped in to fill the void. The people resumed their lives as if nothing had transpired."

"It's the way we are."

"Now the miracle of Chin is receding. He needs to reassert himself, and step things up."

Wise beyond her years, she realized at once. "You are indeed Chin's Lao Tzu. I must be, and therefore am, the Chinese people's new miracle. I want to kiss you, Magus, but I know I cannot. It is no longer about me. It's about my country. And my people."

Crayle smiled as he held up an index finger, signaling Lenny—who'd just entered—to close his just opened mouth. "My plan has come along nicely. Now, here's what we do next to cast your country's future."

Having provided Ling with his best wisdom, he completed his call more than a little worried for her.

Crayle rejoined Chin.

• • •

Together, in their carefully crafted disguises, Crayle led Chin and the team to the site of the Ch'in Xihuangdi Terra Cotta Warriors. Since Chin had moved from a village at the west end of the Yangtze directly to Hong Kong, he'd never visited the ancient city.

With the customary substantial crowd at the site, no one noticed that their new emperor was present. Typical of first-time visitors, Chin remarked that to be present far surpassed the photographs he'd seen. He was wowed.

Following their subsequent visit to the old palace, they discussed placement of Chin, his Imperial Guard, the Europeans, onlookers, and overall security for the upcoming move. Crayle shared surface travel routing and every other imaginable component for which he was such a master.

Chin's comfort level with the plan and his spirits were at an all-time high. With their reconnaissance mission accomplished, the entourage returned to the airport for transport back to Hong Kong.

Rested after the few hour trip, they deplaned and returned to the Chin palace. The emperor could tell that Crayle had more. He asked him for a private meeting. It was just as Crayle had anticipated.

• • •

The two sat in Chin's living room. With Crayle and Micmac's input, it had been designed as a sound and technology isolated facility. The windows employed NSA-proprietary technology lest they be laser surveilled. With Crayle leading the way, they spoke freely.

"The problem is the absence of leadership in the world."

"Every country has a leader, Mr. Crayle. Even here in China. You saw the passing of the baton—albeit by coup—and nothing changed. The people are the same. Their jobs are the same. Their home life is the same. Government benefits—the same. What is your point?"

"That the changing of the guard—even the changing of the style of government, in your case—makes no material difference is my point. The lot of the citizenry never improves."

"It is their lot in life. Some are meant to be on top."

"That common folk must suffer is not inevitable."

"I can't possibly concern myself with 1.3 billion individuals. You must concede that."

"With due respect, Emperor Chin, it's much bigger than are you."

"How dare you—"

Crayle held up a hand, cutting short Chin's nascent tirade. "I've found a way."

"What way? And to where?"

"Bear with me. Around the world, governments are failing and have been for many years. Even dictators have gotten themselves in trouble. Qaddafi, Assad, Hussein. Even elected governments have lost touch with their peoples. Country-by-country, they've tried to buy off their populations with what we call freebies.

"Unsustainable. Socialism: failure in Sweden, Greece, three times in France. Everywhere it's been tried. Communism—socialism's evil twin—failed in Russia, North Korea, Hungary, Czechoslovakia, Poland, the Baltic states, Cuba, and here."

"Then you argue for a right-wing conservative approach?" Chin shook his head. "You are boring me with these politics, Mr. Crayle."

"But I'm not. You just don't realize at this point that you're not bored. And … the excitement is on the horizon."

Chin refilled his Scotch glass. "This makes me more patient." He nodded at the amber liquid. "Please continue."

"The mirror image of the true socialists are the true conservatives. While the former throw riches at problems solving few, the latter do nothing, solving few. Neither approach improves anything. So, using democracy to bounce back and forth between radical or extreme ideologies has borne no fruit simply because the trees of the far left and far right are equally barren."

"The failure of these radical ideologies, as you term them, is therefore inevitable."

"I commend you on your superior grasp of the English language and the logic. Yes, inevitable."

"I know you by now, Magus. You don't pontificate. Where are you leading me?"

"Magus? I believe that's a first."

"And from now on, you may refer to me in private as Yao-wu."

"Very well, Yao-wu. The manifestation of policies in even the once-great United States have deteriorated to the artificial and superficial. Narcissism rules in Washington. Paris, London, Moscow, and the rest are no different."

"And …"

"I have devised a new strategy whereby you, the nascent Emperor of China, can bail out the world leaders prior to their being lynched by their constituents."

"I am privy to the size of their accumulated debt. That would certainly be bigger than me."

"Well put. In brief, you will save the politicians, provide humanity with its best lot ever, and elevate your personal legacy to put you among history's greatest visionaries, and leaders."

"Alright, alright. It's not like you to brown nose, so this is also a first. I—"

"A Summit Meeting."

Chin stopped. He looked first at Crayle, and then at the emblem of his office in the center of his table. His glance returned to Crayle. The magnitude and potential magnitude of such an event rendered him speechless.

Crayle stepped over to Chin, putting his hand on the man's shoulder. "I have pierced the inscrutability of the Chinese, at least as it relates to you. I see in this moment that you understand. You are called upon to ride to the rescue. Leave the details of this meeting and attendee list to me. There's one more little item."

"The other shoe."

"You hold it in your new seat of power. Xian."

"I've given further consideration to your previous comments in this regard and …"

Crayle knew that deference was not an option. For his master plan to work, he had to stand firm.

"There is no choice here. You are going to move the seat of government."

"But—"

"It's perfect. The Summit will be in Xian. Where Ch'in Xihuangdi first united China."

Chin sank into his throne. "Oh."

"The leaders of the so-called free world will attend you as you establish the new social, political, and economic center of the planet Earth. It's no small task, and there'll be many devils in the many details. Are you up for it?"

Chin reached for the bottle, but Crayle snatched it away. "I have a surprise." He clapped his hands and Ling appeared, carrying a crystal decanter. It had been cut to depict an emperor in full regalia, standing, its stopper the face of Chin.

"It's a blend, Yao-wu. A coming together."

"Blends of Scotch are for women."

"For this moment, I acquired samples from the ten most respected distilleries of Scotch in the world. Each is fifty years old from single casks. The best the world has to offer in a single bottle. Replicated nowhere else."

"Symbolic."

"Of what lies ahead."

"I propose a toast," Ling interjected. She'd poured three. "To a much better world, and the peace and harmony it will bring."

Of all Chin had accomplished to rise from a small western village to the top in all China, he felt he was back at the bottom looking up. It was a fool's dilemma. Only a fool would take Crayle's bait, but only a fool would pass it up.

"Xian, it is."

"The Summer Palace north of Beijing is still intact, and Hong Kong shall become your getaway Winter Palace. Deal?"

"Deal, Magus. Deal!"

CHAPTER 31

Chin Yao-wu's second in command, General Li, expressed great pride in his ability to pilot the huge and ungainly aircraft. He'd used it to haul his master's genuine Caterpillar earth-moving equipment from Vancouver, Canada, to construct the Hong Kong Palace on Victoria Peak. Now, just he and Red occupied the flight deck and could converse openly once they'd departed Hong Kong and achieved cruise altitude. Destination: China's former capitol.

"The CATs are in Beijing helping to rebuild the government buildings damaged by our tactical nuclear blast. The one that brought Chin and I into power," Li began. "Those structures will be used for regional functionaries, but the new empire's palace, and government seat, shall reside in Xian. Returned there after over 2,200 years."

"What about the Standing Committee members who escaped Hainan and attacked the palace with the green lasers? Those who survived the Crayle team still live in the Hong Kong Palace dungeon."

"At first I had trepidation about the former communist regime of Po and the others remaining alive. Now, I see potential for them working for me. After Chin. I envision a modified communism.

Perhaps you can help me, Red, to develop a new *ism* in which we maintain total central control and bring in the SARs—Hong Kong and Macau, but utilize the innovation and growth machine that is capitalism."

Of necessity, the young woman known as Red daughter had become wise beyond her years. She answered with care. "I am happy you asked me to join you in this C5A transport. We will move the CATs to Xian, as Chin has directed."

Li wondered to what extent his wife had deduced the operational phases. "And next?"

"Then, we'll fly back to Hong Kong to fetch his Terra Cotta Warriors while the crew uses the earthmoving machines to dig a place for them."

"Yes, space enough for the 8,000 will take them some time."

"But there is a rush, my general and consummate bedmate. You told me last night under the covers. Chin has called on the European leaders for a Summit Meeting at the site. He intends to impress them, then work out new trade agreements."

"Yes. I did say those things. Amongst our other under cover activities. Now, back to the business at hand. Delivering the Warriors will take a couple of trips. We'll have to cart the loaders with us so they can unload in Xian, then bring them back for the next load. But, hear me now, Red. We must be very, very careful with our language among even the working class."

Red paused, then asked, "Why move the Warriors? You won't need them, and you'll be dispatching Chin anyway."

He'd anticipated her question. "We will strike with our Super Drone. Chin will be honored after his untimely demise, and buried with the Warriors defending his afterlife."

"Then you become Emperor."

"I'm thinking ..."

"Please hear me out, my husband. The original Ch'in waged war to create the first China. You are, unlike Chin Yao-wu, a warrior. It is appropriate. And Chin's Terra Cotta Warriors—they can become yours."

Li thought about the possibility, but he said no more on the subject. "Curl up and get some sleep. This promises to be an extremely long day."

• • •

Two hours passed. A small degree of turbulence caused Red to wake. She resumed her place in the copilot's seat, ready to receive Li's latest thoughts on their impending coup d'état.

"As you are aware, I plan to have my technical guru whom you know quite well, Gao Bo-da, employ the Super Drone—that I had intended to use on Hainan in my scheme against the Vietnamese—to blow up Emperor Chin, Empress Ling, and the Crayle team. They plan to fly to Xian in the Emperor's new aircraft, a custom Boeing 787. When it lands, boom! We will deploy the Hainan nuke and all will die."

"But why do you take me? Gao has the technical skills. You usually choose him for this manner of work."

"Gao has a special assignment. He alone possesses the skills to fly the drone to its destiny. It is well that you did not kill him as I suggested previously."

"You wished to test my loyalty. I understood."

• • •

Once they'd landed and been transported by military escort to Beijing, Li was impressed by the progress on the new government facility. "Come. We'll spend the time at my suite atop the Shangri-La China World. You'll love it."

"I have a husband, a very special husband, to love."

Li really needed some rest before resuming the rest of his workday, but knew what awaited as soon as they found privacy. He smiled.

"I considered for a moment moving the seat of power to Shanghai, near my birth home of Suzhou—" Li's cell phone interrupted. He listened, rang off, then turned to Red. "Come, the CATs are finished. We must gather them and the workers into the aircraft."

Within the hour, all of the Caterpillar tractors were aboard and lashed into place, and the workers were strapped into seats along the sides of the cavernous cargo bay. The Li's were back aboard and jets in the queue moved aside at the C5A passed to the active runway. They made Xian in just over two hours, unloaded their cargo, and headed south for Hong Kong.

Li realized that, for once, he'd run out of things to say. "Anything you'd like to talk about? Perhaps your plans to remove Empress Ling?"

Red felt conflicted. The empress had always been Black daughter to her. Ling An-yee. And like herself, an orphan adopted by Chin. They were sisters. But Ling was quite intelligent, had a perfect body, and a beautiful face with the sexually perfect rounded lips. Red had always wanted whatever Black had. Now it meant the title of Empress. In another way, she didn't want to come second. Perhaps once the coup was accomplished, a First Lady like Madame Chiang Kai-Shek. Hmm.

Once in Hong Kong, she watched as Li and Gao loaded the dismantled Super Drone into the cargo bay and covered the components with black tarps. Workers then loaded the first batch of Warriors and, like the heavy equipment operators before, strapped in for the long flight. The last ones aboard were several of the other daughters, who would have a special purpose in the scheme.

Red remembered Li's last words before they landed once again. Gao was still expendable. It would happen in Xian.

• • •

The flight back to Xian took place in silence. Exhausted workers slept in the cargo bay while Li and Red had nothing more to say.

Crafted of dense clay and life-size in height and girth, each Warrior required three normal-sized, strong Chinese to lift it onto a gurney and roll it to its destination in the pit. When the last had been removed and the workers were still at the pit, Li's co-conspirators—Red, Gao, and the daughters—transferred the encased drone components to a purpose-built hangar east of the city for reconstruction. The process, practiced by the daughters in secrecy at Li's air base near Hong Kong, required less than an hour.

"There." Gao clapped his hands, and stepped back to admire his creation. "The bird is ready to fly."

"Yes, Lieutenant Gao," said Li. "Attach the mini-nuke football to its center, and assure me that the remote control signal will travel from my hand to our satellite, and then to the bomb's initiating mechanism."

"You have my assurance. As you commanded, I will fly the bird to the coordinates you specify, you will issue the 'bomb away' command, I will divert the drone from the danger zone, and—at your leisure—you will operate the remote to detonate your bomb at whatever altitude you choose."

Li smiled at Gao's notation that the bomb was his and his alone. He'd considered having lettering on the side, something like *Goodbye Emperor Chin, Mr. and Mrs. Crayle*, et cetera. It would've required more space than available, so he would just go with the Spaulding and Wilson monikers that had been provided at his multi-brand factory in Wuhan, not far from Mao's Villa.

CHAPTER 32

Because of the failure to blow up the European leaders at their Neuschwanstein congregation, Otto Von Prem and his alliance required a new tactic for their removal.

Pattie Norbrunn had provided it. Or so she'd said. She'd put them on the road to the nearby southern Bavarian city, Füssen, where they, along with the Iranian nuclear physicist, made their way by private jet via the North Pole route toward China.

Donning disguises that she'd provided, they'd made a quick stop in Paris to bust loose the top layer of France's elected government. Since no one knew the leaders were sequestered there in the subterranean remnants of the old Bastille, spiriting them out proved relatively easy.

The Aryans hardly had them above ground when the rescued French leaders—disguised as Muslim women in Burkas to avoid facial recognition—began to complain. They didn't like being taken anywhere, they didn't like being taken anywhere by Germans, and so forth.

Von Prem listened in a huff until they'd boarded Pattie's private jet. Von Prem, who preferred action to words when dealing with the

French, drew his '08 Luger, racked the knuckle slide chambering a fresh 9mm round, and pointed it at the nominal President of La Belle France.

Enough said.

The rest of the journey to their Asian rendezvous point was silent, although there did exist minor rumbling about the quality of food and drink.

Behind closed doors in the sole bedroom while Pattie spent time on the flight deck helping the pilot with stress relief, Navid Mohammed poured out his heart to Von Prem and Mengele.

"This General Li provided us a bomb to our underground facility near Fasd. Central Iran. Unlike your mini-nuke duds, our Chinese bomb functioned just fine."

"Because someone benefitted from that outcome," reasoned the Aryan.

"I continue. By apparent plan, it was detonated by remote control. Many died. The explosion was detected easily by the incessant monitoring IAEA and, within two days, egregious sanctions were introduced. Our ayatollah pointed to the agreement we had with the West, but it held no ground."

Von Prem produced a sympathetic response. "I believe it was detonated to make Iran a scapegoat. The explosion of a weapon with an identical signature in west China's Ürümqi city redoubled the incrimination of Iran. Then Beijing, with the same nuclear and seismic footprint. Everyone blamed your country. From my own research and from what you've said, I'm liking Li and his effective boss, Chin, for all of it."

"It looks that way."

"We Prussians like being precise. It doesn't just look that way. Consider, who benefits?"

"You are correct. Chin blamed the communist leaders for their failure to protect the people component of the People's Republic, declared himself Emperor, and named Li as his second in command."

"We shall have our moment, Navid." He stopped for a moment. "May I address you so?"

"Yes. Yes, Otto. You may." He smiled briefly.

"Please continue if you wish."

"Pattie, whom I believe you know quite well, is the one I am certain killed my brother in Monaco. He had travelled there because of a sighting of the French lunatic called Mitim, who masqueraded as the modern version of The Man In The Iron Mask. Believed to be a guest at the Prince of Monaco's palace, and the one who pressed the button on Fasd. Our intelligence fingered—I believe is the spy term—her."

"But you didn't kill her at Neuschwanstein. Why, may I ask?"

"Even revenge can be conflicted. For myself, I needed to kill her. But for my country, I needed to allow her to facilitate revenge of a much higher order. Do you understand?"

"*Stimmt.* I mean, correct. To retaliate against these Chinese and then to lead Germany back to its rightful position in the world order, perhaps even to ensure that order, is far loftier than anything personal. While they made me a fool, that is not why I must destroy them. They and these special nuclear devices that emit no radiation could be used with great effectiveness against us."

"Cut off the heads, they say, and the snakes die."

"Nicely put, my friend, Navid. We will deliver the French delegation, and then ourselves fade away to a rendezvous point with Kaari. A discarded airport a short distance from one of the many Chinese old war museums. One with aircraft."

"Then we sleep. We will need clear heads."

"Indeed, we shall."

• • •

The Aryan plus Pattie entourage landed at a remote airport not far from Xian. There, they offloaded the fugitive French government into a waiting transport, which headed off to meet with Chin. The

Aryans, having pronounced the French free of their care, headed into the closed-for-renovation WWII air museum.

Before they landed, Von Prem encountered Mengele, who voiced her worry.

"I understand your concern," he had responded to her question. "I have chosen to fly the mission for two reasons. Number One: I am the most qualified for this job. I have piloted the aircraft in question no fewer than twenty times."

"But you have never bombed anyone. And you have never bombed anyone with a nuclear device."

"Number Two: My grandfather served in the Luftwaffe under Field Marshall Göring." He pulled a ribbon from inside his leather coat pocket.

Mengele's jaw dropped when she saw the medal.

"Yes. He was awarded the Iron Cross for his courage."

"With due respect, he didn't drop a nuclear bomb, and escape the blast zone before he and his plane were exiled from the sky. Your country needs you. Your race needs you."

"That you recognize my importance to our cause is commendable. Still, I am not flexible on this issue."

Navid Mohammed, master bomb maker, walked along the aircraft, long since restored and kept to a high grade of polish. He'd noticed a partially full case of Meguiar's top-of-the-line car wax as they'd entered the museum. Planes such as these had bombed his homeland during WWII. He smiled, thinking of the aspect of his plan he hadn't shared with Von Prem.

CHAPTER 33

With little to do until the next cargo of Chin's Terra Cotta Warriors had been loaded, General Li and Red took the opportunity to fill in some of the many blanks of their relationship.

"You have not told me of your past," Red began. "Of what *makes you tick*, as the Americans say. We are married. I should know."

"For we Chinese to remain inscrutable, it is not good that we volunteer personal details." He sipped a 25-year-old Scotch from a metal flask.

"It is my role, my honor, and my duty as your wife to protect you. Therefore, I have the need to know."

"How, my lovely Red, can Chin be without you? Very well. I was born in Suzhou next to one of its many canals. There, I achieved my basic education." He stopped. "My early life will bore you to tears."

"Skip to the hot parts. Things I can post on social media."

"That is not at all funny. Posting such pejorative matter would constitute your final act. Am I clear?"

She reached for the flask, and quaffed a gulp. "You would kill your own wife?"

"Execute is the operative term."

"Of course. I understand. But tell me, anyway. In my mind, I will classify it Top Secret/RD."

"The compartment?"

"Red Daughter."

"Of course." He chuckled, but briefly. "Very well. When I finished with high grades—my parents had pushed and pushed Confucian education—I was accepted into an excellent university at age twenty-three. One where important families sent their children. From there, I became an officer. I wished with all my heart to lead an infantry company over the border into North Vietnam."

"I learned of a few incursions there from my own studies. But our forces were always pushed back. I didn't understand. At the time, both China and Russia were Communist. And the notion that all communists must link arms across the globe was a premier tenet."

"Something that looked good on paper. North Vietnam feared that we would just march in and take them over. We had done it before."

"But long before Karl Marx."

"They sided with the Russians, wanting their implements of war. Especially the AK-47's. And an endless supply of ammunition."

"But no warplanes or ships."

"You have studied history well."

"Please …"

"I was put through a crash course in espionage and stationed in Hong Kong. It was there I met the elder Crayle."

"I know about this. From Black daughter."

"It disturbs me that Ling would know. Anyway, his job was to help defeat the North Vietnamese and the Russians, as well."

"But why did the Americans and their allies commit such treasure to a third-world conflict?"

"Under President Dwight Eisenhower, America spawned the Domino Theory. Its primary thrust was that Soviet communism's goal was to unite the world's workers by overtaking countries one-at-a-time. They would institute a communist government, insure the subjugated peoples could not overthrow them, then use the new acquisition to infect that country's neighbors."

She let the word *infect* slide by, noting that Li might not be the hard-liner he appeared.

"Magus Crayle acquired his intellect from a brilliant father. That man, Lieutenant Colonel Crayle, discovered that I was much more an opportunist than an ideologue."

"You killed him."

"Regretfully. He could have helped us in a quite material fashion as now does his son."

"You ... we ... must hope that Magus Crayle never learns of this. You must have destroyed the weapon, especially if it had been issued to you."

"That's an intrigue within an intrigue. In short, I could not. Even though my best interests so dictated, I had to keep it. You see, Lieutenant Colonel Crayle proved to be an excellent intelligence officer, and a good man, as well. In his honor, I kept the pistol."

"Then you have it hidden?" Although Red was committed to Li, gathering powerful information was an indelible facet of her being.

"At the palace. In a place where no one would look."

She smiled and nodded, but couldn't deny the opportunity, and the risk. There was a great deal to think about during the remainder of the flight. No more words were spoken.

Red listened intently as Li made one more material statement just before they touched down. As she'd anticipated, he again declared Gao to be expendable. It would need to happen in Xian.

CHAPTER 34

Since Chin and Team Crayle were still en route to Xian, Li and Red had a little time for any last minute scheming. A small windowless office in the hangar afforded them the requisite privacy.

Li had a thought. "Magus Crayle is as Chin portrays him. Brilliant. And like a brilliant light, he lights the path for Chin, while shining straight into my eyes, blinding me to mine."

"You must see your path, Li. If he brings you such anguish, why not just ..."

"Kill him? I've thought of it. Even how. And the words I would say to him just before."

"Then we must do it, my General."

"Chin would have me shot."

At first, Red bore a distressed look, her brows knitted and her lips pursed. But the next instant produced an epiphany. And a sly smile.

"Then make it his idea. When they reach Xian, convince Chin to send Crayle, along with the rest of his team, to a place where you can avenge his meddling in our affairs."

Her words produced a smile. His. "You remind me, Red, why I need you as my confidant, as well as my wife."

• • •

The Chin entourage arrived at the Xian airport an hour later. After a smooth landing. the group was eager to deplane and set up for the Summit Meeting. The man who called himself Emperor seemed full of vigor and confidence.

"We are here, my dear Crayle." He drew a deep breath as if the air in this locale was itself imperial.

Next to him, his Sun Tzu/Lao Tzu did likewise. "I believe the air is elevated by your presence, Your Majesty."

"Please don't toy with me, my friend."

"My apologies."

Chin continued his thought.

"It feels like I am a reincarnated Ch'in Xihuangdi as I re-institute his royal personage and palace."

"That's what I intended. Residing in Hong Kong, you were a faraway name to your people. Xian is real to them. Xian is legitimacy. The people will rally 'round, especially after you meet with the European leaders."

"Your insights are correct."

"The citizens would not travel this far for a mere usurper. When this day is done, we should all celebrate. Even General Li. Where is he, by the way?"

"How forgetful of me. He asked that you and your team drop by at an old airfield just a couple of miles from here."

"I'd love to see what he's cooking up, but I think I and the team should remain here. As protection."

"Nonsense. My Imperial Guard is quite adequate. I insist that you head over there. You'll be back within the hour, and I will introduce you to a 75-year-old Scotch that I brought along for this grandest of occasions."

"If it will allow you to relax, then we'll go. When you meet with the leaders, calm will work best. They need to leave here feeling that you, and no-one else, is in charge."

"Please, go. And return whenever Li's demonstration—whatever it happens to be—is completed."

With that, the Crayle team jumped into a knock-off Humvee and headed east, enjoying a view of the city's ancient walls as they drove away.

CHAPTER 35

Chin hadn't just been a stock market mechanic in his fortune-building days. He'd made a number of valuable friends, ones he'd added to his Inner Circle or Guanxi.

As he watched the French leaders cross the square and rectangular gray stone tiles outside Warrior shrine, he felt total control. His plan, or was it Crayle's plan, for a Summit Meeting was reduced to this. Communication after communication from all the other countries expressing regrets that they could not meet with China's new emperor. It seemed that 'something has come up' in every country at precisely the same time. Except for France.

The rain and the heat surprised none of the Xian locals. The month of September brought with it average rainfall of just north of three inches with highs and lows measuring seventy-nine and sixty-one respectively.

The men approaching looked as if they had slept hunched together, then had removed clothing that they'd worn for at least a week, taken a shower aboard Pattie's jet, and re-dressed.

"*Bonjour, L'Empereur* Chin," said the man he recognized as the French president. He had little respect for the socialist who'd taken his economy down several notches. Chin would take care not to make similar mistakes.

"*Bonjour, Monsieur President.* And *Ni hao.*"

"*Ni hao,*" the group chorused.

"We'll converse in the language of our common enemy. The English."

They smiled, nodding up and down, and followed him inside the Warrior site. He felt that no words were necessary. Photographs of the troop replicas never did them justice.

"These are the warriors of my great ancestor, the creator of China. As you can see, the parts were excavated with great care. Engineers had to preserve the thousands of pieces left by marauders. They've been identified, remolded, and placed in ranks, with the generals—they're the ones with the hairpiece on top—in the lead. And horses and chariots as well. Perhaps the leaders of France would consider such protection after death."

"We French leaders need the protection in life. To keep it."

"Coming here while the others didn't could turn into a positive."

"*Qu'est-ce que c'est?*"

"You are the only ones to have this honor. And I am turning around our own economy in this brief period of governance. I can offer you a trade deal. Your competitors in Europe miss out."

"We are socialists."

"If you socialists bring work and prosperity, as I am doing here, you become heroes—past sins forgotten. And that man, Mitim, will be forgotten. Without my deal, he becomes King of France and democracy—and any future chances for your party—disappear for several hundred years. You can live in exile or take my offer. The choice is yours."

He could tell they were in territory not of their choosing. "Here. Follow me to *my* pits. My Warriors. You will note that the originals we just observed were life-size, while mine are 20% larger than life."

"From stock market to emperor. I'd say you *are* bigger than life, Chin. Might we walk to view your post-life troops?"

Chen led them the several hundred yards. The pits were dug. Li's workers had managed to install half of the 8,000 clay soldiers. Perhaps he would reward the general. Perhaps another star.

CHAPTER 36

General Li! The drone's aloft! The bird flies!"

Li had just re-entered the hangar's control room, ostensibly just having de-stressed via Red before the start of battle. He strode to Gao's work table still zipping his fly.

"I've assured that, under Emperor's orders, all aircraft remain clear and that all radars are looking elsewhere. Congratulations, Gao. I will observe as you move your creation into position over Chin's new digs."

The lieutenant glanced up at Li's use of an Americanism.

"Some of Crayle's presence in Hong Kong rubbed off, I'm afraid. But the as-yet-uncovered pits are coming into view. I can see the European dignitaries Chin has invited, and the limousines that brought them. And …" He laughed. "… the array of bodyguards they believe can protect them. This shall be my finest hour."

Red entered the room, still arranging her cheongsam. "I agree. And I will share it with you."

"And more. Once we have sent them all to Hell."

"That Black remained in Hong Kong will leave our effort incomplete."

"We'll deal with her later."

The pair stood behind Gao, peering over his shoulders.

"We are at 2,000 yards, General. On my *Go*, press the *Fast Forward* button on your control."

Li raised the device, then blanched in fear. "You have checked the batteries? We shall have but one opportunity."

"Fresh. From our factory in Fuzhou."

The general was at the ready. Red wore the look of primal satisfaction. She could feel the tension in the room. She glanced down to observe that Li was becoming sexually aroused, and touched him.

He almost pressed the button at her touch. His breathing increased.

The drone loomed ever closer to the target.

Those on the ground started to hear its approach. They glanced up into the glare of the sun. Gao had been clever. He'd utilized the age-old technique of approaching from that direction.

Li breathed ever harder.

Red went to her knees, and slid down his zipper.

Oblivious to what was occurring behind, Gao absorbed his general's anticipation.

"*Go!*" the lieutenant cried.

Li pressed.

Gao put the visual into split screen. On the left, the view from the drone forward. On the right, the nuclear bomb falling away. Heading earthward.

The technician veered the craft left, heading it toward safety. "Do not press the *Play* button until I have maneuvered my creation beyond the nuclear blast envelope … please."

The right side of the screen showed the initiation of a commotion. Like a Three Stooges scene, people, including bodyguards, began running into each other. The bomb reached a height of 157 feet when Li could wait no longer. Red daughter saw to that.

The general began to gulp air.

Red furnished the final thrust

"*Play!*" Li yelled in his final moment.

Gao waited a few minutes for the general's return to reality.

"What happened?" an exasperated Li exclaimed. "It didn't detonate!"

"It was what we call a test run. To see that all components function properly and that you could have a personal run through before we do this for real. I kept you in the dark so that you would feel the pressure of the moment. I am bringing our Super Drone back where we shall attach the bomb."

"And its next flight?"

"Yes."

CHAPTER 37

Neither Crayle nor the rest of the team had wanted to leave Chin at the Warrior site. He had his Imperial Guard, and the French legation hardly posed a challenge.

The notion that Li had something important to show him tickled his nervous bone. Spies survived by being skeptical. He'd checked the maps before leaving and pulled their vehicle into a wooded area adjacent to the general's site. He filled in the team on his plan of ingress. It was especially a good idea in this instance since former UDT-SEAL Micmac had the chops for getting in close and getting in quiet.

Following his lead, Crayle's team spread out along a drainage ditch next to the sole square cement pad.

They expected a helicopter to arrive, or one to depart. Crayle observed the large rollup door. Perhaps it would move and a whirlybird would be pushed out. Perhaps Li would be in the pilot's seat.

No sooner had the thought passed than it hit him. The building was of the same dimensions and construction as the one at the Oktoberfest in Big Bear. Where he and Hekka had been captured. A link? Between Li and the Aryans?

The door started up as a whir sounded from the distance.

All heads ducked in unison.

The thrum of the four large propellers seemed to march across the field right at them.

They hunkered deeper.

Li's large drone briefly hovered over the pad, then touched down.

Crayle noted the absence of provision for a pilot as the blades wound down, finally becoming motionless.

Micmac let out a hum as the blades of each motor rotated one over the other until the four aligned sets hung above each of the four fuselages. A storage configuration. Knowing the mechanics of helicopter flight, he scratched his head with a 'how did they do that?'

The team saw several young women run out—one with a small tractor. They hooked up the aircraft and towed it into the hangar.

He recognized the young women. A group of Chin's daughters no doubt brought up from Hainan to Hong Kong, along with their Standing Committee prisoners. Then here.

Li took a few steps out and patted his baby as it rolled by. The flying machine came to a stop inside, the girls chocked its wheels, and then they disappeared from view.

Crayle felt the heat build in his face. He reached for the cargo pocket, feeling Ling's present for him. Li's Makarov Type 59.

"It's time to head back to the Terra Cotta Warrior site and lend Chin any assistance we can with the French."

They returned to their transportation, and heading westward toward Xian.

• • •

Otto Von Prem stood in what he deemed the museum's ready room, wearing a World War II Luftwaffe uniform worn by his ancestor and replete with Iron Cross. He stood at attention for a moment to respect the magnitude of what he was about to do. This was for country and race. Two inseparable concepts, in his mind.

Von Prem was not only a licensed pilot, but also owner of several remanufactured WW II combat aircraft. Behind the Prussian and facing aft—as was the rear gunners lot—sat the Iranian nuclear weapons expert, Doctor Navid Mohammed.

Otto was now the last in the line of the Otto Von Prem quintuplets. Though they'd passed as clones for the purpose of raising funds from neo-Nazis, they had been products of the beyond-limits researcher, Joseph Mengele.

Previous violence at the hands of the Crayle team had killed one through four. For the same reason, Kaari Mengele was the last in line of her own genetically engineered identical siblings. Since this particular plane only had room for two—and the two within were mandatory—she'd been left at the museum.

The New Master Race female prototype—perfect of mind and body—waved as her male counterpart took to the skies.

Von Prem tested the intercom. "Can you hear, Navid?"

"Loud and clear, I believe you say."

"*Ausgezeichnet!* I mean, excellent! We have a ways to go, perhaps you will find the following of interest. In order to rebuild this fighter-bomber, we employed *Die Ungesetzlichen*, those the Americans call The Illegals. Ours were undocumented and from the Middle East. It was perfect. We paid them little and, when finished, eliminated them with no trace. And who would miss them?"

The Iranian remained silent.

"I have on good authority that there will be no Chinese interceptors to get in our way. As you surely have noticed, the Stuka is driven by a single propeller. We would present an easy target."

"What else have you left out that I should know?" the Iranian complained.

"What you don't know can't hurt you."

Von Prem pointed them toward Xian.

• • •

The time had come. Li had given the order and Gao had flown the bomb-laden drone. Toward the ultimate target: Chin. The European leaders would be a bonus.

Gao had handed a remote control to a smiling Li as their bird of prey entered the kill space.

Seconds later, his mood took a major downturn.

All would have gone well and should have gone well had there not been corruption at the Fuzhou factory. It seemed that, before the spate of anti-corruption purges by a recent party chairman, the director of the factory had absconded with a quantity of funds for use at the Macau casinos. Quality of workmanship had suffered, as a result.

The batteries in General Li's remote control had just enough juice to activate the bomb release. Gasping, he watched in horror as the bomb bounced on impact, taking out cars and people in random fashion until it crashed through the Terra Cotta army like an oblate bowling ball.

"*No!*" he yelled. He pressed again and again. "*Blow up!*"

Red wiped her mouth on his trousers, and jumped to her feet. In an instant, she surmised the source of her husband's grief. He had witnessed the cluster of French leaders and Chin himself as they rose to their feet and pointed to the drone receding into the distance.

Gao spun, grabbing the remote from Li. He removed a back plate, and rotated the batteries with his finger. This generally worked if good contact was the problem. It wasn't.

Red pulled a straight pin from her hair. Just as she tightened her jaw, prepared to shove the dual-purpose implement up the back of Gao's skull, they all stopped in place.

• • •

As they passed over Xian, Von Prem peered down through the bomb sight window in the cockpit floor.

There it was. He could see the giant crowd below.

"It is time," he said to himself.

He pulled the dive lever rearward.

Next, he rolled the plane 180 degrees onto its back, effectively nosing it into the dive.

Although the aircraft had been designed for a ninety-degree descent, Von Prem chose sixty degrees partly in favor of the Iranian, but also to minimize the risk of a multi-G blackout.

In the back seat, Navid's heart almost stopped. But he'd mentally prepared himself prior to fastening his safety belts.

Limited to a dive rate of just 370 miles per hour by dive brakes, the shrill cry from the engine penetrated the canopy sending two heart rates through the roof.

The characteristic dive scream of the Stuka could be heard ten miles away.

• • •

What was that screeching sound?

Quickly, Gao returned to his seat and spun the drone's bomb bay camera around.

There, darting straight down from the heavens screamed what appeared to be a World War II fighter-bomber.

"I've studied enough war aircraft history to know that the plane is a German Stuka dive bomber! It's aiming at the pit!"

"You're right, General!"

Gao felt relieved.

Red held the pin behind her back, just in case.

No one realized that the vintage-appearing bomb attached to the belly of the plane was a disguised delivery device for Iran's first nuclear explosive. Xian, China was about to become Navid's beta test site.

• • •

Navid clutched his remote control tight in his hands. As the G forces increased, his vision began to blur.

The Iranian gave a quick smile in the direction of Tehran, and toward the gravesite of his assassinated brother.

He positioned his thumb over the requisite button. The one he had labeled *Paradise*.

Though the Prussian pilot was in top shape, he wasn't as young as he once was. His own vision turned to a haze.

The Ju-87 Stuka had an automatic system to pull the dive bomber out of its steep dive even if its pilot did lose consciousness.

Unfortunately, one of the devilish details of which Von Prem was unaware was the following: during the plane's rebirth, one of the workers, a displaced Syrian, had learned the owner's identity. Von Prem. The young man's grandparents had been bombed into eternity by a German pilot during the world war. The hinges for the dive flaps had come from the discard bin. With the Stuka under incredible stress, and at the last second, Von Prem attempted to pull out of the dive.

Snap!

Snap!

Both flaps sailed up into the sky as if fired from cannons.

Without the flaps, the aircraft appeared determined to punch a hole through the Earth.

"Release the bomb … *Now!*" Von Prem yelled through their intercom.

What he heard back, he didn't want to hear.

"*Allahu akbar!*" screamed Navid. "God is great!"

Von Prem realized. He wouldn't need to pull out of the dive.

Navid pressed.

Then, harder.

He pressed again.

Still harder.

Approximately 100 miles away by now, Pattie viewed the entire operation via her satellite feed. She could almost feel the Iranian's panic.

"No, Navid. *I'm* doing this. Just as I did your brother."

She held up her own remote, and smiled.

"Bye, bye."

• • •

Still nonplussed regarding the strange flyover of the huge drone, the French leaders heard the dive bomber's characteristic scream. They, too, screamed. Their panic reactions caused any notion of a Chinese fire drill to be superseded by their French version.

• • •

Chin jerked up his head as the Doppler effect of the screeching sound waves compressed downward. He didn't scramble like the French, but only wondered who had betrayed him. In his youth, he had visited the WW II museum, and had seen the plane. Of course. The Aryans.

He'd been apprized of their bomb failure at the castle in southern Germany, and those bombs had Made in China written all over them. He took pride in what the young man from west of the Yangtze had accomplished … for three seconds more.

• • •

The descent of the Stuka and its two passengers terminated by atomic explosion at precisely 11:01 A.M. local time. Coincidentally, it was the same nominal time of the explosion years earlier at Nagasaki, Japan.

Pattie rolled over in her jet's king-sized bed.

The pilot, ready and willing, reached for her.

She pushed his hand away.

"First, a little quiz."

His eyes appeared to have been propped open. "A quiz?"

"Yeah. You know, pilot stuff. This should be easy. And I'm the prize. Here goes. When America dropped the big bombs on Japan in 1945, all of the B-29 pilots had a call sign: a word followed by a two-digit number. What was that word?"

He shook his head, and reached for her again. He got his hand smacked.

Then, she smiled. "Dimples."

In bed with one of the most erotic and enigmatic women he'd ever met, he was no longer sure what, or who, would come next.

"We're good on autopilot for another few hours," she whispered into the captain's ear. "Let's do it again."

CHAPTER 38

At Ground Zero, the crowd that had pressed in just to get a glimpse of the heretofore reclusive Emperor Chin numbered over one million.

The air blast hammered them with a force greater than that of World War II's Hiroshima and Nagasaki combined. Estimates had those bombs killing up to a quarter of a million people, half on the first day.

Ironically, this day's detonation occurred 1,900 feet above Xian, the same height as that of the Little Boy bomb over Hiroshima.

The blast from Iran's first legitimate nuclear bomb vaporized everything for a mile. Had the explosive lived up to Navid's one megaton billing, the destruction should have been just over sixty-two times that of Hiroshima—all things being equal.

Still, it sent pressure waves of a phenomenal and terrifying nature. Pressure levels pounded into the landscape, reproducing in the land the sound waves from the sky.

The steel roof of the Terra Cotta Warriors museum disappeared. The temporary plastic roof over Chin's Warriors melted along with the terra cotta to form an unrecognizable plastic-coated puddle.

Newer buildings, built to modern codes, of brick, cement, and steel withstood the blast. They did so far better than their denizens, many of whom either died, or would die, from secondary effects depending on where and how they fell.

The explosion and aftermath demonstrated that Navid Mohammed's claim to one megaton was somewhat optimistic. Still, the devastation through a one mile diameter from Ground Zero, the hypocenter, exceeded those of Hiroshima plus Nagasaki, and was elongated a bit since the Stuka's dive had been only near-vertical. Perhaps in the shape of a flame.

CHAPTER 39

Prior to the detonation over Xian, the Crayle vehicle had not made it very far from Li's personal conspiracy and treachery haven, before it acquired a flat tire. In minutes, which seemed like hours with Lenny shouting instructions, the team had it back on the road. It was like taking the road into Versailles that seemed so long ago.

The ground shook violently as shock waves rippled the ground for a mile. A huge mushroom cloud rose in the distance.

Crayle knew in that instant that there was no point in continuing toward Xian.

He spun the vehicle carrying the Crayles, the MacKays, and the Lipschitz's back toward the drone hangar just before a ground ripple careened it onto the shoulder of the road, and then back on.

Magus Crayle still had the chops for driving fast.

He was well aware that they'd been spared certain death by having tracked to the east of the original Ch'in's massive burial mound.

In normal circumstances, they would have screeched to a halt outside the hangar door, then stormed inside.

Instead, Micmac drew a portable weapon and leaned out a window.

His depleted-uranium creation melted the door just before the vehicle would have slammed into it.

Crayle screeched the Humvee to a halt.

Weapons drawn, they jumped from the vehicle, and followed Phoebe into the office.

There they stood. Just rising from the floor where they'd fallen. Gao Bo-da, Red daughter, and General Li.

An aftershock threw the Crayle team weapons off target.

Li grabbed for his sidearm. He drew a bead on his least favorite man.

"Drop your weapons," Li commanded.

With no other choice, the team did.

No one moved. No one spoke.

It was just the two of them.

Crayle and Li.

"You think you are James Bond, or Jason Bourne. I assure you that you are not."

No one heard or saw Hekka's stealth climb into the overhead.

She could see Li with his gun on her husband.

Since the general's words reverberated, Hekka couldn't make them out. Until she pressed her earflap shut.

"I would ask you to strip down to be assured that you are unarmed, but you will be dead in less time then it would take."

He brought light pressure onto the trigger.

Her move along the beam had been precarious. Barely able to hold position, she felt her moccasin slip from her foot.

The slap as it fell twenty feet to the floor caused Li to spin in order to fire at the sound.

The whoosh of something large and heavy cycling through the air was followed by a thunk. Hekka's ten-inch Bowie slammed into the general's right shoulder.

Eyes wide, he cried out in pain. Li's gun arm dropped to his side. The weapon clattered onto the cement beneath his feet.

Li glared at nemesis Crayle just in time to see him pull the old Makarov Type 59 that he, Li Ya-fei, had used to kill the man's father so long ago. He watched it belch flame.

In slow succession, Crayle pumped all but one bullet into Li's frame, taking care not to hit his face.

The unarmed Gao and Red just stared.

"There, Li. For my father."

The general, writhing on the floor, heard the words. He spoke as Crayle walked to his side. "*My* father was a man of honor. Your father helped the Russians. He helped them aid the North Vietnamese."

Even in dying, the man could fabricate a hurtful lie.

The American spy crouched onto his haunches as he replied. "No. He helped the Chinese who wanted the Russians to lose."

"But—"

Bang!

Crayle pulled the Makarov Type 59 back from under Li's chin, and stood.

He walked over to Red and handed her the empty weapon. "Here. You can use this to remember him by."

With that, he left to the vehicle and, when the rest of his team, watching his back, piled in, drove away from the site.

Revenge required that two graves be dug. Crayle recalled learning the Chinese philosophy from his earlier sojourn helping Chin with the Blackstone Strategy. What a difference a day makes, he thought, as he headed toward the southeast, and the Yangtze River.

• • •

Following the departure of the Crayle team and demise of his boss, an out-of-work Gao lay naked on the floor of the office with a widowed and naked Red daughter pounding on top. She leaned down to press against him as they both reached their climax.

Having manipulated the straight pin out of sight of Gao, she positioned it behind his neck. One more stroke.

CHAPTER 40

The sky full of dirt, debris, terra cotta body parts, and the better part of a million human beings paled into the distance. With transit already secured and the skies devoid of Chinese interceptors, passage out to Hokkaido, Japan for refueling and beyond was a piece of cake. The day faded into night. Few lights glowed below. There was little life. The Iranian nuclear device—its first—had achieved its purpose. As almost an irony, behind to the West there was a glimpse of bright red sunset, in the direction of the Uighur province, Xinjiang. Where the takeover of China began.

"Where am I?"

"You're on Flight 911 direct to the promised land, Lenny," came the infinitely sexy voice over his earphones. "This is your captain, Flori, speaking. Jack said you folks needed a pick-me-up. So I did. You did leave a mess back there in more ways than one. He said you might be hearing from the president."

"Oh, great. How about landing in a country with no extradition treaty, sweet cheeks."

"Sorry, Mr. Lipschitz. No can do. But how about a detour to my old home town, Rio? Copacabana. Ipanema. And the Caipirinhas are almost as good as mine. Hmmm?"

To Magus Crayle, the banter was mere background. He'd avenged his father. He'd finally killed Li. And with the same gun. He owed Ling a lot for that. Still, there was little comfort. A blast from Iran's first nuclear weapon was not what he'd expected when he'd planned the summit meeting at Xian.

"Let's take it on home, Flori," said the former SEAL. "That was some heavy lifting. We all need about eight weeks of absolutely nothing."

"Roger that, Micmac. Setting course Zero-One-Five. Captain out."

Hekka nestled closer into Crayle's arms.

He pulled her tight to him, and placed a soft kiss on the crown of her head. "We don't need complicated right now. Simple works. Agree?"

"Yes, I really do, Magus. This one was almost too much. I feel like we're pushing our luck out to its limits. The next one could be it."

He glanced over at Micmac and Phoebe, locked in a similar embrace. "How about you two? Ready for some serious downtime R & R?"

"I've gotten behind on some serious weapon cleaning. My Glock's gonna gum up if I don't get with it. And Micmac needs to return that tank. It's overdue."

"I did get unlimited miles, though."

As if Lenny's timer had just gone off, he added to the conversation. "I want chocolate. I'll bet there's none aboard. Whine … whine … whine."

"Let's see," said Alona. "I seem to have misplaced my potassium cyanide capsules. Has anyone seen them?"

Receiving no response, Alona realized that the entire rest of the team had fallen asleep. For some reason unknown to her, a smile crept onto her face. She ran her fingers through Lenny's hair as he perched his head comfortably against her shoulder. Yes. They'd all made it. Thank God.

• • •

A couple of refueling stops and ten hours later, pilot Flori put an end to the cat napping of the ops team. Not being one to overdo formalities, she sang. "*Flyin' into Los Angeles. Bringing in a couple of keys. Don't check my bags, if you please, Mr. Customs ma-a-an.*"

The old Pete Seeger tune had a different effect in the present environment. No one lit up a joint, or a bong, or anything else. They rubbed eyes, scratched private parts, and stood up for a stretch.

"*Bom dia.* This is your Captain speaking. Time to sequence you through the shower. One shower. One-at-a-time. Micmac has the details. He built the thing."

"Another of his creations," observed Phoebe. "Probably belches fire."

"Close. You walk into the bedroom and close the door. You disrobe, placing all of your clothes into the item that appears to be a washer dryer. You shower, sailor style, and if you've not dallied, pull your clothes out fresh and dry. Takes ten minutes each. Should I repeat that for the slower folks?" He glanced at Lenny, then sniffed. "You first."

Hekka took the opportunity to enter the flight deck, taking a seat behind pilot Flori. "What's the plan once we make continental landfall?"

"Jack's little airport down the back hill from Big Bear. Why?"

"Do you do requests?"

"Try me."

"Drop the other four off as planned. Us?" She whispered her secret plan into Flori's ear.

The Brazilian smiled. "Stick around so I can ferry you and Magus back to Las Vegas? To finish your vacation? Roger that big time."

Hekka forged a smile. Flori was not only an excellent pilot and the sexiest woman alive, but she was letter perfect for Jack Sommers. Then again, so was his first wife, Marli. Oh, well. She just shook her head and returned to the cabin.

"Alona?" yelled Lenny as he exited the bedroom looking like he'd actually climbed into the washer/dryer combo. "You're up. Sorry about using up all the hot water."

• • •

The battle was done. Both Chin Yao-wu and Li Ya-fei were so much history. The only remainder of the old guard communist leadership knelt before the country's new leader.

In the Hong Kong palace, Empress Ling An-yee sat tall, wearing the appropriate garments, and looking royal and in control beyond her twenty years.

The former head of government, Po, spoke when she motioned at him.

"Your Excellency. I have a proposition. You have the position, we have the expertise you require to manage 1.3 billion countrymen … and women."

"You are communists at heart and soul. China is the new empire with no room for ideologies which exacerbate problems rather than solve them, and which prevent solutions rather than create them."

"You will be, perhaps, surprised. I agree. The masses only require masters. The masters make clear the rules, and we all move forward."

"Communism is the most extreme ideology. You cannot expect me to believe you will evolve at the change of the day."

"Please allow me to speak."

She nodded.

"As a young man, I travelled to Budapest. I witnessed the deviant manner of the communist leaders there and aspired to be just like them here in my own country. After the fall of European communism, I travelled back. I asked a young tour guide—a moonlighting university student—what it was like with capitalist leaders. He laughed. 'The ideology of extreme socialism is gone. The leaders are the same,' he said."

"Interesting." Ling mused. "You noted that it was all about being of the power elite. That ideology was merely a convenient excuse to suppress and repress a people."

"To be honest and forthcoming, leadership here struggled with this issue for years. We'd aligned with communism, which demonizes capitalism. We had no choice but to deploy the capitalist engine in order to create enterprise, innovation, and growth. Jobs for our population. As they say in the West, we threw Carl Marx under the bus."

"Wisely so."

"The Soviets proved over a seventy-year span that Workers of the World Unite was a fool's bargain. Communism demanded that we have total, centralized control, but that same control would cause the people to revolt."

"I think I understand. You needed a way out of the communist absolute, but couldn't find one."

"Precisely. We considered renaming our party with an evolutionary name, but we'd have to get it past the ideologues."

"So you foresaw either a revolt within your party or a revolution by the masses."

"What has happened is perfect. Communism has been destroyed by the Muslim bomb in Beijing. We wish to maintain the order by serving Your Excellency."

"On another subject, Po, you must, according to the custom of the West, choose an Anglicized first and middle name."

"Knowing that you studied in the U.S., I have already done so."

"And ..."

"Edgar Allen."

"I shall consider your offer."

• • •

Flori's landing at the Jack Sommers International Covert Airport on the northeast side of the Big Bear plateau was smooth. The team departed in the usual EMT ambulance, a little crowded, but glad to be back at the cabin.

"Lenny! How about a little help in the kitchen. Someone might mistake you for a perpetual consumer."

"I'm busy, MC. Checking out these novels Jack had put on what are now your bookshelves."

"As you know, Hekka and I spend most of our time at the horse ranch. Keeping this cabin on Jack's property is a great place for us all to congregate. Now, about that help with breakfast?"

"That's what wives are for."

"Hekka's still in bed. Sleeping off last night's sojourn at the Sugerloafer."

"That was fun, seeing Micmac sitting in with his old band. That new chick singer had me needing several napkins just to mop off the drool."

Alona, standing in silence behind the P.I. until now, couldn't let that comment slide by. "You're getting older, Lenny. The drool is nature having its way."

"Hey, how'd you get in?"

"Proximity card, luv. I put it in my hip pocket, wiggle my butt, and I'm in."

"Hey, is Tylenol the strongest you have?" Micmac stepped from the bathroom.

"I'm glad you sang that song again. I heard it for the first time when we met, what, eleven months ago?"

"Yeah, Phoebs. *Life Is Just A Game*. Written by the same guy who penned those spy novels you're checking out, Lenny."

"Is he still alive?"

"He used to come up here to write. Had a cabin not far from the Sugerloafer. Next to the forest. He'd wander into the woods a mile, two miles, whenever he got writer's block."

"Did the mountain lions get him?"

"No. He toted a Buck hunting knife. That's all. Never saw any of the cats. Good thing."

"Just checking out his bio. I'm guessing this guy was a real spy."

"Like us?"

At that moment, Hekka walked into the room with a washcloth pressed against her head. "*Ohhh!*"

As much as the team had learned to preclude Lenny's off-color comments, he'd learned to get them out without hesitation. "Jeez, HC. You look like shit."

She pointed her aching head at Crayle. "Why didn't you protect me?"

"Protect?"

"It is a man's traditional role. We Serrano are big on tradition. You allowed me to drink three pitchers of Buckler. *Ohhh!*" She filled the cloth with ice cubes, alternately pressing it against each temple.

Even though the beer had been necessarily free of alcohol, Crayle knew that any retort to a woman's accusation would prove hopeless. "You have my heartfelt apologies. Speaking of spies, we're close to being done. I've already finished Chin's Redrock Strategy. It belongs to Ling, now. It should keep her in power for the foreseeable and unforeseeable future."

Lenny looked puzzled. "What about your CIA work? You know? For the president?"

"Oh, that. We return the organization to the proper attitude, structure, and methods of the past. The coffee cups, T-shirts, and ball caps with the Agency emblem have to go. The DCIA moniker reverts to DCI. The DNCS just becomes a component of the DO. And no one calls it the CIA anymore. It's just the *company*."

"So the ultra-secret organization becomes exactly that."

"What a concept."

Micmac tilted his chin. "Boots on the ground?"

"You bet. HUMINT makes a comeback. We actually know what's going on. The president, having spent a lot of time at NSA, already has someone whipping them up to max speed on the SIGINT side.

She'll assure that the Science and Technology directorate and NSA SIGINT pipeline has all the bandwidth it requires."

"New presidential dictum: wipe out the bad guys before they kill any more innocent people."

"The president set the pace up front in his administration by wiping out the governmental district of Tehran."

"Here. I'll check the news," Lenny picked up his tablet computer. "Yeah, team. There's been another explosion in Iran. Wow! The Ayatollahs got together to pray during Death To America week. Seems they lit a sacred candle and the damn thing blew up. Got 'em all. There's chaos in the streets of what's left of Tehran. A million demonstrators—this time unpaid—shouting Down with Iran! Up with Persia!"

Crayle grinned. "I got a little head start in my new job."

"I'll say," said Micmac. "Without Iran's leadership and beaucoup bucks, the terrorist organizations will dry up."

"That form of aggression might go away, but the people underground, working to develop the bomb, are even more dangerous. As we've seen with the North Koreans, they'll be able to extort whatever they want if they establish a nuclear weapons arsenal."

"Buzz kill!" said Lenny.

Micmac had something. "I can help with that. I'll get to work on ways to engineer localized earthquakes. Maybe use fracking technology. Bury the aspirations of their nuclear types along with all their goodies."

"Not bad," Crayle responded. "Get started on that. Let me know if you need a little dark funding. But first, breakfast is served."

CHAPTER 41

The morning after she'd enacted her plan to sneak back to Jack's airport and have Flori fly them to Las Vegas, Hekka Crayle reached under the covers for her husband. "Forget our undies, did we?"

He rolled onto his back, his head flopping her way. "Damn."

"I'm getting up."

"Okay." He rolled back onto his side.

"I'm going to do something different today."

"Set a new Guinness record for Bowie-knife throwing?"

"Bingo!"

"I was kidding."

"No. I'm going to go play Bingo."

He laughed. "Breaking quarter horses isn't enough excitement? Or fighting evil wherever it might find us?"

"I'll take *N-34* to *Now! Now!* anytime."

He rolled back. "Want me to tag along?"

"With all due respect, Mr. Danger Magnet, I can handle this one alone."

She was washed, dressed, and gone in what seemed like sixty seconds.

"I guess I have the day to myself."

He pulled the covers over his head for about a half minute, then tossed them away. "Coulda turned out the light," he said to the empty room.

He'd existed for the past several years by finding intrigue whether there was any or not. He suspected foul play.

"My new reality. If she has to get up, I have to get up."

He marched his stark-naked body into the shower and, oh, it felt so good. Toweling off, he canted his head back as if speaking to the nearest *company* satellite and, softly, uttered a challenge, "Find me here, Jack."

Dressed in a little longer than it had taken his wife, he fired up the flat screen TV and waited for it to produce some news. With the bad luck they'd had at the Hard Rock Hotel last time, he'd registered this time at the cross-town Gold Coast.

Crayle turned away just as the television's speakers blurted, "Good morning, Magus. Glad to see you're feeling well and back on vacation. Oh, don't respond. This message is a recording. Beep."

In the time it had taken for Jack's little fun fest, Crayle had retrieved his pistol from under the pillow and had drawn down on the screen, which now sported several totally biased pundits discussing the next election.

He relaxed. Five minutes later he was downstairs catching a cab over to the Hard Rock. A nice breakfast at Mr. Lucky's 24/7 was just what he needed.

And nice it was. Having experienced all of the crouching, running, and jumping exercises in Asia, he decided an after-breakfast walk was just the thing. He set out from the café down Harmon Street to the strip and then north to the Paris Casino. He noted that their Eiffel

Tower showed no signs of the major dustup he and his team had lived through the previous Christmas on the original.

Twenty minutes later, having passed by all of the gambling opportunities and eateries, he exited the adjoining Bally's onto Flamingo Street and headed west. Over the busy Interstate. Back to the Gold Coast. That he'd passed by several sleeping homeless individuals and a mountain of discarded trash reaffirmed his opinion that governments everywhere—even in this wealth center of the universe, Las Vegas—continued to fail in even their most fundamental responsibilities.

Passing the Rio All-Suite Las Vegas Hotel and Casino and Resort—known locally as the Rio, he noticed The Palms across the street. What the heck, he thought. He crossed at one of Las Vegas' multitude of eons-long lasting traffic lights, entering under a porte cochère.

He quickly scanned the typical large gaming room, the Hooters restaurant to his left, and a kiosk displaying a property map. Something caught his eye. Although he was hungry again after his three-mile walk, he headed away from the Hooters to something identified only as the Sky Tube. Hmm. Sounds fun.

Up one floor in an elevator, he stepped into a long hallway with side-by-side people movers in both directions. Along the wall to his right, rectangular windows had been placed at odd locations to let in real light. He stepped onto the first of two sequential fifty-foot-long people conveyers.

• • •

The three men dressed in tactical gear had been put up in the ritzy PalmPlace Residences ever since the Crayles had left Las Vegas for Hong Kong. They'd registered for the minimum one-month lease under a false name, and were there as a Plan B in case Crayle and the others couldn't be taken out in Asia.

They spotted Crayle heading toward the casino by hacking into the facility's surveillance system and employing facial recognition software on the images. Their tepid report to the Monaco palace that the target's wife was not with him yielded an emphatic "*Take him now!*" order.

There they were. He spotted them as they jumped into view. They separated by several feet as they ran onto the opposite-direction conveyer.

They had short automatic weapons. MP5Ks. Nine hundred rounds per minute. Good for spraying death in close quarters. Not good for him.

Crayle reached beneath his shirt for his weapon. Before he could take a shot, three chinks separated by half-second intervals exploded as many windows from their surrounds.

Just as quickly, the three assassins fell to the metal conveyer, dead.

He reached the end of his ride, carefully stepping off, but maintaining the combat grip.

One-by-by one, the bodies were deposited at the end of their ride. The final end.

Quickly, he retraced their pathway, took another elevator down, and walked out of the PalmsPlace Residences as if nothing had happened. Back across Flamingo, he entered the Gold Coast via a back entrance and headed up to his room.

Perhaps he would give Jack the sniper a call. Perhaps he wouldn't. One thing was for sure. He was not going to tell Hekka.

CHAPTER 42

Having just begun a new day in Las Vegas but already dressed for the pool, Magus Crayle heard the phone that he'd purposely left behind when he'd travelled to Hong Kong. It contained a special inscription and, beyond that, no other apps. And it possessed but one ring tone: Hail To The Chief. He pressed his right eye to the camera to answer.

The President of the United States, POTUS for short, sat in the plush rocking chair just nodding his head. "You're all back safe?"

"Every one of us made it out. I believe I owe you an in-person sitrep."

"That you do. But it's, as you can imagine, bigger than that. Much, much, much bigger."

"The erasure of the nominal head of our biggest enemy and biggest potential ally puts the world up for grabs, doesn't it?"

"I need you here. And now. Then, I promise, I'll spirit you in the most secure manner anywhere in the world you choose. We'll video in Jack from the Manassas office."

"With all due respect, every promise anyone has made that we're finished with this stuff has come to nothing."

"I get that. I can promise best effort. How's that?"

"I'll be bringing Hekka."

"Joined at the hip, are we?"

"Joined in every way possible. She knows what it could mean every time I walk out the door."

"Then it's done. Dinner for three at ..."

"Six P.M. Eastern."

"Done." The president rang off.

Crayle provided his left eye to conclude the call on his end.

• • •

In as few words as possible, Crayle explained the situation to Hekka. He recalled his promise to finish out their peaceful week's vacation, interrupted to the extreme by a nuclear and small arms battlefield he had codenamed simply as Xian O'Grady.

Following a quick call to the pilot at McCarran, and a grab of their Boogie bags and the Cobra, the Crayles sped over to the nearby Las Vegas Airport, jumped into Jack's old Falcon 7X, and made Washington's Dulles Airport in less than three-and-a-half hours, onc hour less than commercial. A quick shuttle to Langley, and they were ushered into a room only used for presidential meets. This time, it was Crayle who spoke first.

"You didn't just motorcade over here, did you?" He waved at the un-presidential attire, dust and all.

"Draws attention. We don't need that. Especially with you here. The new tunnel from the White House is slick. We used some folks from south of the border. It seems they can dig for miles and no one notices. My former associates at NSA borrowed the rail plans from a German firm. You might have heard of them." He gave them the name.

Crayle's eyes appeared to be stuck in place. He'd noticed a manufacturer's plate riveted to the maglev vehicle that had transported him from the Aryan cavern *Rotfels* to Eagle's Nest. The name, Alliance International, labeled the secret society who'd kidnapped he and Hekka in Helsinki and had taken them there—he under Neuschwanstein—the anything but Disney castle—and her in the Eagle's Nest complex—Hitler's former home away from home. He glanced at the president. His friend's smile seemed genuine, and he knew Kimbel not to be someone who could be linked to the German radicals. And the NSA had proven over time to have an extensive reach.

CHAPTER 43

It was the very next day. The quick trip to Langley was over and done. A light rain began to fall in Las Vegas, but not enough to dampen the Crayles' spirits.

She lay on the bed naked.

He dropped his robe and stood three feet away. Also naked.

She crossed her arms in an X configuration, hiding her breasts.

"My body used to excite you. It must no longer have that power." She slid her hands down to her developing tummy. "Not now."

He put on a pair of sunglasses, and stepped to the floor-to-ceiling sliding door, visible to the many upper floors in Las Vegas.

She loved the man. But why the shades?

Of course.

She knew.

Hanging around in the spy world told her. He stared straight ahead, but watched her in the door's reflection while pretending to be no longer interested. Spycraft.

Hekka reversed it, and noticed that in his reflection, his interest in her had peaked.

They made love.

They fell asleep.

• • •

Hekka awoke an hour later to someone speaking softly. The man in bed with her.

"What are you doing on the phone, Magus?"

"After that, I'm ordering in."

With breakfast in their room complete, Crayle scored an epiphany. "Let's take in a movie."

"Movie? In Vegas? No one does that. Who even has a theater?"

"There's one right here, in the Queen."

"Since we have nothing better to do other than enjoy our eternal peace, sure."

Thirty minutes later, they entered the theater, picked a movie, grabbed popcorn and drinks, and found a pair of seats. Ten minutes in, Crayle had his second epiphany.

"I've seen this before," he whispered.

"You've seen *Dr. No*?"

"Spy gets the girl. Spy gets the villain."

"Then, spy gets a different girl?"

"Oh, no you don't. Spy remains true to his one and only."

She considered that perhaps she had become a little paranoid, what with all the mayhem. "Tell you what. I'm going to watch the remainder. You reconnoiter some lunch. Text me when you have something, and I'll meet you there at noon."

He processed the request. "I happen to know that there's a Hooters across the street. Great burgers."

"Let me guess. They serve medium-sized drinks in a … C-cup. D-cup for large, and so forth."

He smiled, and walked out of the theater only to return five minutes later.

"I've been requested back East."

"Right after we finally complete our week's vacation in Las Vegas. One more day."

Silence.

"One more day, Magus. Right?"

He glanced over to get a feel for how she really felt. Normally, she didn't provide emphasis by elevating her voice. Normally, she didn't extract her Bowie from its scabbard and flick her thumb over the blade's edge.

"I know. I promised. One more day of total bliss, and I'm off the hook."

He slapped his hand over his mouth.

"Off the hook?"

Hand still in place, he attempted a rescue. "Steak tonight?"

She extracted the movie ticket from his pocket, and sliced it neatly in half. "Morton's?"

"Done."

He almost followed with, "Whew!"

CHAPTER 44

While the Crayle's endeavored to complete their seven-day vacation in Las Vegas, a group of Catholic missionaries had flown into Rapid City, South Dakota. Under normal circumstances, not a surprise for anyone. They'd picked the center of America for a reason, not the least of which was anonymity. Missing from their pre-trip analysis was that, in the American Midwest, those who were *not from around here* were immediately noticed by locals.

That these nuns were all Chinese quadrupled the attention. In private, they spoke their native language. Otherwise, they stuck to English to appear less foreign.

Though nervous about the curious eyes and mobile lips, they were disciplined. They stuck to the plan. They rented a sport utility vehicle, having chosen a Japanese brand because the *they all look alike* crowd might conclude they were of that ethnicity. One U-Haul and a load of cargo later, they made rendezvous north of Rapid City and just outside of Belle Fourche at the geographical center of the United States, and practiced their routine with the trailer's contents.

Two days later, the leader pronounced them ready. It took them a full day to pack up their tent, their special item, and return to the airport.

In three hours, they landed at destination number two.

• • •

The Chinese Missionary Daughters arrived at Maryland's BWI airport just outside of Baltimore. Having processed through customs, they headed for the heavy cargo facility to retrieve their goods. As planned, a flatbed truck was already in place to receive the crated four large and four small tubes, the four propulsion devices, and the requisite connective gear.

The portable airboat, they'd explained while authorizing the trip via U.S. Customs, could be flown anywhere in the world, set up in a couple of hours, and deployed to the benefit of the world's remote poor, who of necessity lined river valleys in Fourth World countries as the sole source of their sustenance. Anyplace with a river or a lake would suffice due to the craft's exceptionally shallow draft.

While the average age of the women portrayed them as too young to be on such an adventurous mission, reality differed dramatically. Their individual educations under Chin's mandated tutelage, and experiences as members of his immediate family belied such a conclusion.

Once they'd reached their destination beside a wide river, the men with the truck arrived, unloaded the several large cartons, received a surprisingly substantial tip, and were on their way.

Now alone, the women opened the cartons for an item inventory.

Within, they located each of the modular 'air boat' components. The official story Red had provided to U.S. authorities was that the tubes were for air boats to aid the poor. She'd specified four motors and propellers with protective shrouding as normal with air boats.

The reality was that the four large tubes could be telescoped out and connected, forming a square. The small tubes would be telescoped and, when connected inside the larger ones, formed a bracing X within the square. With the motors connected at the corners, there came into existence one large UAV drone. A baby bassinet brought along by one of the Daughters would be attached at the center. It would receive the football-shaped mini-nuke. The one Li had intended to destroy the Standing Committee at Hainan, and to initiate conflict with the Vietnamese.

As a reward for their success so far, Red allowed the women to doff the nuns habits to reveal underclothing they felt much more apropos to the task at hand. Assembly into the air boat configuration actually took far less than they had experienced at Belle Fourche, and their boat was a thing to behold.

They'd fastened the four smaller tubes to form a floatable flooring, with two tubes end-to-end on each side as the primary floatation components. Lastly, they affixed the airboat motors, and the four propeller assemblies with their protective screening.

"The two propellers on the front are azimuthing, ladies. They point the boat and are used for steering. The hind two, also azimuthing, are used mainly for propulsion, but can be turned for tight or emergency maneuvers."

The leader spun up the motors for a test run and then shut them down.

The metal structure employed titanium throughout so pushing the craft into the water was an easier task than it would have appeared.

• • •

By nightfall, they reached their next destination and docked inside an old boat house

Red provided some prescient intel.

"We will utilize a rented barge for the remainder of our journey—the one I've dubbed Li's Surprise—in order to get our device close enough to our target."

"Can we have the target now?" Blue daughter asked. "If I am to utilize my whirlybird skills, I need to know as soon as possible in order to check out the airspace."

"And you shall, Blue. Meantime, Gao will spool up and initiate a cyber attack on our target. It will prevent our operation from being compromised. And, with that, I'm taking no questions at this time."

Red still remembered the little unexecuted subplot she and Li had devised. She'd chosen not to kill him at her previous opportunity outside of Xian. When Gao had finished with his attack, she still might need to off him. For job security.

Finished for the day, she took a moment to ponder her revenge. Magus Crayle had killed General Li, the only man she'd been with. It was on careful consideration following the events near Xian that she'd concocted the current plan. The other daughters had been easy to convince. Chin, who'd been the only father they'd known, had been horrifically murdered, she'd said tearfully, and that justified what they were about to do. And to whom they were about to do it.

CHAPTER 45

September beginnings were always semi-bleak in central Virginia. Jack Sommers now headed the Other Specialized Staffs office, following the former head's assassination in France by one Pattie Norbrunn. He sat behind Neil Wohlford's old desk as he always did, applying another three fingers of fine Rémy Martin X.O. cognac. Or he would have had the bottle not run dry.

Jack, a problem-solver extraordinaire, pulled from a zippered case a bottle of Jack Daniels and a bottle of Crown Royal. North American hootch would supplant the French attitude of the former mole. It was fitting.

No sooner had he plopped fresh cubes into his whiskey glass, his cell phone intoned *Hail To The Chief.* First things first. He poured the liquid and took a long pull. He smiled.

"President can't wait," he spoke to the glass as he set it out of the frame for the visual. He pressed the icon for Skype/TS to ensure that no one could intercept the audio or video, and then brought up the visage of President Kimbel Stones.

"Good day, Jack. How are things in the bowels of Manassas?" The president referred to the office location far beneath the civil war battlefield.

Yes, thought Jack. Ingress via the porta-potty elevator was so confined that spiriting in the booze had been a struggle. Still, supplying a urine sample for identification validation had been one of Neil's better moves.

"A good day, indeed, Mr. President. How goes it in the people's political playground?"

"You know I don't banter well, so we'll skip the gossip. Something is afoot, my friend. My old consorts at the NSA have picked up the following. As you know, the Monaco Grand Prix had to be rescheduled to September due to your little assault on the palace a few months ago. I'm hearing that everybody's going to show up and that includes the Illuminé's Elder masquerading as the Prince of Monaco, the pope, who we know to be Illuminé as well, and our old friend, Pattie."

"If I read between the lines, you're wanting me to send a hit team to chop off the head of the monster. That about right?"

"Close. Not just any team, Jack. THE team."

"You're seriously kidding. With all due respect, Sir, they've gone through hell twice within the past month. First Hong Kong, then Xian. They're beyond beat. I …"

"I know, I know. Fact is, this is a one-time opportunity. We also know that Pattie was involved in the recent catastrophe in southern Germany. She's nuts, Jack. She'll kill people until there aren't any more. Now, she's got a taste for taking out heads of state."

"I get it, Sir. And you give the orders. What do you want me to do?"

"As an aside, the good Doctor Rorschach has reprogrammed the DCI and DDCI moles at Supermax. This brain-fucking actually works. They have no memories of their attachment to Illuminé, but have retained all the knowledge necessary to return to work. As of today, they're back in their seventh-floor offices here at Langley."

• • •

A barge, seeming little different from a number of others floated down the 400-mile-long river. The river was the Potomac. Aboard the barge appeared a watercraft, interesting on its own merit. A large pontoon boat lashed tightly to the deck with a number of young and pretty nuns sitting on top, waving their hands and crosses at passersby.

On a signal from one, they all turned to work at dismantling the boat atop the barge. In short order, they transformed it into four large tubes along with four smaller tubes. Four airboat-style, propellered engines sat nearby.

"Quickly. We only have time to assemble, load, and deploy," said the lead nun.

There were no return comments. The rest joined her in the assembly they'd practiced and practiced some more at the Midwest town, Belle Fourche.

An elongated special item had been removed from its hiding place in one of the tubes. The leader placed it on the deck, and promptly sat on it, her cloak obscuring it from prying eyes.

In thirty minutes, the Li drone was complete. Its four-fuselage, square shape mimicked many of the toy drones, but this one was quite large.

Last, the women tore off their garments. For those who watched from other boats and from along the river banks, jaws dropped.

The traditional Chinese garments sported several colors of the rainbow. Slits up each side revealed a lot more leg than would be appropriate for nuns.

• • •

Crayle had just one more day to go to finish his one week of Las Vegas vacation obligation to Hekka. Unfortunately, he'd given his word to Kimbel Stones.

The Crayles made their way once more to Langley. He needed to make good on his promise to meet with the president about the latter's job offer. The RUN-THE-CIA job offer. With respect to his personal life, the answer needed to be no. But you just didn't ring up the President of the United States and say no. He had no way of knowing what else was about to transpire.

Once inside, Crayle asked Hekka to wait in the lobby. That little chess move gave him an excuse to be brief. Civil, but brief. One look and he remembered that the transparent CIA ingress box was, in part, due to Lenny's father, Sammy Silberweiss. That history made the tight squeeze and momentary claustrophobic sequestration more bearable.

His credentials checked out since the glass surround didn't turn opaque, nor did the chamber fill with debilitating gas.

A gregarious young man, likely an intern, escorted him to the bowels of the building.

When they'd reached the open door to the Sound and Technology Isolation Facility, the STIF room, the escort took his leave.

Crayle stepped inside the chamber, and closed the door behind.

"Good morning, Mr. President."

The sole other occupant rose and offered his hand. "I thought we agreed on first names, Magus."

"We did. Great to see you again, Kimbel."

"As usual, the President of these United States and leader of the Free World is on a short leash. Twenty minutes max, I'm afraid. Everything we say is between us and protected by this STIF. Now, about that job I offered?"

Looking into the other man's eyes just made Crayle's task ten times tougher. In his mind, he wanted to say yes. In his heart, he had to say no.

"This world, this country, and those you love would be a lot safer if you agree to the DCI position."

"Mr. President … Kimbel. Given your last comment, I doubt if you could make this any more difficult."

"Hold that thought. Let me get Jack on the line."

It didn't escape Crayle's notice that the president had pressed *Redial.*

• • •

The man entered for a guided tour/orientation. The woman awaiting him in the CIA HQ lobby, advised that she was the administrative assistant to the director of the fourth directorate, Administration. Pattie's badge, a leftover from previous work, sported a name other than her own.

That his contact met him just inside the entry was no surprise. He was the kind who might be suspicious up front, but became less so as time went on. That surprises didn't always come at the beginning wasn't in his playbook.

"Hi, I'm Fran. I'm meeting you outside of the inspection box so I can vett your creds, then usher you in through one of the highest security entities in existence."

The man was a little unnerved and tried to make light. "Have they killed anyone lately?"

"Not today."

"Good."

"Not yet."

Hekka Crayle waited nearby, but didn't notice the pair as she peered through the Langley forest to the Potomac River.

"This won't take long," Pattie assured.

Ten minutes and they were through.

"That is most unusual," he said as he pointed between her breasts. The tight material exhibited the outline of the large cross beneath. "The chain around your neck gave you away. Catholic." He smiled at his capacity for deductive reasoning.

She knew the type. He'd look her up and down, then would bring his exceptional charm and other talents to the fore. She'd be easy, he would think.

Pattie started to feign a protest, but he raised his hand. "It's okay, Franny. I like Catholic girls."

She likened his grin to that of a weasel. "I would bless you, but I'd need help getting my cross free."

Her dimples were all he needed. The STIF room, isolated from all else, would do just fine.

"Oh, I see you may wish to do some administering yourself."

"I'm sorry. I …"

"Hold that thought, although I don't believe such administrating is permitted on government premises."

"Yes. You are correct."

"I notice from the markings on your badge that you are very important. Don't be surprised around here if some of the badges don't bear our actual names. That said, let me take you on your tour. We're going below." She glanced down at his crotch. "To the STIF room."

• • •

Lieutenant Gao sent the Super Drone aloft, controlling it with his special Smartphone.

"Bring it down!" Red ordered. "Crash it on top of the building, then detonate."

"No. No. I'm taking it to a high altitude for maximum dispersion."

The drone responded by climbing ever higher as it flew south.

"Their radars will see it!" He was ignoring her. She tried to snatch the phone from his grasp.

Gao was quicker, turning his back to her.

She looped an arm around his neck, pulled the straight pin from her hair, and thrust it upward into his brain.

He fell.

The phone skittered across the dock.

Into the river.

"*Omigod!*" Red screamed.

She recalled that the new phone was water resistant, and dove after it.

Murky, the Potomac took its time to allow her a visual.

There it was.

Red swam down.

A nearby crustacean, curious about the foreign object, crab-walked nearer.

Red, with almost no air left, wanted to scream "*No!*"

Too late. The bottom feeder's long leg tapped gently on the phone's screen.

CHAPTER 46

The president was in mid-sentence with Jack when Crayle saw her.

On the STIF room monitor screen.

There, not twenty feet from the STIF, she stood with her blouse in one hand, and her bloody, knife-bladed Holy Cross in the other. Her guest lay on the granite floor. Quiet to a fault. But not the one she'd come to kill.

Pattie noticed that the security camera had stopped panning. The necessary advantage of surprise lost, she turned and ran. She'd been a sprinter in college and was still quite quick.

Just as Crayle headed full tilt from the isolation room, it happened.

The sky-burst pounded the ground as if an exploding black hole were creating a new universe.

Boo-woo-woo-woo-woo-woo-woom!

The ostensibly bomb-proofed CIA headquarters shook with incredible violence.

Chunks of ceiling crashed down.

Steel beams protruded like bones from a compound fracture.

One of the large projectiles slammed Crayle in the head, knocking him to the floor.

• • •

Before Jack could respond to the president, the entire underground facility at Manassas shook violently. Items attached to the walls fell. Items atop flat surfaces crashed to the floor.

"What the hell was that, Jack? What was all that crashing and clunking I just heard?"

"We just had a shaker. Happens from time to time. Stuff falls on the floor, I pick it up, and put it back. No big deal."

"And the clunking?"

"Earthquakes cause the security system to enter lock-down mode. What you heard is all the doors being automatically super bolted. No one can get in or out. We still have comms, but that's about it."

"Holy Hell! The wall mount, Super Bowl-capable video in here just went nuts. I'm looking at Langley, Jack. Holy Shit! We've been hit!"

"Can you be more specific, Sir?"

"Some kind of aerial bomb. I'm rewinding a bit … crap! A drone of some kind flying in from the river. Aerial burst. It nearly flattened Langley. STIF room, where I am, is fine. Seventh floor's gone. Most of the rest."

"The DCI and DDCI?"

"Accessing the sign-in … yeah, they were on site."

"We're in a world of hurt, Kimbel."

"Gotta go, Jack. I'll work things from my end. Get the team on the way. Oh, and one more thing. The DCI and DDCI roles? Fail-over time, my friend. To you."

• • •

In the private section of Dulles Airport south of Langley, the Brazilian was out of the hangar and into the air shortly after the Langley explosion. The Navy stud pilot had gone to the head. Flori had Jack's new Falcon 8X under control on a track north for about thirty seconds. That's when she spotted the chopper.

Off to port. She turned.

• • •

Blue daughter, who had the exfil role for the Super Drone team, had the other daughters aboard, but no Gao and no Red. She caught the motion above. She spun her helicopter's tail around and began to flee. Flori quickly closed on her. The future looked bleak and brief. One pass by the business jet and the wash of those huge engines would slam her into the ground.

Flori prepared her flyover. Blue spun her aircraft around and headed in the opposite direction.

Maneuverability was not a jet's strong suit. Not against a whirlybird.

Flori affected the tightest turn possible, pulling heavy G forces.

For an instant, she thought of the Navy pilot rattling around in the head. As long as the toilet tank held, he was only in the dryer component of a washer/dryer combo.

Close now, she screamed in at what a sailor would call Flank Speed.

Blue flattened the collective, sending her craft downward. At the last second, she pulled back on the stick.

The copter tilted to vertical on an intercept course with the Falcon.

Flori saw the move. Brilliant. If she dodged, she'd likely lose control. If she throttled back, they'd collide.

At the last instant, she dropped the landing gear.

"*Ahhh!*" Blue screamed. Her rotor blade tips shattered as they struck the wheels.

Blue knew she was done. Not much held a helicopter in the air in the first place. Her craft tumbled and spun until it slammed into the Potomac.

Upon impact, it erupted like a small version of the bomb that had just struck Langley.

• • •

Back at Manassas underground, Jack answered his red phone. "*Go!*"

"There's a problem in La-La-Land."

Jack Sommers pursed his eyebrows. "Hollywood?"

"No. D.C. and environs."

"Flori! Sitrep!"

"Had a little to-do with one of Li's disciples. Landing gear damaged. Got to set down."

"Doesn't sound good. The Tango?"

"Pulled down. Off the game board."

Jack noticed Flori's voice trailing off at the end. "There's more?"

"I got a glimpse of the pilot. Asian, but wearing a blue Chinese . . ."

"Cheongsam. Right?

"Right."

"Boy, we've been there before. Look, your landing gear is damaged. Set down in the water, Sully style. That plane—and all the goodies I've added—is expensive, so make it shallow."

"Aye, aye, Cap'n Jack."

"I'll get folks out there to pluck you from the wing and close off the area. Hazmat suits and such will work nicely."

"I'm going to be a tad busy, so wife out."

Jack Sommers worried for her. He'd been around the block several times, but she'd taken him places he'd never imagined. And that was just in the bedroom.

CHAPTER 47

Minutes after being struck, Crayle roused.

He glanced into the STIF to the president. Gone. As he checked out the outer enclosure, still no president. And no sign of his path out.

He crawled over debris to an armored door.

It was guarded by an overhead sign.

EMERGENCY EXIT

AN ALARM WILL SOUND

"I think this constitutes an emergency."

He leaned into the door, and it provided no resistance. And there was no alarm.

"Low bid," he muttered as he gazed at his means of egress.

The stairway had buckled down the middle and not only had pulled apart side-to-side in four-foot sections, but had disarrayed itself vertically as well.

With fingers and nails, he crawled ever upward, stopping only to gasp for breath.

Then, a noise.

A brief *oomp*.

The right echelon of stairs collapsed, falling fifteen feet to the well bottom.

He spared his own life by rolling left in the first instant.

He pulled himself up to ground level, and through a door left in pieces in the bomb's aftermath.

Ahead, Hekka lay stuffed into a bomb-detecting device.

When he reached her, he saw no movement.

He heard a moan.

Clumps of acoustic tiles caused him to check above. The ceiling appeared ready to collapse.

As quickly as he could, he extracted her and wrapped her arms around his neck.

Depleted as he was, he toted her outside and placed her in their vehicle.

He blasted their SUV through the main gate, experiencing no resistance. The guards were both scattered. And dead.

Just as they reached the Dolly Madison Parkway, a video popped onto the center display.

Crayle screeched the car to a halt under an overpass.

It was a replay of some kind. It displayed the Li drone heading in, then the bright light of detonation. The vehicle's eighteen-speaker system provided the deafening sound. The subwoofers burst into flame.

If that weren't enough, the severe initial vibration that had permeated the surrounding twenty miles had caused the concrete of the overpass to shatter. That a semi-trailer had been hurled onto the top didn't help.

One huge chunk slammed down onto the roof.

Crayle ducked. The caving roof struck his head a glancing blow. Lucky for him, the cement didn't cave in his head. The hits to the head, now two, took their toll.

"That was close," Crayle said, gritting his teeth to remain conscious as the shaking subsided. He heard no response.

"Oh, my God!"

It had struck primarily on her side.

Her head lay immobile on her shoulder, blood streaming out.

He yanked off his shirt, folded it into a compress, and applied it onto her wound with every ounce of pressure he could muster.

"Hekka! *Hekka!*"

She moaned. Just a little one. But enough.

A siren approached, its volume increasing.

Shortly, an ambulance slid to a stop close by.

"Help!" Crayle yelled through a shattered window. "She's alive! Help!"

One of the four EMTs employed the Jaws of Life to open the passenger door. With his attention focused on his wife, he couldn't see them.

In two minutes that seemed like two hours, the door crunched open. Another two lifted her carefully onto a stretcher after ensuring there was no spinal damage.

As she was being loaded aboard the ambulance, the fourth EMT stepped to the open door, hopefully to get him out. A female.

"Oh, no!" he cried out. "Pattie!"

She smiled, then gave her head a little shake. "No, don't get up. We'll—I'll—take very good care of her."

He couldn't move. "No—"

"Ah, ah. That's okay. And once a few repairs are made—perhaps to her memories—you can come for her."

He felt consciousness slipping away.

"Wh .... where?"

"Oh. Home, of course. She'll be my guest for the Grand Prix."

"Where ..."

A 'he's been hit on the head and doesn't remember' look gathered onto her countenance. "Monte Carlo?"

Pattie returned to the back of the ambulance to help attend to her new patient. Crayle watched. After she had seen that Hekka was properly secured, and appropriate medications infused via a drip mechanism, he watched his forever nemesis step to the driver's door.

At the last moment, she turned, pulling open her red trench coat.

She pointed to her naked body, then held her hand—thumb and forefinger extended in the international 'Call me' sign—and mouthed the words.

Crayle whispered the word *No!* as he fell forward, unconscious.

The ambulance drove away, lights and siren off, bypassing a multitude of smashed vehicles and dead or dying bodies.

• • •

Two days later, Crayle awakened to the sound of his ringing phone in a hospital bed. He recognized his special ring for this particular caller.

"I'm going to kill you, Jack!"

"What? I just—"

"Kill! Do you understand? Kill!"

"How was I to know—"

"Same as before. You snuck us into an op. You knew we'd say no, otherwise."

"Jesus. Calm the fuck down. How'd I know that Pattie would sneak aboard the Royal Princess as crew and try to kill you?"

"I recall an op where you put us aboard another cruise liner, Queen Mary 2. We almost went up in the aquatic equivalent of a mushroom cloud thanks to her."

"But you're fine, aren't you? And those days are done. I've got a task force at Langley going after the BG's, and a crew of British Sixers and French DGSE in Europe. And now Chin and Li are dead, and the group formerly known as the Chinese Communist Party wants back in. I'm telling you, you're fine from here on out."

"I hear you, Jack. It just brings to mind a used-car salesman saying, 'This beauty is fine.' You now what I mean?"

"I'm hurt."

Crayle could hear the sound of Jack's fist thumping his chest.

"But that's not why you called, is it?"

"No. Great news."

"I can't wait."

"Look, I'm sorry. Oh, I almost forgot. After Langley lost most of the seventh floor—the mucky mucks—I've got the helm, as Micmac would say. Tell you what. I'm going to make it up to you two and line up another vacation. No kidding. I felt truly sorry about the last one, so this one's on me."

"Forget that. Where's Hekka, Jack? No, don't answer. Pattie has her."

"Oh, bullfuck. You're just imagining the worst."

"Like hell. I saw her. After the fucking blast."

"Oh, crap. I wonder …"

"Monte Carlo, Jack. Pattie said Monte Carlo."

CHAPTER 48

The weather for the eastern portion of the Riviera was as predicted: partly cloudy, breezy warm, and with any chance of precipitation being held at bay south of Marseille to the west. It was the best Thursday ever for Formula 1 racing in Monte Carlo. Besides the collection of dignitaries and celebrities, the grandstands were full, as were all balconies and rooftops with even a glimpse of the course. Representatives of sports networks rounded out the peripheral entourage with their cameras, Smartphones, and tablet computers.

The morning two-hour practice session opened with thirteen two-car teams. While the Ferrari fans, *Tifosi* they called themselves, outnumbered their competition, the latter did their best to match the enthusiasm. Flags and banners from driver homelands spanned the globe.

The thirteenth team had been added midyear, a purchase and re-branding of a struggling Russian team. Carrying out negotiations in secret, no less a personage than Chin Yao-wu had scored the acquisition, having even kept it from his foremost confidant, Magus

Crayle. It had been intended as a special wedding present for Chin's new Empress, Ling An-yee.

The Empire of China team utilized one carryover driver from the Russian team and a Polish driver who'd recently recovered from a severe crash at the re-instituted French Grand Prix at Clermont-Ferrand in central France. Expectations were minimal given the non-impressive performance of the team's predecessor. That the Polish driver won at the Belgian Grand Prix two weekends earlier surprised even the experts.

Since a very surprising mystery guest had been announced for the event, many anticipated the new Chinese empress might make an appearance. That the cars' liveries were a montage of the various shades of jade added emphasis to the team's new domicile of record.

On a cloudless day, Practice One completed without the usual mayhem on the very tight Monaco city street circuit. No one paid much attention. Indeed, they drank, and drank some more. Many wore their finery with this being the classiest venue of the year. Middle class visitors who'd practically re-mortgaged their homes for the $1,000 tickets were looking fine. While everyone took a breather for lunch, and the mechanics changed to the tires of an optional, softer rubber compound, the royal palace to the west was a beehive of activity.

• • •

A couple of miles west of Monte Carlo at the palace, Pattie Norbrunn sat, hands on lap, in the Yellow Room opposite her father.

"You brought her here."

"This is my home. Until Versailles is rebuilt, and Sylvain and I assume our crowns there, this is it."

"I have no argument there. You've kidnapped and brought Magus Crayle's wife here. Don't you see? She's a ticking time bomb. She may have one of those CIA locator chips you informed me about."

"Vestige? Yes. That's my plan. Magus will track her to the palace via the implant, or utilize his tremendous powers of deduction to the same effect, and then we'll have him."

"Or he will have us. He is ever most lethal." He could see she was not movable regarding her plan. "You intend to kill him here, then."

She slapped her hands together, and giggled. "I do. Magus and I shall make love. That's when I like best to do it."

The Elder wanted to start with, "My little psychopathic daughter" but went instead with, "When the deed is completed, I will see that the two of them are buried at sea. Near the African coast. The Spanish territory, Ceuta. No one will know."

She stepped over to her father and kissed him on the lips. "Gotta go. I must catch Practice Two."

"Yes. Practice Two."

"I am certain you shall be elated to have taken him down."

"Do not forget in your ecstasy that you must take her life as well."

She smiled. "The bait always dies."

She left.

He had a mind to see to Mrs. Crayle's termination right away, but the ubiquitous American spy satellites had without doubt already tracked her to the palace. They probably had her vitals, too, so killing and moving her wouldn't work. The man of intellect, publicly known as the Prince of Monaco, appeared nonplussed for once. What to do?

• • •

Pattie breathed a major sigh of relief as she departed the palace. She knew Crayle would check there first. She left for an hour to check in on her captive. Satisfied, she returned to her royal apartments to change for bed. Stepping from the bathroom, she found her father sitting in her quarters, pondering.

"Uh, oh," said Pattie.

"What is the matter, my dear?" said the Elder.

"The Aryans have reverse engineered the sponge."

"The radiation sponge engineered by General Li's people?"

"Yeah."

"But you told me that you switched the real football-like nuclear devices for fakes. When you went to Switzerland. To transact with the Aryans. After St. Lucia."

Pattie pursed her lips. "The bomb fakes had the sponges on them, so they'd appear real."

"You removed them from the bombs? That means ..."

"I'm afraid so. Our two are regular old atomic weapons, radiation and all."

"It's still no problem. Without real bombs, there could be no radiation for the German fanatics' sponges to absorb."

"The Aryans are very, very clever."

"We must be perfectly clear about this. You possess our two bombs. The Aryans used the sole Iranian device—that country's first nuclear weapon—in China. I have seen the reports. No radiation detected means the Aryans have replicated—or have been supplied, by Li, the technology for—the sponges."

"That spells a potential alliance between Empress Ling and the Iranians. An unholy alliance to be certain."

"Beyond unholy," the Elder observed.

"Might be a good time to call the pope."

"Perhaps. But first, on to a lighter topic. Your view from the Princess chambers is worthy."

"I can view most of my realm from this top floor suite. The peninsula out front with its aquarium perched above a sea cliff, east to the Monte Carlo casino, and west into France. On a clear night, I can see the lights of Nice."

"And I am able to see that you are certainly exhausted from your journeys, so I will be brief. I have just a few important things to say to you."

She rolled from her side to her back, the gauze night gown concealing virtually nothing.

A man of supreme control, the Elder averted his eyes from her body's siren song. "I believe it is time for me to relate some quite relevant backstory. It was during a Grand Prix week, long ago. The finer ladies from Amsterdam arrived to sop up some of the excess wealth. Since you are familiar with the practice, I shall spare the details."

"High-priced call girls, we say in English."

"I was quite a bit younger, and she was the class of the profession. When I went to compensate her, she smiled, much like you do."

"Yes. Momma had dimples, too."

"Quite so. Then she dropped the bombshell. She said she'd stopped her birth control two months before, and was at the peak of her reproductive cycle."

"She wanted to have your baby. Me."

"Correct."

"You could have thrown her out of the country. You could have executed her. Why not?"

"My mind works differently than most others. I told her, should she become provably pregnant with my child, we would enter into an alliance."

"She must've informed you of her ancestry."

"That was bombshell number two. She told me about her relation, the World War I spy, Mata Hari. Your mother claimed to have inherited traits advantageous to the art and science of spying."

"Art and science?"

"Those were her words. For all those years you grew up in Amsterdam, she provided me with intelligence gathered in her bedroom to include our dearly departed Neil Wohlford, former head of the CIA Office of Specialized Staffs and its subordinate entity, the Strategic Solutions Office operated by one Jack Sommers."

"Yeah. The OSS for the first, then spelled backwards for the second one, was cute."

He smiled briefly. "Each year thereafter, I would provide—in a covert fashion, of course—a suite at the Hôtel de Paris for her during race week."

"Did you ..."

"We acceded to our sexual proclivities each day."

"But you didn't marry her."

"Impossible. I was the future Prince and Head of State. Her background would have been scoured for dirt. We agreed to maintain our arrangement indefinitely." Just pronouncing his last sentence brought sadness to his tone.

"What now?"

"It is complicated."

"Tell me."

"Your brother, who is next in line, has fallen for someone of your mother's ..."

"Profession?"

"I could not convince him otherwise ... he will abdicate before the end of the year."

"Then I'm next."

"As I said, it is complicated. You see, I have decided to take a wife."

Pattie, dumbstruck for a moment, retorted with, "No! You wouldn't do that to me!" She calmed herself, realizing that ultimatums don't work. Plotting, scheming, and executing did.

"I pined for your mother since her murder so long ago. I believe you were only fourteen at the time."

Pattie remembered the murder explicitly.

Staring alternately at the wall and at Pattie, the Elder continued. "She helped me bring Neil Wohlford into the Illuminé and had just been with him before ..."

"Did you suspect him?"

"He had an alibi. He'd returned to America the same evening. Your mother was still alive. As you are aware, the hideous crime was never solved, but it is easy for me to suspect a jealous client—she was that desirable."

"So this new wife, do I know her?"

"You do. She is the equally accomplished and beautiful CIA research psychiatrist, direct superior to Doctor Rorschach, and Illuminé mole, Monika Rikki."

Pattie closed her eyes. Monika's face thrust itself into view. The redheaded psychopath of mind manipulation. Then, questions. Had the woman already manipulated her father? Could Rikki turn her father against her? Could she have Pattie tossed from the royal household? Could she somehow get into Pattie's mind?

Those four pertinent questions paled to the reality. Second in line again. That simply wouldn't do.

• • •

Three hours to the west by jet, a lonely and beaten man stood at the water's edge. He'd been here before. To Portugal's Estoril beach, just outside of Lisbon. Then, it had been with the woman he'd grown to love. The sunrise had yet to arrive behind him, so he viewed the final moments of the precious darkness. Darkness, only interrupted by a full moon just above the horizon, and the thousands of tiny sparkles it projected on the breeze-blown Atlantic. Water Diamonds, he had named them. The medium brown sand beneath his feet felt as before. Supple. Moist. He and Hekka had made love here.

In twenty minutes, a tourist van transported him and his operational team to a private dock that appeared from the outside to be more of a drive-in warehouse. Inside, the reason for the deception and large size became apparent.

They filed across the gangway, each carrying his or her black tactical duffel. Ahead stood an impressive array of khaki-clad officers. A bosun's mate performed the necessary three-note salute honors with her pipe.

The Officer Of the Day took his salute first. Then stepped back as the Commanding Officer followed suit.

"I'm Captain Hildebrand. Welcome to the SS Anchovie." He anticipated the surprised looks. "I did a few things during the Cold War. As a reward, I got to name her myself. Since I consider myself an Old Salt, Anchovie seemed just right." He'd been read in and knew the primary on the op. He glanced at the man who must've had a tight link to the president. "And you are Mr. Crayle."

Micmac stepped forward. "I can help here, Magus. Request permission to come aboard?"

"Permission granted."

The Captain scrutinized each one as they passed, wondering what manner of mayhem might be in store. Bottom line? His role was to get this crew in and out, if possible, while maintaining his boat in one piece and combat ready. His years of experience told him that this mission would be a challenge.

"Mr. Roberts, my XO, will see you below. We cast off in thirty, so get your gear stowed wiki-wiki. I realize your personal quarters are kind of tight. So, if you need to meet, you can have the mess decks." He provided the non-mess timeframes of availability.

"Be aware. The crew may step in for a coffee from time-to-time. Your colleague, Micmac, knows the drill. We sailors live on strong, black coffee. I've let the crew know they can come and go, but not to dally … and no questions. Are we all on board with the ROEs as I've detailed them?"

"Aye, aye, Captain," said Micmac.

"And thanks for the ride in," Crayle added.

"Normally, we'd check your weapons into our armory for the duration. The president has said otherwise for this mission."

"Thank you for your hospitality, Sir."

Alona nodded concurrence.

Out of character, Lenny—positioned directly in front of the FBI agent—said nothing the entire time. When the team reached the entry hatch, Phoebe removed her Glock from his lower back.

"When this is over," he huffed, "I'm gonna have a little chat with Kimbel Stones, Missy."

"Good. It's better that he off you than me."

As the P.I. descended the ladder into the sub, she heard, "Whine, whine, whine."

As he'd finished the coming aboard protocol, Crayle noticed something peculiar. Later, below decks in their quarters, he asked Micmac. "The C.O. has one star. As I understand it, in the Navy that's a Commodore—a wartime rank."

"Whoa, you know some shit."

Lenny chimed in. "I can fill in the blank. I grabbed some Wi-Fi time before we came inside. I figured reception would be zero and the U.S. Navy wouldn't be offering free Internet. Today, Kimbel Stones, President of the U.S. of A., re-declared war on Islamic Terrorism."

"Wartime rank equals wartime."

"Bingo."

• • •

Later, underway aboard the Anchovie, the team took a breather in their berthing quarters when a knock sounded. A rap, rap as if with an acrylic hammer.

"Permission to enter." Lenny snickered, then glared once again at his computer screen.

When the Captain stepped inside, his smile seemed out of place. He glanced immediately at the guilty party. "You won't be getting Internet while you're aboard, young man. I've ordered it stowed for the duration. No traffic in. No traffic out."

"That's interesting. Since I've got nothing better to do, how's about having one of your guys show me how that Web on/off thing works?"

The Captain's smile faded a bit. "In the old days, when it wasn't *convenient* to keel-haul certain parties, the captain would have them tied to the deck. Back and forth went the wooden ship, down came the piercing rain, across blew the bitter cold wind."

"Convenient?"

"Since the Anchovie is an older boat, I've considered resurrecting that protocol. 'Lash him to the foredeck' I'd say. 'Take her down to 90 feet' I'd say."

"Message received, Sir. Uh. Ack, as Micmac says."

"Wait. Let's stick to the script," Phoebe interjected.

"The script, as Ms. Bransfield puts it, is this. Mr. Lipschitz? Lead your entourage to the mess decks for a cup of our fine coffee."

"Do you have decaf?"

The now-irritated captain had enough with Lenny. "When we finish an operation, any surplus coffee is turned over to the CIA … for their enhanced interrogations."

"Navy coffee would be more effective than water boarding," Micmac said as he nodded.

Phoebe gave Crayle a wink as she closed the door and followed the others toward the mess decks.

"You don't look comfortable sitting there on that rack, Mr. Crayle."

"Rack equals bed. Noted. Now, what's on your mind, Captain?"

The older man pulled a chair opposite where Crayle sat. "I believe you know where we're headed, but I'll share the little I know so we can approximate being on the same page."

"Ack, Sir."

"I and my boat are here to infil and to exfil, that's all. No combat assistance either in manpower or firepower. The weapons and ammo you brought with you are what you have."

"Kimbel … the president … read me in on the ROEs."

"First name basis with the Commander-In-Chief. Hmmm. If you like the ride, I could use a little positive mention. A boost from the rank of Captain to Rear Admiral, two stars, would bump my retirement significantly."

"But you already wear the one-star Commodore rank."

"It's fake. Not legit in peacetime. If we, sub and crew, are captured, D.C. will say we'd gone rogue. The bogus rank adds to the mythology. That is, a commander fantasizing about being at war."

"You believe he would just abandon you?"

The Captain laughed. "No, no, no. That's for appearances. We'll be released through back-channel communications, at which point I would retire."

"One problem."

"Yes?"

"We really need that Internet feed from above. Being up-to-the-minute with what's happening at our target site is crucial to success."

"We can be tracked if we acquire the Web through above-surface comms … we'll do something else."

"If it has the desired effect, I'm on board."

"ELF. Extra-Low Frequency. With encryption, we submarine types use it a lot. We send and receive secure comms through the world's oceans and seas."

"I'm not sure I understand. How is our location protected that way?"

"Low frequency sounds travel in all directions. Almost impossible to trace."

"Almost is scary."

"I hear you on that one. Our Department of Defense and CIA built systems to track Soviet nuclear missile subs back in the 1970's. Like in the Red October movie."

"Could that technology be used to track us?"

"Not sure. The president before Stones provided that and other hi-end tech to some of our enemies so we'd all have the same chance. He thought it would be like Mutually Assured Destruction Lite."

"His suicide sure put an end to that line of thinking."

"The following stays in this room. Stones' people at the NSA chased down one of the architects of that system. There's a back door." The gleam in the Captain's eye approximated that of a young geek watching the movie War Games for the first time.

Without warning, the Anchovie decelerated to a stop. The two men stared into each other's eyes.

"*Lenny!*"

• • •

The P.I., coffee cup refilled for the third time and eyes bulging like the Springtime squirrels at Big Bear, had just passed the 'No Coffee Beyond This Point' sign when he tripped.

The Captain arrived seconds later, caught his breath, and asked the OOD for a damage assessment.

"Non-critical electronics, Sir. Have 'em back up in 30."

"When you've got it squared away, see if you can locate those keel-hauling ropes, Lieutenant."

CHAPTER 49

Having completed their Thursday practice sessions two days prior, the Grand Prix racing teams scrutinized their lap times with respect to their competition, accomplished necessary repairs, and processed collected data with respect to tire compounds, pressures, and chassis settings.

Since the street course at Monte Carlo included straight segments for short bursts of maximum power interspersed with tight corners, any setup was doomed to compromise. It was a fact of racing life, however, that the best compromise, as well as an excellent performance by the driver, would likely win the day.

Qualifying One—Quali One in participant vernacular—lasted just twenty minutes. Based on best lap times, the slowest cars would be excluded from the rest of the filling-the-grid process.

A second run of fifteen minutes, Quali Two, excluded the slowest of the remaining cars. The best ten on this particular day entered Quali Three—a ten minute sprint to determine the prime starting position: Pole.

As usual, there had been few surprises in performance save for the sole Asian team, which showed unexpectedly well.

• • •

Pattie stepped out of her special hotel room. A messenger approached her and indicated that her father required an immediate confab. She realized that this could be an 'uh, oh' or something good. Not to worry. She could handle it either way.

Being summoned to the palace Yellow Room, as she'd been, had its own cachet. It was the room utilized throughout palace history for entertaining foreign dignitaries. Pattie's mind toyed with her Queen of France persona, but only for a moment. Given the pervasive crowds, it took twenty minutes for the normal ten-minute ride.

"It seems, my dear Pattie, that repairs to the poison gas damage from the Crayle team's previous assault at the palace are taking far longer than planned. I should have declared it an act of war, since Mr. and Mrs. Crayle were not of this country."

"Well, Father, having a population of right around 37,000 here in Monaco causes you to bring in French artisans for such an effort."

"Artisans? Their first assessment when I specify the work is always *c'est impossible!* Always."

"They say it's impossible so they can get a good price, an extended timeframe, and appear to be geniuses when they come in on time and within budget."

"True. True. But my point is both otherwise and pressing. We must present the race trophy elsewhere. What do you think?"

Her consideration took no more than a second, and removed a logistical nightmare with respect to the Crayles. "In the square. The steps of the Hôtel de Paris. The Grand Casino is nearby, and, like the casino patrons, the drivers do take serious risks."

"Hmmm."

"And the lucky horseman statue they all rub is just inside the hotel foyer."

Perhaps, he thought, he was witnessing a break in his daughter's narcissism. "So it will be."

"And I shall present the silver award, and kiss the champion."

He made a mental note to have her pass through a metal detector to inhibit any notions of death dealing. "And your brother shall attend, as well. And I shall make my grand announcement."

"Announcement?" She produced a quizzical look that portrayed her surprise.

"Yes. Once, there was a shot heard 'round the world. Mine will be a *shout* heard 'round the world. I can no longer wait for this Mitim, your lover, to play out his part. Wherever he is, let him rest there."

"Wait, wait, wait. He and I were married, if I remember correctly, by you and the pope. At the Roman Colosseum. King of France, Queen of France? Are you getting Alzheimer's?"

"Wait and see. I want to surprise you as well as the rest of the world." He touched her arm, then stepped from the room.

"Not good," said Pattie to herself. "While Sylvain remains sequestered on Sainte Marguerite, our whole thing is falling apart."

She took a moment, glancing up at her father's portrait, framed in gold. In that instant, her way forward became clear.

"Sorry, Papa."

• • •

Pattie made her way through the crowds back to the Hôtel de Paris. To the special room she'd reserved long before. She assured that the door was well secured before turning to her captive. "Sorry to have left you for so long. Daddy needed me."

She set her large purse next to a water pitcher and bowl.

"Now, if you promise you'll behave this time, I'll let you go potty again."

Hekka Crayle, spread-eagled on the bed with her wrists affixed to the wrought-iron headboard and her ankles similarly fastened to the footboard, nodded. She felt she'd been in this place for a week now and the routine was always the same.

Pattie took a seat across the room in a period Monegasque armchair and pressed her remote. The spooled reels attaching her captive to the bed slacked off.

Watching the woman climb from the bed and move across the room reminded Pattie of a human-form fly testing the elasticity of a spider web. The four black lines played out, following Hekka into the bathroom. Although Pattie had ordered the door removed, the two could not see each other.

Pattie heard the familiar sounds and then something else.

"You're doing it again. I told you last time, the window doesn't open."

She pressed another button and the powered reels activated, yanking Hekka from the bathroom, across the bedroom, and back into her standard prisoner configuration on the bed.

"When Magus comes for you, we can't have you running free around the country. You must stay right here, for now. That's how bait works."

"Mmmm," Hekka responded through her gag.

"Bait must be dangled. And so shall you be."

• • •

Aboard the SS Anchovie and sitting ninety feet deep just off of Monte Carlo, Micmac, with his extensive SEAL experiences, took the lead with Crayle and Phoebe right behind. The trio followed the specialist the captain had designated to send them on their way. On their way to Crayle's insertion. The three could tell that the specialist wanted to accompany them in the worst way, but this needed to remain a Crayle team operation. If they were discovered, some political stooge somewhere would disavow any knowledge of the operation.

Phoebe noticed something special about this man. His security badge labeled him as X. That's it, just X. Then she noticed that the man's clearance tag was nearly as brief: TBD. To Be Determined. This high level of inscrutability extended to his Asian-Hispanic blend of ethnicities.

He responded to Phoebe's eye query. "You can call me Carlos Ajima. Or anything else."

"I'm guessing you're sort of like the Triple-X character in the movies?"

"Not quite. I got the X thing right the first time. It took him three."

"The X thing?"

"Don't ask."

Just in time, she glared at Micmac, who judiciously didn't follow with, "Don't tell."

After necessary instruction, even though Micmac had some serious experience with the make and model of submersible they'd use, they donned diving gear and were inserted into the vehicle, powered up, and heading toward the otherwise innocent city, Monte Carlo.

Their transit consisted of underwater conveyance from the submarine to an out-of-sight position beneath the overhanging balconies of the beach-side Fairmont hotel. Micmac and Phoebe gave hugs and watched Crayle exchange his diving gear for an Italianate set of clothes he'd brought in a plastic bag.

The MacKays watched as he struggled across the stack of boulders placed there to prevent erosion, and then he disappeared.

"God bless you, Magus Crayle," Phoebe said.

"Roger that. And *veni, vidi, vici*," Micmac added. Feeling rather than hearing the question mark, he translated. "I came, I saw, I conquered. Julius Caesar."

"Here, sailor. Gimme a kiss. We *are* in Monte Carlo."

He did.

"Okay. Infil done. We're outta here 'til we pick 'em up."

"That's right, Phoebs. Both of them."

• • •

At all Formula One events, the public address system is critical in keeping fans informed, and in handling individual disasters such as lost children, wallets, purses, or other non-expendable items. There had been numerous broadcasts that day, but the next one caused Magus Crayle to stop in his tracks.

"This message is brought to you by the Helmi Poppi Dating Service—we bring people together. If you're interested, please stop by the Save The Horses of Namibia booth opposite Tobacconist Corner for further information."

That was it. Few even knew about Hekka's mother, let alone her nickname, Helmi. He didn't like having no options. Yet, there were none. To find and rescue Hekka, he had to locate Pattie first. He noticed a circuit map on the sidewalk a few feet away, and trekked toward the seawall at the exit from the Fairmont tunnel.

There he located a fifteen-foot-high white tent with the faux charity's name above the opening. He stepped inside to come face to face with someone dressed in a nurses uniform. Approximately five inches taller than Pattie. He glanced down. Five-inch white spiked heels.

Pattie had him. A silver-plated Beretta 92F nine-millimeter with a royal seal on each of the solid gold hand grips greeted him when he looked up.

"My thing with you isn't personal, Magus. But I remember our early operational time together. We could've been an item. I want you to understand something. Sex with all those other men was nothing like what we could have had. I know you think I'm crazy. I'm not. That said, *woo-hoo!*"

She tossed the pistol straight up into the air.

Crayle's eyes tracked it upward as he raised his arms. His only chance.

Pattie lunged, catching him in the mid-section, knocking him back, and over the sea wall. With her arms and legs wrapped vice-grip tight, he couldn't resist.

The two splashed down just as Crayle's head banged hard against a channel marker buoy that'd been towed in for repairs.

The initial chill sent shock waves to his brain. He fell unconscious a second later.

• • •

A couple of onlookers had seen the pair tumble into the Mediterranean. Pattie, sopping wet in her nurse's uniform clung to an equally soaked Crayle as the men pulled them to safety.

"Even a rich man can have too much drink, fall, and hit his head," she sputtered. "Please, help me take him back to his hotel. I'm sure he will compensate you very well."

They did and, for their troubles, now resided in a hotel room closet.

• • •

Pattie's unconscious nemesis came around fifteen minutes after she'd dispatched the good Samaritans. She daubed a facecloth filled with ice cubes on his face and neck, as might a nun in a Catholic hospital. She didn't speak until his eyes regained their piercing blue clarity.

"It wasn't one of General Li's bombs at all at Xian. I still have a couple, by the way."

The groggy, blood-adorned, and bandaged Crayle looked puzzled. He spoke in a whisper. "Then whose? Who else has tactical nukes?"

"It was pure Iranian this time. The physicist was aboard the dive bomber piloted by one of those Otto guys. Navid Mohammed was the name. Brother of Hamid." She made the sign of the cross. "They're together, now."

"So, unlike his brother, this Navid was able to *choose* the Paradise option."

"That's not how it went down, Magus. Under Neuschwanstein, I filched Navid's remote. Sure enough, it was a knock-off of one like this," she held up hers, "from the CIA. Probably a gift from Chin via General Li. I put the two devices together, grabbed his detonation codes, and disabled his device. That's why nothing happened when he pressed *Play*."

"You watched somehow, and then it was you who detonated the bomb."

"It turns out, I needed Chin gone. And Li. After the two flaccid bombs I substituted at Neuschwanstein, them supplying more real ones to the Aryans or others … that would be a future wild card."

"Navid's bomb didn't get Li."

"Well, shoot."

"I did."

"Hmmm. I owe you one."

"And what about Ling? She stayed home at the Hong Kong Palace. What about her?"

"She just gave her first speech as Empress in charge of everything."

"Thanks for the update. I've been out of touch."

CHAPTER 50

As was typical for the Formula One circus, excitement and tensions had fed on themselves incrementally right up to race day. Sunday. The weather for the race had been reported to be cool, still breezy, and otherwise perfect for what was about to occur.

The only possible fly in the ointment—a storm west of Corsica had been pushed out of its stagnancy by a Rhone Valley Mistral, and could quite possibly arrive before the action on the course had completed. Normally dangerous, the probability of injury, death, and destruction moved up significantly if such a storm made its way in. None of that potential for mayhem bothered those in the premier gambling establishment on the planet.

It's official name was *Casino de Monte Carlo*. Everyone referred to it as the Monte Carlo Casino. You were afforded entry to glance about, if dressed properly, but only permitted into its quite secure high stakes component if the staff recognized you and had already vetted your current state of wealth.

The paparazzi couldn't get enough of her. Lights inside the famous Monte Carlo casino sparkled off her alabaster, floor-length, diamond-encrusted gown and matching clutch purse. Patricia G. Grimaldi she wanted them to call her.

She gave a pull on one of the antique slot machines as the photographers jockeyed for just the right shot. Her lips produced an *Oh!* Just as she released the handle.

Clunk, clunk, clunk.

"*Sevens!*"

Euros poured from the belly of the beast. She glanced down as the coins overflowed the tray. Then, back at her admiring crowd. A smile that produced her trademark dimples was all they needed.

Click.

Click. Click.

Click, click, click.

"I feel throughout my being that this is meant to be my day. When someone wins the Grand Prix, I have won, too."

"You aren't wearing a ring," observed a journalist from France. "Perhaps, if the unmarried driver from Germany wins ..."

"Ha." She admonished the man with a waving finger. "Perhaps I am already married, and will be the next Queen of France."

The tabloid component of the press corps was off and running. They could care less whether it was true or not, but were highly seasoned at making it seem so. Besides, it was more believable than The Killer Nuns From Mars story that'd run the previous day.

"As you are aware, the race runs for precisely two hours. I have much to accomplish before I greet the winner on the steps of the Hôtel de Paris across the square." She blew a kiss. "*Au revoir, mes amis.*"

Her exit proved as gracious as her repartée.

• • •

Back in the hotel, Pattie Norbrunn examined her countenance in one of the ornate mirrors. It was clear that she had begun to lose the smooth lines of youth and acquire the rough surfaces that reflected experiences. She'd spied and killed. And killed. She didn't appreciate that her deteriorating countenance, in effect, told her story. Or at least that she had one.

She looked up once again at the man seated across the table. The only other conscious, living person in the small, sparsely furnished quarters.

His stare back was more inquisitive than condemning. Perhaps she could blame him for the facial lines.

"You aren't struggling to free your wrists," she said. "This Velcro is special. It is single-use CIA Velcro." She nodded at the two strips super-glued to the table top and their two opposite-gender mates strapping him down. "I want you to struggle, Magus. I want you to hurt."

He listened to her voice. Somber. Depleted.

"I could have drugged you as I drugged your mate." She nodded at the bed pressed against a near wall. "When I am finished with you, I will have her mind manipulated by Doctor Rorschach. He will make her love me instead of you."

Crayle applied all of his strength upward. He rolled his wrists left, then right. No use.

The spy, killer, and resident psychopath unzipped a black-sequined clutch purse and withdrew a compact. Holding the bottom between thumb and three fingers, she placed her other hand on top. "The last person to see this was my husband, Randy. Did you know him?"

Crayle hadn't. But he knew precisely how the Deputy Chief of Mission at the American Embassy in Paris had been killed. In Zurich. And by whom.

She read his thoughts. "I wrote RLP on the fogged bathroom mirror afterward. It stood for Randy's Little Psychopath. It was the least I could do in his memory."

"Killing solves nothing. You are done, Pattie. Finished … or *finis*, as Lalumière would put it. But if it makes you feel better, then do it. Kill me." He nodded toward the motionless body. "Let her go. She's not like us. I dragged her into the world of espionage and the political insanity that attends it. I didn't know who I was, or that I'd ever been a spy. Let her go."

Pattie shook her head in slow motion. "Nevertheless, you brought her in. When you are deceased, she will be free. And she's so beautiful. I envision a happy and long life. For her. For us."

Crayle thought about another bout with the restraints, but realized the hopelessness.

The young woman only a couple of feet away started to twist the compact's lid. Another half-inch, and the razor-edged blade would protrude from its side.

Her gaze moved from his ice-blue eyes to his neck.

She would draw a clean red line there. From left to right. Then the blood would flow. As it had with her Randy.

It would be a victory to watch this man expire. He had destroyed everything she'd ever hoped for. Her position at the embassy. Her prospects as its next ambassador's wife. Queen of France—gone.

Slowly, she twisted the lid. She glanced down to see the thin blade protrude.

A smile forced her point dimples out of hiding.

Her thumb slid to the side. It pressed the release. The lid popped open, revealing a mirror. Pattie slowed her breathing as she examined her face. Bringing the compact closer, she verified that her makeup did nothing to diminish her natural beauty.

With her head held straight at Crayle, but her eyes down, observing every move in its mirror, she drew the device to her own throat.

"You are right, Magus. It is my time."

She walked to the bed and watched Hekka for several seconds, then used her compact to sever the straps that splayed her on the bed Da Vinci style. "Your wife will awaken soon." She returned to her former seat.

"Let's work together. As we did long ago. The stakes are much, much higher now. The Elder, and his pope, must be stopped."

"Nice try, Magus."

"You hate him. Free me, and I'll see that you get to take him out."

She stared at him for several seconds, then down at the table. It seemed that she'd been overcome by a gray cloud. Looking, but not seeing. A lifetime played in her mind as would a slow-motion video. In the background, in the depths of her soul, burned the single word. Revenge. "You'll keep this promise?"

"Hekka has to go free. Then, yes. My plan is foolproof. And if you have to take me down after, so be it. But Hekka goes free. That's the deal."

"With him gone, I become Crown Princess. My half-brother becomes Prince of Monaco. That's not enough."

"My plan includes your brother. You become the monarch. At the top."

She sat back, then grabbed her head with both hands, shaking it back and forth. She stood and walked across the room to its oaken door. With her back against it, she banged her head. Once. Twice. Three times.

"Just release these bonds. We'll leave together. When we're safely away, I'll have Hekka picked up."

Pattie stopped the head banging, and stared blindly across the room. At a copy of a Picasso. It was the woman who seemed formed from a number of sections. Connected in space, but not emotionally.

Crayle recognized her disheveled mental state. "My word is gold. You know that."

Pattie snapped back to her operational self. "Let's do it, Darling." She told him nothing about her planned aftermath of her father's death. How she would take the magnificent Magus Crayle to bed, and then she would kill him. One orgasm after the other.

"In a short while, I shall be Princess of Monaco, Head of State."

"You will be the new Grace Kelly."

She strode to where he sat, jabbed him with her drugging utility, and yanked his straps free.

He realized that this was likely his only chance. Before he could even stand, the drug took effect, and his head thunked onto the table top. Satisfied, Pattie addressed the immobile Crayle.

"Princess Grace has to use the restroom. Remember your promise, and remember that I have the only gun."

• • •

Not many fishermen get to reuse bait that has already met its mission. The petite nun with dimples led Crayle's sedated wife the hundred yards from the hotel service entrance to her destination. Hidden from the gathering crowds view, she secured Hekka for the grand finale. With the help of a cellphone flashlight app, she assured that her captive could go nowhere.

"Now that I've explained it to you, my darling Hekka, what do you think? Do you love the Grand Prix as I do? The words mean Grand Prize, by the way. I love it. I've always loved it. And no matter who wins this year's race, I shall have my own grand prize."

With hands and feet bound and her mouth covered with royal blue duct tape, Pattie's question waxed rhetorical.

A Caterpillar yellow crane arm extended fifty feet above the streets of the golden city. Those in the grandstands, balconies, expensive boats, and top decks of hotels below craned their necks and shaded their eyes. Observations like "I'm keeping my day job" and "I can't even stand a high dive" threaded through the crowd.

A black shroud adorned the basket at the top of the arm, perhaps to keep the sun from the camera lens. What the crowd couldn't see was a remote-controlled camera atop the shroud.

• • •

With the race about to begin, Pattie needed to hurry. Shortly, the race course would be closed. It meant that getting from where she was to anywhere else would require walking around the course periphery, which translated to the city of Monte Carlo.

With that imminent threat in mind, she used her universal remote to lower herself to the ground, taking care that no one saw or suspected that her high-profile captive, Hekka Crayle, was still inside the shrouded basket. Using her CIA remote once again, she returned the boom skyward. She reckoned the motion, plus the occasional battering by gusts of wind, might be somewhat beyond terrifying to Mrs. Crayle, but easily convinced herself that the end really did justify the means.

• • •

The race had begun. Even on the top floor of the hotel, Crayle heard the commotion. He'd tried every possible means of escape until his trips back and forth to the door and window of his effective cell were interrupted by a nice young woman, who had simply unlocked the door and stepped inside.

"Ms. Grimaldi requires that you be released in order to continue her game of cat and mouse. She said pussy and mouse, but I believe she meant the former."

With that, she exited the room and disappeared before Crayle could catch her.

• • •

The Anchovie had broken its run silent, run deep status to rise to ninety feet in preparation for the hopeful exfiltration of Magus and Hekka Crayle. At a pre-arranged time, Micmac and Phoebe would venture in with one of the submersibles to the rendezvous point, and wait. At the moment, they had a little time to kill, and a lot of tension to dispel.

• • •

Two hours after its always auspicious beginning, a wave of the checkered flag ended the competition. The crowd cheered and collectively breathed a sigh of relief only exceeded by the drivers themselves.

The view from the Hôtel de Paris entrance was special. The casino to the right. The circular fountain dead ahead. The Formula 1 winning race car and driver now steps away. The adrenaline-rushed crowd of fans. The precious journalists.

And then the spectacular fireworks display commenced, exploding the skies above the Prince's domain.

"God bless this place," quipped the atheist Prince. He smiled toward the man on his left. His special guest.

Pope Innocent returned the evil smile and the comment with the sign of the cross.

CHAPTER 51

Captain Hildebrand had always been a fan of the special operations people. While his own abilities had pushed him toward Annapolis and ultimately a boat command, still the rough and tumble of real-life John Waynes carried a lethal romance of its own. These men got close and personal. Now that he had Micmac and Phoebe in the Anchovie's Control Room, he took a moment to engage Micmac in some conversation.

"Since you were a SEAL team member and swam and performed ashore, I thought I'd give you a tour."

"Thanks, Captain. I'd like to see how these things load up and fire torpedoes."

Phoebe stood, ready to join the men.

The OOD stepped in. "I'm afraid this is a dues-paid tour, Ma'am."

"Oh, I'll just drop down and pay my dues. You can rename this area the Head Quarters."

The OOD turned to Micmac with a grin. "By your leave, Sir."

"See. I'm right," said Phoebe. "All sailors are alike."

The Captain smirked at the OOD, then turned his attention to the request, gesturing at a set of switches and knobs. "It's easy. You open the outer doors … here … select the tube … here … load the tube … enter a firing resolution … and fire. This one under the security cover arms the weapon."

"That's it? It's all automated?"

"You bet. Fewer crew needed because of the refit updates. More environmentally friendly."

"If you don't direct the torpedoes, they just shoot dead ahead?"

"Or astern for the after bunch. Speaking of which, I'd like to show you the after torpedo room."

As they exited the space, Micmac snapped his fingers. "Left my phone back there. Go ahead. I'll catch up."

"Okay, but watch your head. Spaces are tight. Sometimes folks forget."

The Captain and Phoebe moved on as the former SEAL, UDT, and weapons specialist returned to the control room. Micmac found the phone exactly where he had placed it.

"Time for a little diversion," he said to himself as he saw the hour that Crayle had specified approach.

While comms that included his phone were still disabled, the compass app still worked. "There. Straight at the harbor," he whispered.

Micmac took a deep breath, then began the sequence specified by the Captain. He chose Tube 7 for good luck.

One of the crew spotted him touching the controls and notified the Captain.

In spite of Phoebe's attempts to get in his way, he stormed into the control room just as Micmac pressed *Fire*.

"What did you just do?" the Captain demanded. "Officer Of the Day! Arrest this man! Take him to the brig." He turned and pointed at Phoebe. "Her, too!"

Feeling that his career had just entered into its terminal stage, the Captain started toward his quarters and his special bottle of well-aged Kentucky bourbon.

"Uh, Sir?" said Micmac.

"What?!"

"The torpedo?"

• • •

Magus Crayle made his way out of the hotel only to be confronted with the huge post-race throng. He scanned all he could see from his vantage point, but could not spot anything out of the ordinary.

"*Wait!*" his brain cried out. All of the cranes supporting overhead camera shots had been taken down. Except one. And unlike the others, it was topped with a shroud that defied a view inside. The camera itself was perched atop the enclosed basket, apparently controlled remotely.

Assuming whatever or whoever was inside was not a camera operator, he rushed through the mob, being struck incidentally by several Ferrari red-and-yellow flags before he reached the crane.

Crayle stabbed madly at the controls on Pattie's CIA remote.

• • •

The Prince of Monaco, seconds into feeling his own rush, just did catch his breath. What seemed like an underwater detonation just offshore sent a column of water more than a hundred feet into the air. That it was the forced, abort destruction of a torpedo rather than a component of the celebration was unknown to him.

"It reminds me of the Jet d'Eau in Geneva," he quipped to the gathered crowd. "A wonderful place. But today, I feel that the most awesome locale in all of the universe … is right here."

Applause.

"Monte Carlo."

Explosive, rigorous applause, hoops, and hollers.

"It is time to present the trophy."

The Italian driver, who happened to be an honorary member of the Aryan Alliance and resembled a much younger, yet brown haired Otto Von Prem, stepped forward.

• • •

Crayle, still convinced that Hekka was trapped high above, continued his manic frustration in trying to get the remote to retract the crane's boom arm back to Earth.

He jumped when a large, athletic man tapped him on the shoulder. The man's Roman-accented English was readily apparent.

"I can help. I have the master device."

Crayle was in a high stakes card game and out of cards. He nodded.

The worker glanced up at the crane's boom and entered the 5 stenciled on its side. One more button, and the boom descended to ground level.

"*Grazie, Signore. Grazie mille.*"

"If I can help …"

"No. We're … I mean … I'm fine. Better you get over there and celebrate the Ferrari win."

The man smiled and jogged away.

• • •

Pattie stepped forward at the hotel and presented her silver trophy, with its notable bulge, to the Italian. After the young man had it in his hands, he stretched it aloft in true champion style.

• • •

Having been released from the brig to the Anchovie's submersible solely for the hopeful exfiltration of Crayle and Hekka, and having just made landfall under the Fairmont hotel's zig-zag balcony outcroppings, Micmac and Phoebe surfaced. They climbed onto the rocks, and what they next saw caused both to gasp.

Climbing over the boulders to the West end of the hotel were Crayle and Hekka. Each one appeared about two steps past dead, but helped each other as if at least one of them needed to survive.

The MacKay team crawled and clawed to them, doing their best to help. Sun Tzu had said something about the ground on which one chooses to do battle, but that provided little help here.

Because all attention remained focused in Casino Square above, no one gave them notice. Getting the Crayles into their dive gear presented just one more tough, but surmountable challenge.

With all aboard, Micmac took the helm and dove their submersible to thirty feet. Just minutes later, and along with the pair they'd rescued, they entered the SS Anchovie via the same attachment hatch they'd used for insertion.

• • •

As the post race festivities continued, the Prince stepped to the podium and raised his hand to quell the subsequent cacophony.

"Since today goes to the victor and his team, I will be brief."

Requiring no justification, the crowd erupted once more.

"I have an announcement."

A quite pretty redhead with long, wavy tresses emerged from the shadows and stepped to his side.

"May I introduce Doctor Monika Rikki. My announcement is that we are, as of this date and time, engaged to be married."

The crowd exploded into all manor of applause and commotion. Journalists needing to escape and file their monumental scoop got nowhere.

Contrary to the situation at hand, Pattie seemed completely at peace with the state of affairs. She stepped over to Monika and kissed her on the cheek. Mafia Kiss-Of-Death style.

With that, she curtseyed and backed into the hotel lobby. A quick change later, and she was out the back wearing a red and yellow Ferrari version of an Adidas warm-up suit.

She checked her go-bag for her remote.

"*No!*" she cried. "*It's gone!*"

• • •

Out front, Luigi Benedetti accepted his first place trophy with a wraparound smile. Barely five-foot-five, he was the man of the hour. He glanced first into the eyes of the Prince of Monaco. Then to the pope, immaculate leader of all Catholics such as himself. He produced an earnest bow to each man, then heard something completely out of order.

His winning Ferrari was positioned directly behind him with the other two top cars in Parc Fermé. It fired up. Impossible.

He whipped around, careful to maintain a grip on his heavy prize. There sat Pattie Norbrunn, revving his engine.

She started to move.

The crowd parted and cheered, believing they were experiencing a new aspect of the show.

Luigi's mouth fell open. "No!" the driver cried. "It takes three months just to understand the steering wheel!"

Pattie's face and dimples turned to her task. Escape.

Luigi started after her. He went to set down the trophy, then realized that it would be stolen in an instant. The driver realized that it was not his car anyway, nor would it fit the new specifications for next year. He decided to enjoy the moment.

Pattie plowed through, fans and press diving this way and that. She spun the multi-million-dollar car around the grand fountain and headed onto the still-closed course.

The Italian tucked the prize under his arm, made easy since it closely resembled a football.

But the crowd didn't notice. It filled in behind the departing Pattie and cheered.

Down the hill she went, right through the Fairmont hairpin. Down, down, down to the beach road.

She turned right and bored through the famous tunnel under the Fairmont overwhelmed by the crushing sound waves from a Formula 1 Ferrari at 175 miles per hour. Deafening.

Cameras flashed at her from the side.

Her dimples lasted through the end of the tunnel and into the infamous left-right chicane.

• • •

Back at the race-end celebration and following the mandatory interviews of the three podium finishers, the winning driver once again lofted high the heavy silver trophy.

With a precedent set by a former German World Champion, he leapt into the air—pulling his feet up behind—smiling from ear-to-ear.

It was the last thing he did.

• • •

Magus Crayle and Hekka were back aboard the Anchovie. Crayle set the device he'd found under his hotel room chair, Pattie's remote, down on a table and asked, "Where are Phoebe and Micmac?"

Alona bore the bad news. "Brig."

"What!" said Crayle.

"It's true. He just let them out to exfiltrate you two, assuming you'd rescued Hekka."

Then he remembered the 'Why not fire a torpedo at the end of the race as a diversion?' He had meant it as a joke before Micmac and Phoebe had infiltrated him ashore. He turned to the Captain. "He didn't."

"Affirmative, Mr. Crayle. Fortunately for those ashore, we were able to abort it in transit. So, let's get you stowed. The OOD will button us up, and we're gone."

Crayle noticed Lenny pick up Pattie's remote and, fearing the worst, snatched it away. It was the right thing to do.

Unfortunately, in so doing, he pressed the catastrophe-inducing *Play* key.

Oblivious, Captain Hildebrand felt he was once again in control of the situation. He enunciated the requisite commands.

"The Med's a bit shallow here. Take her down. Zero-Nine-Zero depth. Heading Two-Seven-Zero. Flank speed."

CHAPTER 52

Having just returned from a bathroom break, the captain stepped to the center of the Control Room, observed the Crayles, then turned to his own team. "I have the Con. Let's take her down to One-Seven-Five. Come right to One-Eight-Zero. All ahead full!"

The subs electric motors spun up in an instant.

The Anchovie leveled off at one hundred seventy-five feet.

• • •

Sometimes, little mistakes have big consequences. The bomb Pattie had manufactured into the race-winner's coveted silver trophy, and had intended to activate at a safe distance with her remote, detonated.

• • •

The race winner, the Prince also known as the Elder, Pope Innocent, Dr. Rikki, Pattie's half brother, and the entire crowd all melded into the scenery as did the Hôtel de Paris, and all inside turned into a molten mist.

The nearby casino blew sideways off the hillside, toppling down onto the pool-adorned roof of the Fairmont Hotel, as if the two grand edifices were destined to be together.

Money that might have flowed freely into the surrounds turned instantly to ash or melted.

Boats moored in the harbor transformed to splinters cast upon the waters of the Mediterranean.

Helicopters blew out of the skies.

The fireball that had replaced the Hôtel de Paris symbolized and actualized the burning of all of the prime perpetrators prior to Hell. Perhaps, a warm up.

Effects of the detonation to the west of the city were immediate. The royal palace, sitting atop a leveled granite escarpment, crumbled first.

Perched on the upper edge of the escarpment in front of the palace, the *Musée Océanographique de Monaco*—the Monaco Aquarium—shook violently and then toppled from the heights into the Mediterranean.

Its surprised denizens, free at last, swam in desperation from the stricken principality at flank speed for a freedom previously unknown to them.

• • •

Although attenuated by the water, the shock waves still struck the Anchovie with tremendous force, tossing everyone aboard off their feet and into bulkheads, machinery, electronics, and other non-friendly impediments to good health.

"Holy shit!" shouted the Captain. "What the Hell was that?"

"It wasn't your torpedo, Captain. One of Pattie's bombs, I'm guessing."

"Nuclear?"

"I'm afraid so."

"See if you can stoke some more coal," the man-in-charge said to the chief engineer. "And brace, everyone. Until we're out of these waters."

• • •

As if the first hit wasn't enough, a reflective pressure wave off of the French maritime alps slammed the water above and behind, and squirted the sub forward like an errant over-sauced hot dog squirts from the end of a bun. The boat was slung sideways, up and down, and rolled stiffly to starboard.

The brute force of the event threw Lenny—the only one who hadn't followed the 'brace' order—against a bulkhead.

"Isn't there some kind of speed limit in harbors?" he complained.

Had Phoebe been present, she would have considered filching the OOD's .45, except that his hand had already gone there.

"Captain? … Captain?"

"Yes, Mr. Crayle."

"Please, check the brig. Or I can do it."

"Officer Of the Day! Send someone down to the brig. Make sure they're okay. What just occurred just might have rattled their cage."

"Aye, aye, Captain."

"Commander."

"Sir?"

"Aw, hell." He threw a quick glance at Crayle. "Release the prisoners. We'll straighten this out once we've passed through the Pillars of Hercules. Out in the Atlantic. We'll surface there, establish comms."

The Captain had predicted problems when the Crayle team had come aboard. What had just happened far exceeded his expectations.

• • •

With the exception of the team's previous assault that rescued the Crayles from the Monaco Palace, no one had attacked the Principality of Monaco since World War II. Its military was but a showpiece, and the police didn't give tickets or even check license plates, be they European or Middle Eastern.

And there never were earthquakes, tsunamis, nor conflagrations of any consequence. Prior to this day, the place could've been renamed Monacoland and presented itself in the Disney tradition of a fairy tale.

The explosion had vaporized the Hôtel de Paris and all inside. Instead of the spectators on the Fairmont rooftop's terrace being rocketed skyward as with conventional explosives, they had been distributed heavenward as a fine, scalding mist.

The Monte Carlo city structure, built to withstand the weight of pocketfuls of thousand-Euro bills, blew West and North into the surrounding French countryside.

The five megaton destruction hurled chunks of buildings as far as the French Cannes to the West and the Italian Ventimiglia to the East. Structural I-beams became the lances of the gods as they rained onto the hapless, innocent environs.

And the Elder? He'd watched the winner jump in the air in jubilation. He'd craned his head in defiance of any God that might be looking down. In the next instant, he'd felt a sudden jolt, and then had vaporized in the thousands of degrees heat. His burial took place in the next millisecond as earth and hotel piled on. It would be his only monument.

Due to Pattie's radiation-enabled nuclear device, the area would be uninhabitable for decades. The Grimaldis—all dead—would never rule again.

• • •

Back in their quarters aboard the Anchovie, Hekka dropped in on Lenny and Alona.

"What happened to Lenny's head?"

"He bumped it," Alona said.

"She clobbered me."

"Okay, okay. He wouldn't behave. He whined again."

"I'll tell you both what. We have a few hours before we pass Gibraltar and can come up for air. Why don't I leave you two alone so you can get some rest, or have sex, or something?" Happy with her rhetorical suggestion, Hekka departed.

"Now there's an ROE that I can live with," concluded Alona. "C'mere, you little twerp."

In another stateroom, Crayle sat alone. Safely out to sea and unaware of specific lives lost, Crayle searched for words to apprise the team that Pattie appeared to have won yet again, and that they had failed once again. It was time to quit.

• • •

Devastation included not only the obliteration of the Principality of Monaco, but as with all nuclear blasts, extended into the hills to the north and along seacoasts, left and right.

To the west, the French Riviera mainstay, Cannes, had taken a beating after the previous atomic blast at Marseille. Perched high on a waterfront hill, it's old town had received severe damage while protecting the harbor and rest of the town from destruction.

This time, due to the blast at Monte Carlo, it was the east side's turn. Apartment buildings and yachts situated along the shore were worst hit. Fortunately, the building demarking the beginning of Napoléon's post-Elba march back to Paris withstood the onslaught. Its black silhouette sign still pointed the way.

Offshore, the island of Sainte Marguerite, where Sylvain Lalumière currently resided, became the proverbial sitting duck.

• • •

Although it was expressly difficult to find solitude in an old submarine, Crayle managed a deal with the captain. Just thirty minutes in the man's quarters, and he would ensure a good word with the president.

He thought of Chin Yao-wu, a man he'd come to know over the past few years. A self-made multi-millionaire posing as the reincarnation of the uniter and first emperor of a grand country of a grand people.

Then, the pope. Insidious to say the least. Perhaps another poseur.

Pattie and Lalumière. In their own minds, the king and queen of France.

And finally, the illustrious Elder, wearing the façade of a duly installed monarch of one very small, but very important principality.

They were all finished. Gone for good. In Xian. In Monte Carlo. The events had served as their Final Masquerade.

CHAPTER 53

At long last, the team simply relaxed in the mess decks aboard the USS Anchovie as the boat pushed its way toward the west exit of the Mediterranean Sea. Just as Lenny prepared to complain about the absence of decaffeinated tea, the captain stepped in and took a seat.

"It looks like we sustained damage from the explosion at Monte Carlo. The force of a five megaton weapon slamming the water like that …"

"Lucky we didn't all die," Lenny whined. "The sooner I get off this rust bucket, the better."

"We have the capacity, on this rust bucket, to release you as we would a SEAL team, into these frigid waters at … say … 200 feet," said Captain Hildebrand.

Lenny opened his mouth.

Alona was quicker.

She grabbed an item from her handbag and stuffed the small American flag pennant she'd brought along for good luck into the opening before he could utter another word.

The P.I., of course, immediately withdrew the muting device with, "Look. I'm sorry. Here, I can make it up to you, Captain. No charge."

The referenced captain chose not to avail himself of all the remedies that flew through his head. "Very well, Mr. Lipschitz."

"Captain, Sir, I noticed on the wall in the con room that you spelled the boat's name wrong. Nothing personal, I'm just making up for that coffee spill."

"We don't have walls here, we have bulkheads. Next, the Navy knows how to spell anchovy. When this boat was refitted and modernized a bit, I personally suggested we spell it Anchovie to give a feminine feel, since watercraft are referenced in that light. Are we clear?"

"Yes, Sir," interjected Alona. She returned the flag to where it did the most good.

Feeling as if he'd entered into an unwitting engagement with an imbecile, the captain excused himself.

• • •

The captain returned to the mess decks in a half hour. He'd had a chance to cool off. Two glasses of fine Bourbon helped.

"For the remainder of this cruise, I'm your Captain."

Hekka sported a quizzical look. "What exactly is a captain, Sir?"

"It goes like this, Ma'am. The captain of a boat or ship is the commander of that vessel. He doesn't necessarily have to have the rank of Captain, which is equivalent to full Colonel in the other services. And Captain in those services ..."

"Thank you very much, Captain Hildebrand. So," she said as she turned to her husband. "A Mediterranean cruise, Magus. What a wonderful idea. I couldn't have guessed."

His tongue went to his upper left molar. Before the memory restore, such a behavior didn't happen when he waited for more shoes to drop. He had just held his breath. So much for getting your old self back. Hmmm. Time for a little offense.

He looked deep into her eyes. "And what better way to take advantage of a Mediterranean cruise … than to restate our vows."

She looked back into the bluest eyes she'd ever seen. As was her style, a nearly imperceptible smile reconfigured her lips. "To the sounds, not of a traditional wedding band, but to the hum and thrum of an American submarine, let's do it."

"I believe the Captain is up for it."

They grasped onto each other's ring and turned to the man in charge.

"Magus and Hekka Crayle. Do you promise to live in peace and harmony … and return to Las Vegas to complete your one-week vacation?"

Crayle's smile disappeared, and his head snapped back to her.

"How the hell …"

CHAPTER 54

They had all been to this place before. After surviving their previous European escapades, the four couples were married here by the now-deceased pope and the current U.S. president. Now, in the aftermath of Xian and Monaco, it seemed more like a safe-house than an underground cathedral for spies. Jack stood at the front of the prime chamber ten feet to the side of the pulpit as if closer would entice a lightning bolt.

"I have a couple of special surprise guests to bring in. Here's the first."

A tall door opened over to their left. The man who entered was indeed a surprise.

"Yes, ladies and gentlemen, Doctor Pirmin Rorschach."

The white-bermed researcher had been set up with his own wireless microphone. That wasn't all. On his arm, someone else they all recognized.

Hekka was dumbstruck, but recalled the memory loss problem.

"An unexpected development with my research. I have discovered a cure, a memory loss cure, that will apply to Alzheimer's."

The woman next to him released his arm and approached Hekka.

"He has done it. Hello, my dear."

Emotions weren't enough. Tears weren't enough.

They embraced.

"But there's more," said Rorschach.

"Yes, my darling daughter." Helmi nodded. "We've fallen in love."

The new hush surpassed complete silence by a quantum.

Not only did Hekka not faint dead away, she found the strength to get her trembling lips to comply with appropriate words. "Let's do it now!"

"I … I …"

"Vell … vell …"

"No excuses."

The rest of the team found no words, and would find none.

"A good Boy Scout is always prepared," said Jack.

A door on the opposite side of the room opened and out stepped none other than President of the United States, Kimbel Stones. "Hi, everyone."

"All please stand."

All but one stood. Magus Crayle had taken a beating in his battle with Pattie. He'd passed out and banged his head on the periscope. His sutured gash had been bandaged and taped, but due to a concussion, he lay strapped to a gurney, much like he had entered into this fray some twelve months before.

A huge stained glass pane behind the pulpit turned black. And then an image.

"Good afternoon and bless you all."

Crayle mumbled just loud enough for Hekka to hear. She turned. "He said: that's that cardinal. Pope Zoran's number one man. Do something, Jack."

"He's today's second big surprise, team," said Jack. "Cardinal Alighieri was our plant in the Illuminé's Vatican team. He had to stand by while Zoran murdered the other cardinal. The German one, Fratze. For a greater good."

Alighieri waited for Jack to finish, indicating that communications were bidirectional.

Then, the greater surprise. "Let me make this more efficient." He emerged from the same door as used by the president.

"As it turns out, I am quite religious. And with the abrupt exit of Pope Zoran, I have been chosen, by God via the Cardinal electorate, to take his place."

Jack couldn't suppress the grin. "Ladies and gentlemen, I give you Pope Alighieri. He hasn't selected a pope name yet, but I hear that Pope Jack is not in the running."

"Wait a minute," Lenny interrupted. "We just got here. It takes weeks or months to crown a new pope. There's the smoke ..."

"It is a new age, Mr. Lipschitz. With the concurrence of the College of Cardinals, the smoke scene at the Sistine Chapel was accomplished with graphics. They all agreed that we needed to keep Zoran's true backstory and Illuminé involvement quite secret. Be advised that the Vatican holds more secrets than a U.S. Secretary of State's email server." He chuckled at his attempt at humor. "May I continue?"

With no objections, he did.

"Today is an auspicious day. Besides its well-known meaning, it is the anniversary date for Mr. Crayle. Jack informed me that one year ago, a man was transferred to a cabin in Big Bear, California, to begin his recuperation from a violent crash and attempt restoration of his lost memory."

At that point, Flori appeared through a side door, carrying what proved to be a well-decorated and quite large cake. She presented it to Jack, who read the writing on top. "Happy Anniversary to Magus Crayle. From Hekka, Phoebe, Micmac, Lenny, Flori, Alona, and Jack." The names had all been written in the handwriting of the various team members.

Lenny stepped forward and, with a pastry chef's writing tube, added two words. "Today's third surprise is that, in his new position, Mr. Sommers here was able to track you down in the CIA's very hidden records department, Magus. As much as we as a team hate coincidences, there is one that is undeniable."

"Oh, God," Phoebe moaned.

Lenny looked over at the gurney. "Just this morning, Jack tracked down your actual birthday. I'm not making this up. I checked and double-checked," he waved to the side, "With Jack's help, and the president's clearance. Today's it. September 11. You've come full circle. Since your crash."

"Lenny!" made an abrupt exit from Jack's lips, as usual. "Get on with it!"

Crayle's memories extended to all of his operational days at the CIA, but not to his childhood. The crash date would have to suffice.

"Come on, folks. Gather 'round Magus," Lenny said as he moved over to Crayle's side. A tear formed in his eye. "September 11 is also your birthday."

A rumble moved through the group. It was clear no one in the room but Jack and Lenny knew.

Crayle looked at the P.I., then at the cake. Then at every member of his team. Then Jack. "You're sure?"

"One hundred percent."

"Finally."

"Wait, wait, wait. There aren't any candles," Jack observed, punching Lenny in the shoulder.

Hekka smiled. She knew how much this meant. "How many candles, then?"

"Doesn't matter," Lenny answered. "MC's way past where you get more than one. And rather than wasting my time running all over trying to find just the right onesy candle, I utilized a keepsake I've carried around since my childhood. An M80."

Micmac recognized the nomenclature. "When I was young, an M80 was the ultimate firework, Lenny."

"Not to worry." He flicked a Zippo lighter that had belonged to his father, and lit the fuse. "It's okay. I buried the M80's business end. Fuse'll go out when she hits the frosting."

"Lenny! Those fuses are waterproof! It'll—"

Foomp!

Luckily the cathedral was soundproof. There was no reaction from the president's Secret Service guard just outside.

The new pope's frock of purest white took a colorful beating.

A blob of cake fell from Jack's eyebrow.

"Oops."

The M80, true to its billing as a Fourth-of-July incendiary device, had exploded, sending cake everywhere. No one was spared. Crayle, wearing only the patient pajama bottoms, got it the worst. "Is nowhere safe?" he lamented.

Before anyone could reach Lenny and take his life in the most painful manner they could conceive, he stopped them all with a few words. "Hey! People! Forget something?" He pointed to Permin and Helmi. "The wedding?"

Those six words saved his life.

The president glanced at Hekka's mother. "The doctor here didn't do anything unprofessional while you were under his care, did he?"

"Vee cite zee doctor-patient priffelich on zat kvestion, Herr President."

Helmi nodded concurrence.

Crayle threw a glance the P.I.'s way, just in case he had anything to add.

"Alona and I cite lawyer-client privilege before you even ask."

The ceremony by the new pope and the president was brief, indeed. At its conclusion, it drew as much applause as the few in attendance could muster.

As usual, Lenny would have done better by saying nothing. "Hey, y'all. There's still some cake left."

Rorschach produced a scalpel. "It's all I have."

Hekka extracted her ten-inch Bowie. "Try this."

Lenny grabbed the first handful before the rest joined him in the food fight.

Later, they all agreed that the pope and the president had pretty good aim.

All in all, quite a day. Of one thing, though, all were certain. These two, the good doctor and Hekka's Finnish mother, would live happily ever after.

Phoebe extracted her weapon from its holster. She licked the frosting from her Glock. "Can I kill him now?"

Jack wiped his face with a surgeon's mask. "Everybody out. At this point, Magus and Hekka could use a little quality time."

All agreed. And left.

The two waited a couple of extra seconds.

"This could be difficult."

"Lay back, darling."

He did.

She reached across him, and pulled straps across his chest and abdomen, pinning his arms to his sides.

"Hey …"

She pressed her lips into her trademark, minimalist smile. "We just undo this … and unzip this …" She removed his trousers and pulled his belt free. As a tease, she slid it side-to-side through her lips, then wrapped it around his waist, buckling it just above his hips.

Before he could assess, she climbed atop her husband of nine months and eleven days, and reached down.

"There. Now, a little backstory. Before I trained the quarter horses, I tried a little bucking bronco activity. Like in the rodeos."

She checked for a sign of acknowledgment, but received only an open-mouthed stare. "Here goes." She slid her right hand under the belt and lofted her left into the air.

"*Now, Magus. Go!*"

EPILOGUE

For many players in a global game of political conquest, the past year represented tumult, mayhem, and an ultimate and requisite death. Those who survived would carry forth deep wounds—some healed, some healing, some everlasting.

THE CHINESE

The Chinese Empress, also known as Black daughter and by her birth name, Ling An-yee, had become, upon Chin's demise, sole ruler of all China. The view from her Hong Kong palace bedroom onto the city below was, in the absence of the usual fog, beautiful. It was the sight across Victoria Harbour that caused her to take a deep breath.

There was Kowloon with its bayside Tsim Sha Tsui and the rest, but beyond she could see all of her country. Pushing petulantly eastward to intimidate Japan and Taiwan. North to meet up with a Russian nation on the brink. To lapse back into a Soviet-style state, or to bow to the czarina. What would that mean for China? For her?

And with Li dead, the propensity to intimidate the Vietnamese also died. Perhaps friendlier ties and a steady stream of the delicious and aromatic fish sauce. But what about Red daughter? What about the others who had followed her lead into the attack on America's spy central at Langley?

Too much to think about at the moment. She spoke into her phone. "Yellow? Bring them to me in the throne room … yes, from the dungeon."

Five minutes later she took her throne just as the two eunuchs opened the large, golden doors.

The men moved in, heads bowed, halting the appropriate fifteen feet from Empress Ling.

"Chairman Po," she spoke. "Your incarceration is complete. We shall move forward with our new plan for China. Mr. Crayle was the emperor's strategist. He is no longer available. The Communist Party having been disbanded, your title of Chairman is no longer meaningful. Fear not, you shall have a new one. You shall be *my* Lao Tzu."

The nascent Lao Tzu straightened, only so he could bow even deeper.

She stepped down from her throne and walked to within three feet of the man. He received an outstretched satchel and peered inside.

It was her look that instructed his next move. A single glance from her to the other remaining Standing Committee members, and he had his orders. And they made perfect sense. The young woman, no matter how strong, could not abide any burgeoning conspiracies from old alliances.

He turned, withdrew the weapon, and shot down those he'd worked with so closely, and trusted, for so many years.

Yes, she owned him now.

THE GERMANS

The head of the German government sat calmly behind her desk. In light of recent events in China, she lofted a pint glass of the finest Schnapps and quaffed it in one continuous gulp.

Von Prem had been recognized leaving the Neuschwanstein Castle, and, from there, surveilled to Paris, and then on to the airfield near Xian. He was dead. And with him, she anticipated, the Aryan movement.

Good riddance, she thought.

At that moment, her prime minister stepped in, locking the door behind him.

She was her own woman. With a reserved smile, she unbuttoned her tunic.

THE FRENCH

The French government—doomed by corruption, incompetence, and lethargy—lay either with Chin's warriors beneath the rubble of Xian, or as mere vestiges of themselves outlined on sidewalks and other hard surfaces. France now had no one at the helm. To fill the void, perhaps Jean-Marc, who'd been saved by the same mother and son in St. Lucia who'd saved Micmac and Pattie. They'd been elated at having rescued not just one man, but two men and one woman in the same day. Here he was. Although he'd been protected since his rescue by the Queen of Sweden, he was after all was said and done, French.

THE SWEDES

The Queen showed up with the Lalumière son attended by her honor guard and army. Her first official act: the end to socialism. There would be jobs, and growth, and enough wealth to completely refurbish the royal palace. She's even coined a new term. Monarchic capitalism.

There was only one fear. The Norwegians, Danes, and Finns were still caught in the socialistic quick sand. But it was not them. She feared the Russians the most. And not the president with his bare chest, horses, and hunting rifles. Rather the czarina. There had been some serious history back a ways. The queen needed to be on guard.

And finally, the queen entertained visions of installing Jean-Marc as Louis XX, King of France, with a suitable—and indelible—alliance between the two countries. It might be a great idea to have the new pope place the crown.

THE VATICAN

The atheist masquerading as a Catholic, Pope Innocent, had been brought by the Elder to Monaco to bless the Formula One race—a quite cool move by the Prince—and was dispatched to heaven or hell to face the music. Cardinal Alighieri, the pope's number two and Christian mole, had taken the helm in the Vatican.

There would be a purge. Of non-Christian insurgents. And the new pope would keep his alliances tight with the American CIA. And he would always wear white underwear.

THE AMERICANS

American President Kimbel Stones survived the bomb attack on Langley. Of all the rooms in the main building, the STIF room was the strongest. He'd stopped for just a moment while passing the corpse that Pattie Norbrunn had caused, then retreated back through the covert tunnel to the White House. Fortunately, the vacuum-enabled high velocity transport hadn't been damaged by the blast.

THE CRAYLES

Crayle had almost forgotten. He placed a call.

"Doctor Rorschach. We had so much going on at the cathedral and, even with your unexpected appearance, I didn't have a chance to give you the good news."

"There can be no better news than my betrothal to my Helmi. Hmmm?"

"The news is still good. No more Monika Rikki. She died in Monte Carlo. And more good news. The president has indicated that there will be no replacement. You get to run your own shop from now on … reporting directly to me."

"I haff no vords."

Crayle should have expected that the magnitude of his news would excite the doctor, causing a characteristic lapse into Teutonic English.

"It's good news. What's wrong?"

"Mine vite maus chust got avay from me."

There it was. The most important event in the Swiss psychiatric researcher's entire career, and he stressed out over a lost white mouse. Crayle couldn't suppress a laugh, nor his final thought.

"Don't you just hate when that happens?"

THE CRAYLES – LAS VEGAS

The Crayles survived festivities in the CIA underground cathedral and, having said *au revoir* to their friends and team mates, returned for a fourth try to the Las Vegas Hard Rock Hotel. This time, Hekka took no chances.

"Don't struggle, Sweetheart. Just a few more shots ..."

A security man and a manager, both summoned by a frightened waitress, approached from the hotel. "What's going on here?" the manager demanded.

"We're doing a magazine spread. Okay ..." She turned back to her husband. "... now, struggle."

With his mouth taped shut, he couldn't talk. With the rest she had done, he couldn't move either.

"It's authorized by ..." She gave the name of the property's top manager.

The two men said, "Oh," shrugged and retreated.

When they were out of earshot, the pool manager whispered, "I wouldn't be caught dead in that rainbow bright Speedo. You, Teddy?"

"You had somethin' to put in there. You just might," chuckled the security man.

Hekka watched until they were out of range. She turned back to Crayle.

"Smile."

"Mmph. Mmph," Crayle complained, pulling at the handcuffs and leg restraints.

"This is the last day of our one week of peace and quiet ... the one you promised. Oh, look! I've dropped your phone into the pool!"

THE FRENCHMAN

What might've been viewed as a thousand-yard stare was better characterized as a 230-year stare. That long ago, Sylvain Lalumière's ancestors were guillotined during France's post-revolution Reign of Terror.

Minutes after detonation, the blast from Monte Carlo slammed his island prison quarters, crumbled many sections of the Fort Royal, and popped his iron matrix door open. A tablet computer had fallen to the ground just outside, along with his jailor's body.

Apparently, the man kept a news app up whenever he wasn't checking the stock market. Lalumière watched through cracks in the screen the unfolding story of the former wealth mecca just east.

Headshots filled the screen of likely notable human losses. Formula 1 drivers, crews, and potentates. Spectators ranging from the rich to the near rich. There was the pope. And finally, the Prince of Monaco, and his two children. There was no parenthetical outing him as also the leader of the world's most secret, and dangerous, society—the Illuminé.

Lalumière had never seen the son, and didn't care at all about him. But recognition of the daughter was immediate. The photo had been taken recently. There she sat, legs crossed in a dignified manner, and wearing a dress suitable only to royalty. The diagonal sash demonstrated that her father had finally given her recognition as his out-of-wedlock child.

The impact of what had occurred moved quickly from his mind to his heart. He'd not felt that much pain in his entire life. Crazy as she might have been, she owned a sizeable piece of his heart.

"Pattie," he moaned. After several minutes, he glanced away from the screen. He saw something else. Probably nothing. All the same, the box *was* blue with a gold fleur-de-lis. Napoléon's crest.

Pattie had left it for him. Of that he felt most sure. Slowly, he broke a wax seal and removed the lid.

Inside, tissue wrapping paper of the same color and with the same crest as the box concealed what appeared at first to be a round object.

He extracted the item, smaller than a baseball, and peeled away its shroud.

His heart stopped. For only a moment. Then began to throb.

There it was. What Pattie had promised she had, in her own special way, delivered.

Peering back at him and sparkling in the sun, the Black Diamond. The final arbiter of the heir to the French throne.

His smile was genuine. He knew her thinking. If she, her Prince of a father, and the pope were to somehow fall off the game board, all knowledge of their marriage and status as the French king and queen would have been lost. With this—he held it aloft between his eyes and the setting sun—he would take Versailles … and La Belle France.

He stepped back into his cell, laid onto the comfort of his Sleep Number bed, and spoke the following words, "If only Jean-Marc could've seen this."

ME

I hadn't known Pattie Norbrunn very well, nor for very long. It was her nature not to be known. She never became close with anyone. When she crashed into the sea in Monte Carlo, and splashed down in the Mediterranean, and was confirmed by the submarine commander via visual imagery as very dead, that was the end.

What she'd learned at her mother's knee, and in her various schools, had led to a quite exceptional life. But none of the knowledge or experiences could have saved her in the end. Her cunning, her quickness, her resourcefulness. Nothing.

Of course, in college, she *had* been on the swim team …

THE END

ABOUT THE AUTHOR

Committed to international affairs, political intrigue and espionage, novelist Dennis Bowen has researched his stories in more than 60 countries. That Bowen engenders realism and spice in his thrillers due to his wartime service, and his defense and intelligence community background, led one reader to remark, "Bowen knows his stuff." *The Final Masquerade* follows *The Water Diamonds, The Blackstone Perfection, The Crystal Seduction,* and *The Redrock Quarantine* as Book 5 in his International Thriller Series. When not traveling the globe to research his next book, he resides on the Southern California coast.

Twitter: http://www.twitter.com/DBowenThrillers/
Facebook: http://www.facebook.com/DennisBowenThrillers
Website: http://www.dennisbowen.com/

THE
VIRTUE TRANSITION

BOOK 6:
INTERNATIONAL THRILLER SERIES

Available: Fall 2017

CHAPTER 1

"I met someone."

The man seated across from the stoic woman said nothing. Like her, he stared down at the paint-chipped and splintered picnic table.

That three little words could cause so much damage was unknown to them. Their last three little words had been "I love you" spoken at their wedding.

Silence followed by more silence.

She stood and turned, exhaling, depleted.

She watched the nearby lake as its waves lapped at the water's edge, but heard nothing.

Even the birds in the eighty-foot pine tree not ten feet away waxed quiescent.

A distant buzz, probably teens playing with toy aircraft, penetrated the gloomy mood.

"It … it …"

"I want to hear," he whispered. "Tell me."

A gust blew past, tossing a loose paint chip to the ground. That covert team member, Lenny Lipschitz, had applied cheap paint over the original redwood as a gesture of friendship didn't matter.

To Hekka Crayle, the table symbolized their relationship. Once strong. Once steady. Now, coming apart. Unraveling.

"I need to know," said the man she'd grown to love. To fight alongside. To fight for.

"I can't, Magus … I … uh"

The percussion of the next moment stopped the discussion dead.

It nearly stopped *them* dead.

One of five armed drones had plowed into the tree, gusted there by the wind. There, to explode.

Crayle yanked Hekka's arm just in time. He rolled right.

Damaged, the tree shook, then emitted an explosive sound of its own.

Two seconds later, another loud crack. The tree leaned. The third crack was final.

The crashing pine missed the Crayles. Barely. It hit the log cabin dead on.

"*Micmac! Phoebe! They're inside!*"

They glanced back in the direction of the attack.

Two of the four armed drone escorts had splintered and fallen from the blast.

Switching to Plan B, the other two opened fire. Caliber .22 rounds arrayed inside their fuselages provided a barrage of deadly potential.

The Crayles fought to protect each other from the fusillade.

Inside the cabin, former SEAL/UDT veteran Micmac and current on-leave FBI Agent Phoebe had been working on a covert ops training video.

The explosion outside should have blown the sliding door and adjacent glass window into deathly shards. Bullet proof, bomb proof, they held strong. The roof, however, had not been strengthened to stop a huge, falling tree six feet in girth.

The two dove away from each other. An instinctive ploy such that one or the other might survive.

Having landed in the kitchen, Phoebe forced open the side door and skirted the cabin.

Pinned by the couch that had slammed the wall, Micmac heard his ops game continue unabated with its own gunfire and explosions.

The last thing he heard before passing out—two booming shots. He smiled. His world went dark.

Phoebe had limped alongside the cabin to its rear. She took in the drones fixated on Crayle and Hekka. Micmac had heard Phoebe's .45 caliber Glock speak.

FBI colleagues referred to her as Annie Oakley for her deadly accuracy.

Two shots. Two drones.

Offshore, a camouflage-dressed man fired up his boat's three Mercury outboards and sped off.

A similarly clad cohort flew a sixth drone, its video streaming into her Smartphone complete, into the waves. The diminutive woman smiled, threw her drone controller into the lake, and ducked out of sight.

Crayle would never forget the flag hanging from the craft's stern.

He rolled his head to the right. To where his pregnant wife had landed.

Gone.

Having slammed his head against the picnic bench, he fought for consciousness.

A light snow began, the season's first.

He begged a desperate pair of eyes for clarity instead of the fog.

No Hekka.

"Where …" he gasped. "… where …"

www.ingramcontent.com/pod-product-compliance
Lightning Source LLC
Chambersburg PA
CBHW020609310726
48979CB00008B/1401/J

* 9 7 8 0 9 9 7 9 1 4 7 0 2 *